Amelia's Secrets

An Historical Novel

by

Maggie Carter-de Vries

authorHOUSE®

AuthorHouse™
1663 Liberty Drive, Suite 200
Bloomington, IN 47403
www.authorhouse.com
Phone: 1-800-839-8640

First published by AuthorHouse 6/26/2008

ISBN: 978-1-4343-9479-8 (sc)
ISBN: 978-1-4343-9478-1 (hc)

Library of Congress Control Number: 2008905435

Printed in the United States of America
Bloomington, Indiana

This book is printed on acid-free paper.

Acknowledgments

This book was not created by this author alone, no book is; it takes a multitude of talented people devoting hours of their time to a project in which only the writer envisions the ultimate outcome ... until at last, it lies before you swathed in its glorious covers, smelling of fresh ink, its pages crisply begging to be opened and read.

I thank the following people for their generosity; without them I would not have reached my goal to tell this story: the staff of Amelia Island Museum of History, who allowed me the privilege of perusing their files and records, and bothering them by telephone for months on end; Nassau County Library, who allowed me the same and taught me to use the antiquated microfiche machine in the corner—amongst laughs and groans. While at the library I happened to meet Claire Shephard (descendant of Ferdinand C. Suhrer). What a surprise! Thanks, Claire, for the hours of comparing ancestry notes, documents and photos. Also, I would like to thank Hal Belcher, author of *The Original Section of Bosque Bello Cemetery*, who aided me in locating those resting in peace. Hal, your help was invaluable! You don't know how frustrating it was to be standing in the middle of the cemetery and not being able to find what I needed. After dialing your number on my cellphone, like magic you walked me right to the spot! A special thanks to Judge Robert "Bob"

Williams for sharing his courtroom knowledge, without which I would have not been able to properly and accurately portray this important chapter of the book. To Beth of Mansbridge Editing, my tireless and exacting copy editor, for correcting misspells and other typos, I could not have achieved this without you. Last but not least, a special and loving thanks to my husband, Dutch, for being my computer guru, and for being understanding of the long and lonely hours while I hid away in my ivory tower to complete *Amelia's Secrets*.

Chapter 1

Katie Comes to Town
September 1883

"My God, have you heard?" The cry resounds round the town not unlike the echo of the vibration following a cannon shot.

Centre Street

Heads shake in disbelief when the nasty little details are passed from one to another, juicy tidbits, true and not being added, I imagine, as the day passes into night and the life's blood trickles from an innocent man.

Or is he?

But hold on, I am getting ahead of myself. I must first lay down the pattern of the days in the lives of the townspeople of Fernandina, Florida, that led us to the tragic day of Thursday, February 7, 1884, at exactly 5:20 p.m. and that final, infinite moment culminating in uncontrollable rage and murder.

Like a pebble is dropped into a pool, so each of us touches another's life. Could one or many of us have changed that moment? Or did many of us create it?

*

My position as clerk of the city council is a worthy position but, I must say, can be on occasion monotonous and today is one of those days. The call to order has been made. Charles Lewis, chairman, is present; so are Jones, Johnson and Higginbotham, but Acting Mayor Suhrer is absent, as are others, and I myself am chomping at the bit for the items of business to be over.

But it continues: payment of the long list of bills necessary to keep our fair city of Fernandina sailing smoothly. And it will go on for some time. I am more restless and eager than usual to be out of here today.

The steamship *State of Texas* arrived yesterday bearing not only bales of cotton, barrels of spirits, cases of cedar, syrup, barrels of oranges, bundles of shingles and miscellaneous other packages of merchandise, but also a certain young lady of undeniable charm and beauty. Miss Pauline Meddaugh has been on a trip to New York with her mother and her mother's friend, Katy Stark, for some time and I have been anxious for her return. An evening tea to celebrate their setting ashore is planned for 6:00 p.m. today at the Mansion House Hotel.

This will be the beginning of the social season for Fernandina, since many families have been returning from summer vacations. I hear that T. J. Eppes, a conductor on the Transit Road, and his new bride, Katie, who arrived last Thursday from Archer, will be there. Everyone says she is the most beautiful woman they have ever seen. She will have to be breathtaking to take my eyes away from Pauline!

Finally, the commission meeting has adjourned and I am away at last!

*

The Mansion House Hotel is awash in every color imaginable. Ladies seem to float in on the arms of their escorts, pert little hats slanted on their coiffed heads. They wave to and laugh with friends not seen all summer.

All eyes turn and time stands still when T. J. Eppes and his new bride walk through the doorway. Dressed in shimmering pale green, long black hair cascading to her waist and dark eyes to match, Katie is a vision of beauty never seen here before. She exudes a sense of innocence and sexuality that affects men and women, young and old alike. She is a magnet; you are drawn helplessly to her and yet you want desperately to push away. She holds her hands out shyly to you in greeting and friendship, but the women want no part of her and the men seem both afraid and excited. Jealously is a strange, cruel thing. It harbors feelings we never knew we had.

The first meeting, the first introduction into this close-knit society, will be the beginning of what will come. You are either accepted or you aren't. Being of proper birth and station gives you certain rights but does not always grant you entrance into our little society.

Mrs. Meddaugh and Mrs. Stark, seeing what is happening, step forward, guide Katie by the arms and introduce her around the room. They become her mentors through the next months: making sure she receives invitations to teas, card parties and socials; keeping her busy while T.J. is out of town—which will be often, as conductors on the railway travel many miles from home. Which is how he met Katie in the first place—in a stopover in her hometown of Archer, Florida.

The ladies drift together by mutual agreement to the parlor for tea and gossip when the men gather on the verandah for brandy and cigars to discuss local politics, shootings and the likes.

The major topic of conversation is the recent shooting of Mr. N. G. Levan, a partner of the firm of Levan, Upson & Co.—which has a shingle mill in operation a short distance from Italia—by Mr. William MacWilliams, who runs the brickyard. It seems that Mr. MacWilliams had written an insulting letter to Mr. Levan on account of an employee in the shingle mill who was recently employed by MacWilliams. On Monday afternoon last, Mr. Levan went to see Mr. MacWilliams about the matter. Hot words ensued on both sides, until finally MacWilliams grabbed Levan by the throat and the two men scuffled, during which Levan had an ear cut and was stabbed in the leg. When Levan became aware that MacWilliams was using a knife he cried out to bystanders, and the two men were separated. No sooner were they inches apart, when Mr. MacWilliams drew a pistol. But a bystander, Mr. J. C. Wilson, grabbed it when it exploded and the shot entered Mr. Levan's side. No weapons whatever were found on Mr. Levan. Justice Mahoney, of Callahan, issued a warrant on Tuesday, and MacWilliams was arrested and brought to Callahan, where his preliminary examination took place. MacWilliams was placed under $1,000 bond for his appearance at the next circuit court.

Although Mr. Levan was alive yesterday, his injuries will probably prove fatal; the attending physician stated at the examination that his condition was exceedingly critical. Mr. Levan is regarded as a peaceable and law-abiding man, and one of the best citizens of the county. His neighbors hold him in universal esteem. The whole county is abuzz over the matter and as to the contents of the mysterious letter, which is yet to be revealed.

Conversation changes to other topics such as the sale of the city's horse and cart at auction last Saturday. The purchase of the horse, at $145, was by Mr. C. H. Swann, and the cart went to Mr. P. Kelly, resulting in a $15 loss to the city. Also, sadness is expressed over the loss of Governor Bixham's only daughter, Mattie, at age eighteen, last Saturday in Tallahassee.

The sound of the cicadas increases with the darkening of a late summer storm rolling in across Amelia Sound. The aroma of cigar smoke drifts across the verandah, mingling with the musical laughter of the ladies in the parlor. Soon it will be time to depart, and my much-looked-forward-to walk home with Pauline to North Sixth Street.

We stroll arm in arm down Centre Street, past stores usually bustling with activity, now quiet for the night. I ask Pauline her opinion of T.J.'s new bride. I am astounded to hear the usually gracious and kind Pauline repeat gossip of a most vicious nature overheard at the tea.

T.J. and Katie met on one of his many stopovers on the rail line last summer. It appears that our Katie is a social climber, having learned that T.J. is the grandson of Judge Eppes of Monticello, Florida, and the great-great-grandson of our late President Thomas Jefferson.

"Can it be," I ask Pauline, "that this is just gossip? You know how ladies can get their feathers ruffled when a pretty new chick enters the flock."

Twirling her parasol, Pauline takes a moment before answering. "Katie's family came from South Carolina after the war and were farmers. Her uncle, her mother's brother, is the main support for the whole family."

I mull over this information, wondering what part of South Carolina since I also am from there—the only surviving child of Joseph and Amilia Whitner, of Marion. Everyone calls me by the nickname of John, given me by my mother at an early age, she said, "So I won't have to call you Junior." This family joke among the three of us always made my father laugh.

We continue to walk in companionable silence, drinking in the salty fragrance of the night air.

The storm has passed us by, as it frequently does, preferring to play havoc instead on our neighbor across the river, Cumberland Island. The lightning still flashes in the distance, causing the inlet to light up, showing the whitecaps dancing like fairies at a moonlight ballet.

Pausing in front of Pauline's house, I lean forward and whisper softly in her ear, "Come walk to St. Michael's with me and sit in the gazebo. You have been gone so long and I have missed you. There's so much I wish to tell you. In truth, I long to spend more time just holding your hand, looking at your beautiful face and stealing at least one kiss."

"You know I can't," she whispers in turn. "I promised Mother that I would come straight home if she allowed us to walk without a chaperone. My word is my honor. But I will see you Friday night for the Harvest Ball at the Egmont Hotel."

"All right," I answer, but a kiss I will still have and a kiss I promptly impart upon her unsuspecting lips. Lips as sweet and soft as dew on a rose petal. If she had slapped me it would have been worth it, but she did not, and I whistle a tune and dance a little jig home to the Florida House on Third Street.

The Florida House, built by the Florida Railroad in 1857 and now owned and operated by the widow Annie Leddy, is right nice. For a decent price you get a room and breakfast, and also dinner if you want to pay extra. There is a parlor with a piano for gathering in the evenings. Lady friends are allowed to visit in the front parlor, which is tastefully decorated. Smoking is allowed only on the back porch, not on the front verandah. Miss Annie says smoking out front gives folks a bad impression of the establishment. Not wanting to provoke the Irish wrath of Miss Annie, I retire to the back porch with the other male boarders after the evening meal, lean my chair back, prop my feet up on the rail and inhale deeply on my one vice … a sleek, aromatic Cuban cigar purchased this morning from J & T Kydd.

My friend, C. A. Key, gentleman, scholar and principal of School Number 1, jumps over the rail and settles into the chair next to mine. He is full of excitement over his trip to Cumberland Island and his meeting with Mr. Morris, who is heading up the project of building the palatial mansion "Dungeness" for Mr. Carnegie of New York.

"You should see the place, old boy!" he exclaims. "It will be truly grand when it is finished."

Ever since President Grant visited three years ago, things around here have been booming. All this building here in Fernandina, what with the railroad, private schools, Lyceum Hall and the theatre. Now millionaires are building summer homes over at Cumberland and Jekyll islands! More tourists are coming every season, not only from Georgia but also as far away as from New York and Philadelphia, spending money and making our fair city grow by leaps and bounds.

"Come go with Doc Palmer and me tomorrow morning to Cumberland and see for yourself. Mrs. Carnegie invited him and his wife to tea to discuss medical care of the family and workers during construction, and me to temporarily tutor the children. I'm sure she would not mind your coming along."

I take a long pull on my cigar and let out a slow, lazy smoke ring before answering. The thought on one hand of not meeting with Pauline in the morning, and on the other, the excitement of the trip to Cumberland Island to see firsthand the beginnings of the magnificent Dungeness is overwhelming. It is my nature as a curious man, to want to know how things are done, why and how. Therefore the decision is naturally made for me to accompany them on the trip to Cumberland the next day to view the laying of the foundation of the mansion, and to make my apologies to Pauline in the evening.

*

The morning sun rises over the inlet, burning away the damp smell of the night's salt air. A light, balmy breeze blowing in from the sea gives the ferry an extra push toward Cumberland.

Doc Palmer, Sarah, C.A. and I are enjoying the early morning ride, the conversation ebbing and flowing like the tide, as it does among friends with moments of quiet when nature unfolds scenery of startling beauty. Florida gators sun themselves on sandy banks. Egrets within easy reach go about their business of leaning forward, arching their long beaks down into the blue water, searching for breakfast to take home to their young waiting not so patiently in nests among the tall trees lining the river. Seagulls hoping for a morning treat escort shrimp boats, and merchant ships head to exciting ports near and far, waving flags of distant lands. They passed us earlier, causing much conversation and speculation. Yes, the port of Fernandina is a dynamic place, bringing much prosperity to the island of Amelia and surrounding towns of Yulee, Callahan and Hart's Road.

My thoughts wander to my friend Emil who has a bakery and grocer business, Angel & Friend, on Centre Street. It has prospered to the point of necessity of hiring two more employees these last six months and a Negro just to clean up and make deliveries. With three small children at home, his wife, Florance, only comes in late at night to do the fancy cake decorating that she alone has the skill to execute so well. His sister, Bertha Angel, is a widow with six children (she is the daughter of Judge John Friend) and is Emil's business partner since her husband was assassinated by an employee last year.

Now, that's a story I should take time to tell you here and now. Charles Angel and his wife were a part of a large group of industrious German settlers including me, Ferdinand Suhrer, John M. Waas, and many others who hold public office, establish businesses and are a part of each others' daily lives. Waas's first wife, Elisabeth, passed away in 1864 and he returned to the same village in Baden, Germany, and brought back a very beautiful, much younger wife named Regina, who died in childbirth on December 16, 1881. According to Waas, she made a deathbed confession that the child was not his but that of Charles Angel. Grief-stricken over the death of his young wife and child, Waas carried this hatred for his boss in his heart for many months and on March 19, 1882, he sent a note to Charles to come around to his house to speak to him on a personal matter. When Charles arrived, John confronted him about the issue. Charles vehemently denied anything to do with his wife and turned to leave. Waas grabbed his shotgun from behind the front door and shot him in the back. Charles died from the wounds later that evening. Waas, tormented by the deed he had committed, went behind his house, took the shaving razor from beside the washbasin and slit his wrists, therefore committing suicide. He took to his grave the tormented thought that he had been cuckolded by Charles Angel. Now, personally, Charles was a friend of mine, and though to this day the talk still has not died down, I will never believe any wrongdoing on his part.

Well, enough of maudlin talk on such a beautiful day. We are nearing the docks at Cumberland. I can see the wild horses running in the distance. Their manes and tails flow straight out behind them as their long legs stretch out in the freedom they enjoy without fear of being tamed by man or nature. As we near the dock I am awestruck, as I am every time I visit Cumberland, by the serene beauty and tranquility of the island.

Lucy Carnegie, holding a parasol over her head to ward off the bright morning sun, is waving merrily to us from her carriage. She is a petite, dark-haired, pretty woman and surprisingly young-looking considering she is the mother of nine children.

Leaving the strict social life of Pittsburgh behind agrees with mother and children alike. A number of Carnegie children are playing a game of tag, racing around the carriage, laughing and screaming, red cheeked as they try desperately to stay out of reach of whoever is "it" at the moment.

Her dark eyes sparkling, Lucy holds out her hand in welcome. "You know there is always a place at the table for you, and I could stand some catching up on grownup news and gossip. Let's load up the children in the buckboard and we will ride in the carriage. Miss Bella is making fresh mint julep, lemonade, and oyster stew and cucumber sandwiches for lunch. She'll be mad as a hatter if the stew gets cold."

Laughing out loud at the thought of Bella waiting for us at the door brandishing a soup spoon at our heads, Doc hands Sarah up into the carriage and we are on our way at a fast trot.

"Tom will be joining us," Lucy says, "then he will take you over to Dungeness for the grand tour. It is being built on the original site of General Nathanael Greene's summer home by the same name. That home was completed in 1804 by his widow, but nothing stands today except the gardener's house. Our Dungeness will be so much larger and grander and, as you can see, we need it with all these children! Nine in all, with Coleman just three years old and little Nancy about to turn one next week. Our oldest, William, is now sixteen and following in his father's footsteps. Then of course there is Frank, Andrew, Margaret, George, Thomas, and Florence. There is never a loss for a playmate or a helping hand around here, that's for sure!"

My respect and admiration for Lucy Carnegie continually grows and deepens. Not only does she rule her large household with a hand of steel and a genteel smile, but she is also an astute businesswoman, buying and selling property and holding mortgages. Quite an accomplishment for a woman.

Arriving at the house we find Thomas sitting on the verandah, balancing Master Coleman on one knee and Miss Nancy on the other while he puffs on a cigar and rocks back and forth. Calling for the nanny to take the children, he extends his hand in a warm welcome and leads us into the dark, cool interior for a delicious lunch and a vivid, detailed description of the third Dungeness to be built—the first being built on top of an Indian shell mound.

The first, he tells us, was built by the English general James Oglethorpe and was a hunting lodge. Revolutionary War hero Gen.

Nathanael Greene, who commanded the Southern Department of the war, built the next. He also owned Mulberry Grove Plantation near Savannah, but died in 1786 before he was able to complete his plans. His widow, Catherine, married her children's tutor, Phineas Miller, and they followed through on Greene's designs, building a huge four-story tabby mansion with six-foot-thick walls, sixteen fireplaces and elaborate gardens. The British occupied the mansion during the War of 1812.

After lunch we saddle up and head toward the building site, leaving Sarah behind with Lucy and the children. On the way, we stop for a few minutes to pay our respects at the grave of Gen. Henry "Light Horse Harry" Lee, Revolutionary War hero and old friend of Nathanael Greene. Lee, in failing health, came ashore at Cumberland as he was returning from the West Indies and asked to be taken to his old friend's estate. After a month of illness, he died on March 25th and was buried on the island. His son, Confederate general Robert E. Lee, had a tombstone placed over the grave, and often visits his father's final resting place.

Coming upon the construction site, I am taken aback with the enormousness of the work in progress. There must be hundreds of workers going about the task of demolishing the old Dungeness in preparation of erecting the turreted Scottish castle with a pool house, squash court, and golf course, and forty other buildings that will house a staff of approximately twenty. This is to be the family's winter retreat; I wonder what their home in Pittsburgh is like.

I am an amateur photographer so I busy myself setting up the tripod and flash, not wishing to miss this moment in history. After introductions are made, Andrew Peebles, the well-known Pittsburgh architect, and Tom strike a pose, one hand each on a shovel in front of the site.

Tom explains to us, "The Army Corps of Engineers are building jetties at St. Marys Inlet, so I traded off removal of the blocks of tabby for use in the jetty construction. I will be using the small pieces in road building on the island. There will be a short one running through the groves of oranges, bananas, plums, olives and sago palms, from the boat landing, and a second road running due east for about a mile straight to the beach."

Tom tells us how he came about purchasing the Cumberland property from General William George Mackay Davis, a friend and distant cousin of President Jefferson Davis. As the turn of events came about, General Davis's son, B. M. Davis, moved his family from Fernandina to the Dungeness property three months after the agreement to purchase and a terrible tragedy occurred. According to the *Florida Mirror* of March 13, 1880:

> A terrible accident occurred yesterday at Dungeness. Mr. B. M. Davis, son of General W. G. M. Davis, the recent purchaser, had the misfortune to shoot and kill his eldest son, a bright little fellow of five years of age. The family had just moved over from Fernandina the day before, to take possession of their new home. ... It has spread a cloud of horror over our little community, and all tender to the bereaved parents their heartfelt sympathy. It is needless to add the parents are almost crazed by this terrible, heartrending disaster.

"It seems," Tom says, "that Mr. Davis decided to shoot some robins from the front porch for breakfast and accidentally shot and killed his son. He himself died nine months later, compounding the family tragedy. Both are buried here at Dungeness Cemetery. As any gentleman would do, I gave his father rights to visit their graves anytime he wishes, and promised to maintain the cemetery in the future."

This is evident by the freshly placed flowers blowing gently in the balmy air at each gravestone as we walk past.

He adds, "An article in *Lippincott's Monthly Magazine* published a thrilling article about Dungeness, written by Massachusetts freelance writer Fredrick Ober in 1880, that attracted Lulu and me to Cumberland Island. We had hoped to renovate the original Dungeness, but upon inspection, found the old walls to be in such a sad state of deterioration after the fire and twenty years or so of neglect, we decided to tear it down and rebuild. We estimate approximately one and a half years to complete the main house, the lodging at Dungeness Landing for Captain Baker—of our yacht *Missoe*—and the dock and roads."

Saying, "That's a long time," I stop to look around, becoming speechless at the enormity of his undertaking.

"In the meantime, Lulu and I will continue to live in the small cottage built years ago by Nightingale and the boys in the carriage house. Before long we will regretfully have to stop tourists from stopping over. The Fernandina hotels ferry over fifty to sixty at a time to tour through, but you of course are welcome at any time."

He and Andrew roll out the blueprints for us to peruse. The main building measures 120 feet by 56 feet and two stories high with an attic. Gracing the east end will be a tower 100 feet high. The exposed outer walls are to be faced with light-colored granite, with the main roof, the dormer windows and the pyramid of the belvedere to be covered with Vermont slate.

The combs of the higher portions of the main roof are to be topped with ornamental iron castings. The main entrance of the mansion will be on the north side, opening into the vestibule of 10 feet by 11 feet, with a marble floor with ornamental borders. To the left of the vestibule will be a grand hall, 21 feet wide, extending nearly the entire width of the building. The parlor, on the east side of the grand hall, is to be 19 feet by 24 feet, with bay windows opening onto a broad veranda, which extends around the entire east and south sides of the structure. Opposite the parlor there is a large dining room, 18 by 24 feet, connected to the pantry and china closets. At the north end of the grand hall is a small gun room with a lavatory. Next to the gun room, accessible from the hall, is a large bedroom with an attached bathroom. A 6-foot wide corridor leads from the grand hall to the kitchen and scullery.

The second story contains the family's living apartments, guest rooms, a library and reading rooms, while the attic has six bedrooms.

The windows of the first two stories of the main building will be of the best quality of polished plate glass, while the window of the main stairs and grand hall will be of ornamental cathedral glass. In the basement are the servants' quarters, a cellar and a strong room. The laundry will have hot and cold running water. Lucy has ordered a roller mangle for the laundry. Dumbwaiters connecting all floors and a system for ringing servants and electric lights are to be run by a gas-powered plant located on the premises.

I am amazed at the detail and thought that has gone into the design of Dungeness.

After I convey this to Tom, he cocks his head, smiles at me and says, "Nothing's too good for my Lulu and the family. Their comfort is my utmost concern. With nine children, Lulu's mother and her brother William who is going blind, and her sister Florence to care for, we have quite a large brood."

I had known about Tom from talks with Emil. He told me that Tom had much rather spend time at home and traveling with his family than taking care of the business he owns and operates with his brother Andrew, Carnegie Brothers and Company, a steel-related business in Pittsburgh.

Pulling out his pocket watch, Tom indicates that we need to head back to the cottage for afternoon tea or Miss Lucy would have all our heads for being late. This of course is said with a twinkle in his eye and a grin on his face.

After a leisurely repast of more of Lucy's famous mint juleps, lemonade, and finger sandwiches, we regretfully take our leave with schedules set for tutoring and doctoring, and promises for neighborly visits.

It has been a busy day and we settle down for the hour-long ferry ride back to Fernandina, answering Sarah's many questions about Dungeness, enjoying the sunset over the St. Marys River and the sound of the soft and gentle slap-slap of the water against the sides of the boat.

Chapter 2

The Fire

September 11th

Egmont Hotel

The Egmont Hotel is blazing with light and color when I arrive for the annual Harvest Ball. G. W. Kettelle, owner of the hotel, has hired a colored jazz band from Jacksonville for the occasion and the music is exceptional. Looking around for Pauline I am surprised to find her in the company of Katie Eppes. Both ladies are turned out in style. Pauline is a vision in a creation of ice blue, tight at her tiny waist—that I could easily span with my two hands—and a froth of white lace at her throat. Katie is the exact opposite, dressed in a low-cut dress of red satin. Black lace panels cross under her breasts, thrusting them upward. Her satin slippers, also red, are tapping restlessly in time to the music.

"T.J. has gone off to Gainesville and abandoned me," she says, making a moue with lips so red I am sure she must be wearing rouge.

"No he hasn't," snaps Pauline, "you know he's working and will be back in three days."

"But I want to dance, and no one will dance with me because I am married and my husband is away," she retorts, "and it's not fair. I'm too young to sit over there." She points at the row of chairs against the wall where the married women, widows and dowagers sit, heads together, laughing and chatting—probably about husbands, children and Katie's low-cut dress.

The band starts playing a waltz and I hold out my hand to Pauline. We excuse ourselves from Katie. A few moments later, looking over my shoulder, I see her sitting at a table, talking to Major Suhrer, manager of the Mansion House, and his wife, Eva Rosa, who is casting her eyes about the room as if looking for someone.

"She's in safe hands and off ours for now, so let's enjoy ourselves," Pauline whispers in my ear. "Mama said I must be sociable and spend time with the poor thing and introduce her around, since we are close in age. Poor thing, my foot! She's trouble, that's what she is, you mark my words!"

Her words cause me to misstep and we accidentally bump into another couple. Apologizing to them, I swing Pauline back into rhythm and she continues her conversation as if nothing has occurred.

"We went riding yesterday and she flirted outrageously with every man, old and young alike, that we met along the way. Embarrassed me to no end! I hate being seen with her. Mama says she's just friendly and eager to be liked. She's eager with the men, as far as I can see, but not so with the ladies. She's making lots of enemies—not friends—with them! T.J. is not going to be happy about her social activities."

"Slow down, Pauline," I say, "I'm sure it's not as bad as you think. She's a beautiful, vivacious, young woman, new to our town and eager to fit in. I'm sure she would not do anything to cause harm to her or T.J.'s reputations."

I twirl Pauline around the dance floor, pulling her closer than protocol allows, feeling the rise and fall of her firm breasts against my chest. "Let's change the subject, shall we? I had much rather talk about you and what you have been doing, other than keeping company with Katie, the last few days. And I have so much to tell you about the new mansion being built on Cumberland!"

The rest of the evening spins by in a kaleidoscope of music, food and drink, without incident until almost midnight when the call comes for the last dance of the ball. A flurried murmur arises when Katie insists on dancing the last square dance with one of the young waiters at the hotel—not seeing what harm is in it. An end is put to the matter; G.W. grabs the young man by the shoulder and escorts him through the kitchen doors while informing him it would cost him his job.

Katie sullenly asks Ferdinand and Eva Rosa to escort her home. Never has such a rule of society been breached! Total silence fills the ballroom as the trio gathers their cloaks and hats and departs. G.W. instructs the band to strike up the music once more and things return to somewhat of a normal finale of the autumn ball.

*

The next day dawns with dark clouds threatening like a hangover after a previous evening. I cannot shed the feeling of a heavy foreboding ... of something bad and evil permeating the air around me. It does not make sense, since my evening with Pauline ended very nicely indeed. "Oh well, I will just have to shake it off," I mutter to myself as I lather my face. Sharpening the razor on the strap attached to the side of the gentlemen's mirror, I count my usual lucky number of seven strokes. Call me superstitious, but I have done this every morning since I began shaving, and today is not the day to make changes.

The aromas of Miss Annie's homemade biscuits and country ham meet me at the head of the stairs as I make my way down to breakfast. The other gentlemen boarders are already halfway through the morning meal when I head to the sideboard for coffee before seating myself. Of course the topic of conversation is Katie Eppes's faux pas of last evening. I elect not to join in. I hurriedly eat, give my usual morning praises to Miss Annie, grab my hat and head out the door.

The dark clouds have given way to a sunnier, slightly overcast day, chasing away the earlier gloomy feeling. I smile, making my way toward work. "Well, that's much better!" I say aloud.

Entering the city commissioners' chambers, I spy City Clerk William Wood deep in conversation with John Wilkerson, one of Fernandina's black policemen. As I draw near, William motions for me to join their conversation, which is a debate as to whether or not the *Western Texas* actually had power enough to tow the disabled steamer, *Newport*, 160 miles into Savannah, as has been reported. The *Texas* herself weathered a hurricane for two days and sustained some damage, the captain of the *Newport* asked for assistance and Captain John Risk of the *Western Texas* reportedly towed her into Savannah. I responded that if Captain Sunberg of the *Newport* reported it to be so, then it must be, however unlikely it may seem. Having said that, I left them to their debate and headed for my office.

The weather is unseasonably hotter than usual for September. The temperature is still hovering in the nineties during the day. The linen suit jacket I had donned before leaving just a few minutes earlier is already damp with perspiration and clinging to my back. After hanging it on the hall tree along with my hat, I sit at my desk in my shirtsleeves, calculating the upcoming offerings for tax sales of city properties. Time passes quickly. I neatly list items in a row, as required by Mr.

Wood. Suddenly I am startled by the sounds of a multitude of church bells clamoring furiously. Running to the open window, I scan the downtown business district. I see nothing toward town, but north, toward the harbor is a déjà vu of September 2. Fire trucks are rounding the corner. Another fire! The tall peak of the Dell House is plainly visible and burning fiercely.

Losing no time I sprint out the door and join in the bucket brigade. The roof is very steep and all efforts to reach it are in vain. Some men are removing furniture, others are wetting down the two-story addition on the back of the house in an effort to save it. But alas, this also is in vain. Only the furniture can be saved.

Mr. Wood's newly built cottage, completed within the past two months, and Mr. J. J. Acosta's home, recently purchased closest to his, are next to fall victims to the fire. This would be the second loss for Mr. Acosta to fire, the first being in May to his home on Escambia Street. If Mr. Acosta's house is not saved, then the rest of the block is doomed, including the residence of Clarence Maxwell since they are situated so near together. The Mansion House Hotel is in serious danger as well!

Men scramble on top of the Acosta house, sweat streaming down their soot-blackened faces. I am among them as we swelter under the extreme scorching noonday sun coupled with the blazing, intense heat of the fire. Exhausted, we struggle on; the water supply is dwindling and has to be brought in buckets from the adjoining block. Luckily the wells at the Mansion House hold out. The struggle is likened to a fierce battle with the combat moving but never ceasing nor letting up. The cistern in Mr. Hammond's yard, luckily, is full from the storm of last Saturday and Sunday. The Baptist church on Alucha is now blazing like an inferno. My arms are aching, the blisters on my hands are broken open and bleeding, but I can't stop, I must go on.

First Baptist Church

Women bring wet rags to tie around our heads and water to drink and we continue on. Bucket after bucket, we pass up and down. Minutes are hours and we continue on. Then the cry goes out! Everyone scrambles into the street as the walls cave in. The church is destroyed. It is finished. The fire truck moves in to water down the already hissing mass. Danger is past of any further spread of fire with the fall of the church.

Exhausted, I sit slumped against a palm tree with my head in my hands. I am too numb to move. My once white linen suit is now a blackened mess of soot, water and sweat but I don't care. I am more concerned about the loss of my friends' properties and that of the city of Fernandina, following so soon after the most recent fire and the one of 1876. The new business district building code demands all brick buildings. Looking at the destruction around me, I think this is a mighty good thing.

Pauline and Doc find me here, assist me to my feet and to his office to clean and bandage my hands and a burn on my leg that I am not even aware of. That's how tired and exhausted I am.

"Where did the fire start?" I ask Doc.

"It seems that a spark from a smokestack of Oaks Planing Mill, situated two hundred feet across from the Dell House, must be the cause. We will know more later, I am sure," he answers as we walk to his buggy. "Right now it is more important to get you home, cleaned up and to bed for some rest. I am going to give you an elixir and some extra liniment to put on those burns. I will come by later this evening to check on you and the other men at Miss Annie's, who also needed medical treatment after the fire.

"It is a noble thing you men and women have done this day," Doc says. "Without your untiring labor and endeavors, the convent of the Sisters of St. Joseph would surely have been destroyed, and many other homes and buildings suffered worse ruin."

Putting his arm around a sooty and bedraggled Pauline, he gives her a hug and the three of us slowly head down Centre Street. First to Pauline's house, and then on to the Florida House where I am grateful that Doc gives me a quick, tepid bath, and I fall easily into a deep sleep until suppertime.

The feel of Doc's cool hand awakens me from a dreamless, dark slumber. My body refuses to turn over. Every muscle screams in agony. My hands are heavily bandaged and I cannot use them to push myself into a sitting position. Doc reaches behind me and lifts me as I swing my legs over the side of the bed. God, how my body aches!

"Whew, I believe I'd best leave the fire fighting to Hook & Ladder Company," I tell Doc. "Sitting behind a desk, putting pen to paper does not condition me to fight fires."

Doc laughs his deep bear of a laugh at my comment. He unwraps the bandages, cleans and treats the wounds and rewraps my hands. The leg wound is not as serious but my face is badly sunburnt and my hair singed. Looking in the mirror I can't decide if I want to try to go downstairs for supper, for fear of frightening Miss Annie, or stay in my room.

"You don't look any worse for the wear than the others," Doc says.

So I decide to go on down.

Miss Annie has outdone herself in preparing this evening's meal. A virtual feast of fried chicken, boiled shrimp, roasted new potatoes, sweet corn, and St. James's Custard.

"We all have a lot to be thankful for," she says. "We lost homes, businesses and a church today, but not one life. God has been good. Let us give thanks."

We bow our heads and hold hands. Different religions, different nationalities bound together; fighting a fire today, praying together this night.

This bond is what I most enjoy about my new life in Fernandina. Nowhere else have I found different races, religions and even sexes working side by side like here. Women own property and businesses. Blacks hold elected office. In fact, the black population outnumbers the Caucasian. Everyone works toward the common goal of improving our community and what is good for all. It's not that we don't have servants and laborers, mill hands and lower-class citizens. We do. It's just that all in all, it is different here.

Even crime is sporadic. When it happens it usually is rare, profound and shocking—or petty. Ranging from the murder of the supposed lover of one's wife, to thievery of watermelons down at Centre Street Market. Again, as I said, crime is rare and swiftly dealt with.

I remember when President Ulysses S. Grant, as a parting gift, gave Mr. Ferreira a box of Havana cigars during his visit of 1880. Ferreira stowed them under the seat of his buggy and a gang of young boys, seeing him do this, stole the cigars, smoked them and got mighty sick. So sick, as a matter of fact, that Mr. Ferreira did not have the heart to have them punished further.

Chapter 3

The Wedding
September 25th

Looking at the destruction around me, I can hardly believe it has been only twenty-four hours since I followed these same footsteps to work. Workers are removing the charred remains of the businesses and homes that were destroyed. Property owners are at hand to recover anything of value. I hear the excited cry of a woman and turn toward her. She is clutching tightly to her breast the picture of a family member not touched by the overeager flames. Furniture overflows the sidewalks waiting to be put into storage until a new home can be built or rented. The same is true with business equipment and merchandise. Bags of oats sit sadly beside gaily-colored bolts of satin and ladies' hats with ribbons and feathers blowing in the breeze waiting their turn to be loaded onto wagons. Again neighbor is helping neighbor. I wish there was something I could do, but my hands as so badly burnt I will not be able to hold a writing pen at work for days to come.

Entering my office I cross over to the window and after failed attempts, call my office attendant to open it, allowing the morning breeze to enter. The salty scent of the inlet mixed with the odor of the shrimp boats and fish docks is welcome for a change. Anything is better than the horrible smell of burning buildings.

I sit here frustrated, staring at all the work that needs to be done, but I have no choice. It will have to wait. As I stand up to leave, my boss, William Wood, walks in and drops down into a chair facing me.

"We've lost our new house," he says, slowly shaking his head. "But thank God that Alice and our daughter Ethel were in Jacksonville shopping for Fannie's wedding, with her and Mrs. Meddaugh. Some of the furniture was saved and we have some insurance on the house, but not enough to cover it all. This is a hard blow after losing my stationery business to the fire of September 2."

Coming around the desk with a hand extended, he sees my hands and instead places both of his on my shoulders. I am surprised to see tears in his eyes.

Returning to the chair, he says, "I came in to thank you for all your efforts to help save my house yesterday. I saw you on top of the roof with the bucket brigade."

"We all did our best," I reply. "I saw you as well. When all hope was gone for your own home you continued to fight the fires shoulder to shoulder with the rest of us. It is a day that will go down in history as a black day in Fernandina because of the fire, but a day to be remembered for the valor of our citizens."

"Quite true," he answers while heaving himself up slowly like a tired old man. "There's not much you can accomplish here with your hands all bandaged up. Why don't you take the rest of the week off? Spend some time with Pauline—or is she too busy with Fannie's wedding? It's coming up in a couple of weeks, isn't it? Fannie's bound to be a bundle of nerves about now."

"You're right," I answer with a laugh. "Pauline, her mother and sisters have nothing on their minds these days except the wedding. It's to be at the Presbyterian church on Tuesday evening, September 25, and to hear them talk, it is the only social event of the year. With your permission,

I do think I will go over to my tailor's and check on the progress of my suit for the wedding."

So with a nod of approval from William, I take my leave and head into the blinding sun and broiling heat of yet another unseasonably hot September day. Walking toward the waterfront I can feel the welcome breeze of early morning picking up again. I make a left onto South Fourth Street, to my destination. The suit is rechecked for fit and will be ready Tuesday week, as promised.

My stomach reminds me that breakfast is long past, so I catch a ride on the trolley to the Idle Hour Restaurant and Summer-Boarding House at Amelia Beach, where I know I can get a good hearty sandwich along with a tall, cold draught of lager.

I never tire of visiting my friend, George Sweeney, proprietor of the Idle Hour, who always has a tale to tell of his travels aboard the Mallory Steamship Line where he served for many years as the stevedore. Today is no exception. A number of locals and a few lingering tourists crowd the cottage when I arrive. George is spinning a tale to a rapt audience while his wife and eldest son are passing between the tables with trays laden with food and drink. Without missing a word in the story he is telling, he nods his head in my direction and points to a table in the corner. George has lived in the Jacksonville and Fernandina area for about seven or eight years and it has been only two years since he built the Idle Hour. He has made a host of friends in that short time, due to his tremendous sense of humor and generous and accommodating nature.

After placing my order, I take a long, hard pull on my cold lager. With a deep sigh of contentment I kick back and relax, letting the sound of the pounding surf lull me into peacefulness I have not known for the last couple of days.

Not realizing I have nodded off, George slaps me on the shoulder and sets my food in front of me. "Hey, John, what brings you out on a workday?" he asks, not noticing my bandaged hands.

When I sit straight up, my nose senses the delightful aroma of the roast beef sandwich. I hold my hands up for him to see. "I can't do a thing with these for a few days, so William gave me the rest of the week off," I reply. I clumsily pick up the sandwich and dive ravenously into the delicious fare: rare roast beef piled high on homemade, thick-sliced bread coated with mustard.

I order another lager to wash it down, and the dessert of the day, blackberry cobbler. "After eating all this I will have to walk back to town! But I think I will wait until my food settles and it cools off a bit. The weather has been so terribly hot this year."

"Yes, it has," replies George. "That's why we still have tourists staying over. It is too warm up north to return. I'm not complaining though, the money is good. But the wife has not been well this summer and is planning a trip to New York before the holidays. We hope the cooler weather and a family visit will set her to rights again."

"I'm sorry to hear that. Will the two of you be attending Fannie's wedding?"

"Yes, we are. Wouldn't miss it for the world." He laughs his good-natured laugh. "Well, I best be getting to work. I have been lollygagging enough for one day. It was good to see you again."

Standing up and gently shaking my hand, he heads toward the back of the room and into the kitchen, stopping to talk to first one and then another customer along the way.

When the last morsel of the best blackberry cobbler I have ever eaten enters my mouth … rests there until it melts down my throat … I regretfully stand up and take my leave. Feeling well-fed and equally well-rested, I head back into town at a leisurely pace. It being approximately a three-mile walk to the Florida House from Amelia Beach and the weather being so hot, I want to take my time.

The clatter of horses' hooves and the sound of a female voice hailing me turn my attention toward the street. The vision is dressed in a pale yellow dress, cut low as usual, with matching parasol, and her long, dark curls peek from her bonnet.

"Well, well," Katie Eppes teases, "so Miss Pauline let you off the leash today, did she?"

"I'm never on a leash," I respond too sharply. "And what are you doing out driving alone without a chaperone? It's not only bad for a lady's reputation but is not safe as well."

"If you're so worried about my safety, why don't you come ride with me?" she retorts. "Or are you afraid for your reputation? Or will little mousy Pauline be jealous?"

The challenge in her sparkling eyes almost tempts me to take her up on the offer. I have already divested myself of my jacket, and my shirt is sticking to my back as the sweat runs down it in rivulets. But I know better than to tempt the ire of my friend, T.J., in accepting, and the wagging tongues of the community at large. They are already wagging enough at his wife's escapades—even though I honestly believe they are mostly innocent. Like her offering me a ride now, in plain daylight, for all to see. Nothing to hide.

"I have just eaten a large meal at the Idle Hour and intend walking it off," I respond. "I do appreciate your kind offer." I tip my hat and start to walk again.

"Kind offer, my foot! You are drenched to the bone and have a considerable distance to go. You will have an apoplexy in this heat! If you are afraid of what people will say, then hop on the back, for goodness sake. You don't even have to converse with me. I will pretend you aren't even there." The challenge is offered.

What a predicament to be in, but I am soon relieved of any decision making upon the arrival of Doc Palmer, who is starting his evening patient rounds.

"Madam," he says to Katie as he tips his ever-present Panama hat.

Nodding to me, he motions to his buggy and I hop aboard with a feeling of relief.

"What luck, you are on my patient list for this evening. This will give us a chance to go by the office to change your bandages instead of doing it at your place. If you don't mind stopping with me at a couple of other patients' homes first?"

"Not a problem," I readily answer.

Tipping our hats to Katie, we canter off.

"You've relieved me of a very awkward situation." Looking at his grinning face, I can tell he already knows this.

"You had the look of a wet chicken being led to the block when I rode up," he says, and breaks into a hearty chuckle.

After Doc makes his rounds and rebandages my hands, he drops me off at the Florida House. Feeling restless and not at all hungry for the evening meal after such a large lunch, I decide to mosey over to the saloon for a game of cards and a few drinks with friends before retiring for the night.

The place is hopping; again, a larger than normal number of tourists for this time of year and the usual mix of sailors and locals. There is music and ladies of—well, let's say not quite ladies—is a better way of putting it. The saloon sits on the corner of Centre and Second streets, and farther down Second Street is Miss Lizzie's place. That's where gentlemen go for pleasure of another sort. Mostly sailors and out-of-towners. Higher-class gentlemen and locals prefer to take the train to Jacksonville to a more high-class establishment where the girls are prettier and cleaner, if you know what I mean. Most of Miss Lizzie's girls have been with her for quite a while and are long in the tooth. Every now and then she gets in a young, new one, but not often. They don't usually find their way to small towns.

*

But one has found her way—Mary. I can't keep my thoughts from her this night and my feet turn in the direction of Miss Lizzie's instead of home. I don't feel like I'm committing a wrong against Pauline. A man can only take so much of stolen hugs and kisses. A man has needs that cannot be fulfilled by his intended before the wedding night. Mary fulfills those needs.

A black manservant, Miss Lizzie's answer to a bodyguard, opens the door, ushering me into her presence.

"Well, well, look who returns," she says, fanning herself with her ever-present ostrich fan that some sea captain gave her many years ago. "Let me guess which of my girls you come calling on tonight." Her heavy makeup makes several more tunnels and creases around her mouth, nose and forehead when she breaks into a laugh. Bright red rouged cheeks glow brighter and the fat around her hips jiggles as she stands up adjusting her dress, bellowing up the stairs for the available girls to come.

Down they come, skimpily clad, in all shapes and sizes. Blondes, brunettes, ebony Nubians, and sassy Europeans, all eyeing me like I am on the auction block for the taking, not them.

Turning to Miss Lizzie, I query, "Where is Mary? Is she not available tonight?" My palms feel sweaty and my heart palpitates, for she is my only reason for being here.

"Of course she is, but she is the pick of the litter and only comes down if I specifically send for her. So it is her you wish again? I should have known. Angel, git back upstairs and tell Mary to make herself ready, that I am sending a gentleman up."

Miss Lizzie slaps Angel on her bottom, sending her back up the stairs while holding out a wrinkled hand to me. "And you, fine sir, that will be double the price, payable in advance if you please."

With trembling hands I willingly render the requested fee. Taking the stairs two at a time I am quickly at Mary's door.

Beckoning me into the candlelit room, she whispers, "I hoped it would be you and not some smelly sailor or that fat old businessman who sweats all over me. Where have you been so long?"

Moving over to make room for me on the bed, she never takes her eyes off my face. She slowly slides her one lacy garment off her slender shoulders, baring breasts impossibly large for such a young, nubile body.

Nipples like ripe strawberries beg to be tasted. I can hardly stand the tightness of my trousers any longer. Seeming to read my thoughts she leans forward and quickly loosens them.

Shucking trousers, shirt and shoes, I quickly taste her all over. I can't get enough. Her body feels like silk but I cannot feel her with my hands all bandaged and I am frustrated. She smells like flowers after a morning rain. I roll her over on top of me as she guides my throbbing manhood into her smooth, hot wetness. Her flowing blonde hair ripples around her face, cascading down onto my chest as she moves in rhythm back and forth. It is agony and ecstasy! The pleasure is too much and over too quickly.

Rolling over on my side, I gasp to catch my breath.

She caresses my face, smiling. "It is okay, it has been a long time. Rest while I bathe you with lavender water. Then we will take our time the second time. I guarantee you your money's worth."

And that's exactly what she does.

*

I manage to ease past the door of the Florida House before the break of dawn, and fall into a deep, dreamless sleep, totally exhausted, totally satiated.

Waking up smiling to a bright shaft of midday sunlight pouring through my window, I bound out of bed while whistling a tune. The next few days will be a round of bridal teas, bachelor parties and the likes leading up to the big day of the wedding. Pauline will be occupied with her mother and sisters and I will have a lot of idle hours on my hands, with the exception of the bachelor party.

An idea occurs to me: seize the opportunity to take a short trip up to Jekyll Island. I quickly pack an overnight bag and tell Miss Annie where

I am going, send a note to Pauline and hop aboard a steamer headed through the Cumberland Route.

The riverboat has two decks. For dancing, the captain has cleared the top deck and there is a colored band on board for that purpose. I might see if there is an attractive and willing young lady to dance a waltz or square dance with me later on. Meanwhile I am content to sit in a deck chair and watch couples stroll by arm in arm while the steamer glides effortlessly through the water.

After a brief stop at Cumberland Island to disembark passengers, we are soon on our way again and the band strikes up a square dance. The passengers are in a holiday spirit and we are soon kicking up our heels to a second set. Time flies by and soon we are at my destination.

Jekyll Island, being only seven miles long as the crow flies, is much smaller than Amelia and Cumberland islands and far less inhabited. That is why I enjoy taking short retreats here. Rumor has it that several millionaires from up north are looking at buying property here and building winter homes, just like the Carnegies are doing on Cumberland. Well-known names like Vanderbilt, Goodyear, Macy, Pulitzer, Gould, Whitney, and Crane. But so far nothing has developed. We will have to wait and see. In the meantime I will continue coming to my favorite little boardinghouse by the wharf, do some fishing and hunting (wild game is in abundance) and while away my time in total relaxation.

Sunday, the day of my departure, has come all too fast. I have not fished nor hunted this trip, just rested and read. My hands have healed well enough for me to return to work tomorrow and, to be truthful, I am ready for my regular schedule again. With only slightly more than a week to go until Fannie's wedding, I won't be seeing much of Pauline until it's all over—except at the various social events. We will have little if any private time together. If this is what we have to look forward to, I shall suggest we elope when it comes our turn. What with the caterers, florist, dressmakers, minister, invitations and the list goes on and on! Oh yes, let's don't forget the house hunting, furniture and so forth. It all gives me a massive headache! But alas, I'm sure her parents won't hear of it. The size of this wedding is nothing to compare to the wedding of Pauline's eldest sister, Mary Ruth, to Frank Waas three years ago. Held at the Methodist church with a party at her parents' home afterwards, it was a huge social event! Fannie wanted a smaller, more intimate affair, but it seems to me it keeps expanding by the day. Me? I just stay out of the way! Do what I am bid, when I am bid.

Arriving at my domicile I find a note from Pauline to join her at Fred Lohman's for a late supper of his famous clam chowder, so I hurry to freshen up and head over there.

"You should not be out so late by yourself," I admonish as I slip into a chair opposite her in the quiet and cozy establishment. Even though I must admit I am excited to see her, and all alone to boot.

"Aren't you glad to see me?" She gives me a pouting look. "You have been gone for days while I have been stuck here running errands here and there for Fannie. I have missed you terribly."

We linger over the clam chowder and hot tea, catching up on the last few days, trying to avoid the topic of the wedding, until finally I tell her we must go. The hour is far too late for us to be out alone without a chaperone. I do not want to compromise her reputation. Luckily we don't pass anyone else on the short walk to her house. I give her a quick kiss on the cheek, spin her around toward the door and wait until I see her safely inside. The things I most admire about Pauline are her spunk—like coming out tonight—her intelligence and her beauty. Life with her will be anything but boring!

Sleep soon overtakes me, for it has been a busy day. I drift off thinking about returning to work tomorrow and also the excitement of the next evening's bachelor party. We will be heading to Jacksonville by train on a private dining car. The entertainment of the evening is a surprise. Not even the groom knows what's in store for him on his last night as a single man.

*

Well, it is Tuesday, day of the wedding.

The party? We were all sworn to secrecy as soon as we boarded the train. As much as I would like to share with you the wondrous bachelor party, alas, I cannot. At another opportunity to make a similar trip I will take you, the reader, along with me. But a gentleman's word is his honor and cannot be broken. Let's just say it was a night to be remembered by all.

My new suit was delivered yesterday and fits like a glove. An hour before the wedding I admire myself as best I can in the small bureau mirror in my room … turning first this way, then that way trying to get a full look. Miss Annie has a pier mirror in her room. I will ask if I can use it for a final look prior to leaving. I splash on a tad more cologne, run the comb through my hair, don my coat and head downstairs.

Miss Annie is obliging and leans against the doorway admiringly as I stare in awe at my reflection in her seven-foot-tall marble-based pier mirror.

"My, my," she says, "you will outshine the groom himself in that suit."

Setting my hat at an angle on my head, I give her a hug and squeeze and out the door to the Presbyterian church I go. I have waited until the utmost last moment to dress so I would not have to sit down and take the chance of wrinkles in the lingering, oppressive heat. It takes but a few minutes to walk the five blocks and I am soon inside the cool interior of the church, which is already almost filled to capacity. The soft organ music combined with the pleasant fragrance of bridal flowers, which decorate the pews and altar, set the scene for the arrival of the happy pair.

As the organist begins the wedding march, Reverend Yerger takes his place at the altar and the wedding party starts down the aisle. Beginning with the matron of honor, Mary Ruth Meddaugh Waas, then my Pauline and Fannie's other sisters as bridesmaids, all look gorgeous in matching dresses. The groom, Hugh Boring, and his man of honor are waiting up front, none the worse for wear from last night, that I can see. Everyone stands as Fannie walks in on the arm of her father. She is dressed in a flowing, princess-shaped satin gown with bits of gold woven through. She is so extraordinarily beautiful it takes your breath away. She seems to float down the aisle toward her beloved. As her father hands her to him, the look on their faces when they turn toward each other is a joy to behold. The wedding vows and prayers are soon said, the music begins and the newlywed couple, clasping hands, is facing us, coming down the aisle starting their lives together. What will their future hold? It is both a solemn and joyous time.

The wedding party and guests adjourn to the Meddaugh home one block down Sixth Street for the reception. The photographer is taking photos, so I have to wait for Pauline to arrive from the church. We find an abundance of food, punch, champagne and bridal cake. Waas Bakers prepared the wedding cake and other confections, and if they are as good to eat as they are in display, the guests will be well pleased.

I must say it is a *Harper's Weekly* style wedding, without a doubt. All the preparations were not in vain! From the invitations engraved on notepaper with the smaller card enclosed for the at-home reception following the wedding, to the wedding gown and bridesmaids' dresses.

Yes, the groom is handsome and stylish in his black Prince Albert frock coat, gray trousers, pearl waistcoat cut high, high collar with a white linen shirt, red cravat and plain gold scarf pin. He is wearing a stovepipe hat and carrying a pair of gray gloves. No gentleman, from the groom to the usher, is to wear his gloves. Just ask *Harper's Weekly*!

Making an entrance with Pauline are two of her sister's friends from New York who, to my astonishment, are sporting the new style that is all the rage in England, of cropping the hair all over the head. The hair is then formed into little loose rings, which look charming on some younger teen girls, but I must say not on many older ladies. I pray Pauline does not crop off her luxuriant tresses in favor of the present fashion mode.

After introductions are made, Pauline is able to break away and we slip outside to enjoy our champagne and cake. We rock gently on the front porch swing, nodding pleasantly to guests as they enter and depart. It is a relief to feel stirrings of an evening breeze slipping in from the river.

"I am so happy for Fannie but I am going to miss her terribly," she says, and sighs against my cheek. "We made an Indian promise when we were little girls never to marry, to always be together. We pricked our fingers with one of Mama's sewing needles to seal the oath," she laughingly recalls. "I know it was a silly child's thing and could not be kept. But still I will miss having her around every day. She and I are closer than the other two. She made a solemn promise to me last night that if she has a little girl she will name her Pauline, after me."

I am thinking I will be glad to have Pauline to myself for a while, but Pauline's next words cause my heart to fall.

"Mama is booking passage for us to New York soon. She says she needs a rest from all the hustle and bustle of the wedding. Mrs. Sweeney is still feeling poorly and is also leaving in a week or two for her health. Did you see how pale she was at the church today? Mr. Sweeney had to take her straight home after the ceremony."

On and on she prattles about first one thing, then another, as the night comes to an end and I must take my leave. The newlyweds have been long sent on their blissful way.

"Come, walk with me, Pauline. I have sat far too long and my legs need stretching."

When I return from the house with her wrap, we set out toward the harbor. The town is still bustling. People passing us in buggies laugh and call out good wishes for Fannie, and ask about the wedding. Grabbing Pauline's hand I turn down Third Street at a fast pace, going toward St.

Michael's Church. Our destination is the gazebo and solitude, away from prying eyes and ears.

"I've never seen you look lovelier than today," I whisper softly as I pull her close into my arms. "Your eyes sparkle like the stars and your hair shines like the full moon on the inlet at night. All day I have been aching to hold you like this."

Drawing her closer, I lightly kiss each arched eyebrow, down each cheek and along her pulsing temples. Her head drops onto my shoulder, full lips part slightly for my mouth to take and I do. At first lightly tasting her like the sweet nectar from a flower, and then a raging hunger takes control and I pull her down onto my lap, nestling her closer, tasting her hungrily. I touch her smooth arms where her shawl has fallen away. Moaning softly, she fervently returns kiss for kiss, turning to cup my face in her cool, soft hands. Moving my hands up her arms I venture farther than ever before, across her rapidly rising and falling breasts, her moans urging me on. The mood of the wedding and the champagne, the starlit night coupled with our love for one another, all have carried us to a level of passion we have never been to before. I know we must stop but I want to go on and on touching and kissing her.

All of a sudden we are startled out of our embrace by the sound of approaching voices. Another couple has the same spot in mind and makes the decision for us. Hurriedly, Pauline stands, grabs her fallen shawl from the gazebo floor, straightens her tousled hair and we hastily make our departure.

Under the streetlamp I can see her cheeks are still flushed from our ardent lovemaking. "I cannot walk you home in your present condition. Let's go down to the waterfront," I tell her. "The night breeze will cool us both down. At least on an outwardly appearance."

In full view of the public while walking down Centre Street, we do not hold hands. We are the utmost of proper etiquette.

After we settle ourselves on a bench at the waterfront, Pauline turns to me with a mischievous smile on her face and says, "Promise me you won't tell any of your friends what Fannie and we girls did last night while you were at the bachelor party, and I will tell you. It was crazy … and a little scary."

With my interest piqued I make her the promise and she proceeds to tell me the most interesting of tales of witchcraft and fortune telling I have ever heard!

Seems the girls decided to go to Old Town to have their fortunes told by an old voodoo priestess, a descendent of the Famous Felippa who it is claimed for many years practiced black magic, healed the sick, made love potions and supposedly caused bad things to happen to evil people.

The young ladies slipped out of the house and arrived for their midnight appointment at a tiny hovel with what looked like an herb garden off to one side. After stepping into the house, they could not see much because the only light came from a low-lit fireplace, which had a big iron pot with something that stank very badly boiling in it. The old woman motioned them to come forward and they almost bolted back out the door when they were able to see her better. She was dressed in what appeared to be cast-off rags trailing to the earthen floor and her hair was a greasy mixture of gray and black.

"Her face was almost as black as the pot in the fireplace … her high cheekbones and black eyes seemed to see right through you. But kind of hooded, like the old crones and witches you see in drawings of Halloween. Her skin was leathery and wrinkled like old parchment paper, but the color was dark like mahogany. I almost expected it to crackle when she moved," Pauline said. "There's no guessing her age, she could be a hundred and she could be Felippa still alive after all these years!

"Fannie was first. The hag poured some powder in a cup, stirred in liquid from the pot in the fireplace and bade her to drink it. You should have seen Fannie's face. It was awful! Then the old woman drew a bag from around her neck and tossed something that looked like bones and rocks on the table, mumbled in a strange language and looked at the palms of Fannie's hands."

"Well, what did she tell her?" I asked—not that I believe in all that nonsense.

"She said, 'You will marry the morrow' (which everyone knows) 'and you will have four children, one girl you will name after your sister, Pauline, one son you will name after your husband. You will travel and live in another state. You will become a widow and not remarry.' "

Tears well up in Pauline's eyes and her voice begins to quiver as she continues her story.

"Isn't that an awful thing to say to a bride on the eve of her wedding! I wish we had never gone there. But Fannie laughed it off. She said it was just guesswork, to make money. You'd think the witch would have something romantic to tell a bride on the eve of her wedding. Surely she earns more money that way!"

"What about you? Did you have your fortune told?" I tease her.

"Yes. I did not want to," she hesitantly answers, "but Fannie insisted we all do it in the spirit of the evening." I drank the same old nasty brew and she told me that I would marry handsome you and have lovely children and live happily ever after."

(Which was not the truth, but my darling did not want to tell me that the old crone saw a different future for Pauline that did not include me. This would all come out later, much later.)

"Well, I'm glad everything turned out all right from your midnight lark. You should have gotten a love potion while you were there for my friend C.A., for I think that's his only hope to finding true love."

Poking me in the ribs for making fun, Pauline turns in my arms, gives me a pretend slap on the face and starts off for home at a fast walk.

"You should not make fun of such things," she retorts over her shoulder as I try to keep up. "Do you know that voodoo is still practiced in Old Town to this day?" She stops to catch her breath beside the huge oak tree in front of Judge Friend's house. "Just like we go to church on

Wednesday and Sunday and special holidays, so do the voodoo cult. People in Old Town are afraid to venture out on the full moon." She whispers in my ear of blood sacrifices not only of animals but also of humans, dancing and chanting, rituals in unknown tongues and placing unspeakable curses against enemies.

"Come on, Pauline, you can't really believe in these things."

Looking her straight in the eyes I can see the fear lurking there. I damn her sister for taking her there last night. Not caring who might see, I pull her close to me, feeling her heart beating rapidly against my chest. I know that indeed she does believe. Stroking her arms I continue to hold her until her heartbeat and breathing slow to a normal rhythm.

"Pauline, I too have heard stories of Felippa the voodoo priestess of years ago. Only those who had reason to fear feared her. She was also respected for the good she did in the community. She was an excellent midwife, attending most births and making them as painless as possible. She saved the lives of many mothers and babies. Haven't you heard how she worked tirelessly during the malarial epidemic? This woman you went to see last night was just some old fortune-teller who makes a living palm reading and pretending to see the future. It was all a ruse. Felippa lived here in the late 1700s and early 1800s, and has not been heard about since around 1817, according to what Miss Annie has told me."

I can see color creeping back into Pauline's cheeks as she peeks up at me from under dark eyelashes and smiles a timid smile.

"Oh, you must think I'm a fool to be taken in so easily, but if you had been there I think you might have been, as well."

"I have no doubt, my dear, you may be correct, but I have no intention of putting it to the test. I shall leave our future up to our own making on a daily basis. I like the pleasure of your spontaneous little surprises. Remember the gazebo?"

Tilting her face up with my left hand under her chin, I quickly cast a glance around to see if anyone is about before I plant a firm kiss on her trembling lips. "There, isn't that better? Now let's get you home before your father calls me out on a duel for ruining your reputation, or your mother has the vapors because she has to plan another wedding before she wants to!"

The rest of the walk home is in companionable silence and needless to say, Pauline's father's presence is evident by the red glow of his cigar as we approach the house. Bidding Pauline good night, I settle in the adjacent rocker to her father and light up my own Havana.

I hold James Meddaugh in the highest of esteem and the utmost of respect. A merchant by trade, at the age of thirty-six he moved his family to Fernandina in 1862 from St. Augustine, accepting at that time the position of Nassau River Inspector of Customs. Since then he has established his own grocer business, is one of our most prominent citizens and is also the tax collector.

Hard-working and industrious, born in New York of immigrant parents, he has determined that his daughters be as well educated as his sons Fredrick and Charles. He intends the girls to be able to survive in a man's world.

Besides being involved in civic affairs, he is devoted to his six children and wife. He also has a generous nature and kind heart.

Small talk eventually leads us to the subject of my and Pauline's relationship and much to my surprise he is not as eager as I had thought on a wedding anytime in the near future.

"You have to understand," he says while standing to lean against the stair rail, "this in no means is a slight against you. It's just that Frances and I feel that Pauline needs to further her education. After all, she is merely sixteen. She will be journeying to New York next month and will possibly remain there for the school year."

Taken totally by surprise, I rise so quickly from my rocker it knocks against the wall and my cigar falls from my hand. "But sir, hasn't Pauline a say in the matter? We love each other very much, and of course we will respect your wishes but we do not wish to be separated! The St. Joseph's Academy for Girls here takes day students, and offers, as you well know, exceptional instruction for young women, including French and sewing."

"We have taken the academy into consideration, but feel that not only does it not offer the type education we wish for Pauline, we also wish for her to spend more time with my relatives in New York. She will be returning home for holidays and the next two years will go swiftly, mark my words. True love will bear the course."

After he bids me good night I stare mutely at the closed door. Heart and legs of lead won't let me leave the porch.

"Psst, psst," I hear coming from the side of the house.

Stepping down, I see Pauline crouching in the shadows.

"What are you doing out here, sneaking around in the dark, eavesdropping on conversations?"

"They can't do this to us, they just can't!" she says, beating her fists against my shoulders. She looks up at me. "Let's run away! Elope to St. Marys, Georgia. We can get married and they can't do anything about it!"

"Calm down, Pauline. I don't like this any more than you do, but we have to think logically, not with our emotions. You know we were going to wait a year anyway, so two years won't be so bad. Not really, will it?"

Holding her close against me, I stroke her long, silky hair that has been brushed the required one hundred strokes, part of the evening's preparation for bed. She smells so nice. It's difficult to think of a long separation when each daily parting is painful as it is.

"I know, but to go to New York to school, so far away from you is the part I don't care for—and I don't like New York. It's cold and dreary, not sunny and warm like here, and the people are not, well, let's just say they are not like here. Besides, who will help Mama with little Sophie? Or are they sending her too? Oh, it's just too much to think about! They have ruined a perfectly beautiful day."

"Pauline, you must not work yourself up so. You have to go in before they come looking for you and find you out here in your nightshirt in the middle of the night! Things will look better after a good night's sleep, I promise. I will call for you tomorrow at seven o'clock and we will talk further."

For all my attempts to console Pauline, my feet are dragging the six long blocks home.

Whatever will I do all these long months without seeing her smiling face, hearing her laughter, holding her, kissing her, sparring with her over various and sundry subjects that cross her sharp mind? Not only is she my sweetheart, she is also my friend. We do so many things together.

Apparently that's what her parents fear; we are spending far too much time together. Pauline is independent, mainly to the credit of her father, and good girl that she is, she is similar to Katie Eppes in the dislike of Victorian rules governing women of today. Such as chaperones when we are out for a Sunday ride or walking at the beach.

We have freely flaunted the rules of society too often and it has caught up with us in the worst possible way. Well, maybe not the worst; they could have sent her to school in Europe.

Lost in thought, I almost am run over by a buggy careening sharply and turning the corner on two wheels, driven by Louis Horsey, his coattails flapping behind him like a madman. Clinging on tightly to the back, bouncing up and down, eyes round as saucers, is a little black boy of about eight years or so.

Startled to see me, Louis jerks back on the reins, almost losing control of the horse that is foaming at the mouth from the midnight race.

"Hurry, hop on, there has been an accident at the rail yard and I am delivering some morphine to Doc!"

I swing onto the buggy seat beside him and we speed away. Louis explains that Doc had sent little Moses, now clinging perilously to the back of the buggy, to awaken him to bring morphine from the pharmacy to the accident scene of a railroad employee who has been crushed after falling between two trains.

Upon our arrival Louis jumps down and immediately begins to assist Doc while I vault toward the nearest bushes to vomit. God, what a mess his legs are in! There is blood everywhere! Moses is standing beside the screaming man, holding his hand. The boy's eyes are still wide in an ashen face and he says not a word. It dawns upon me this is his father. Heaven forbid the child should see such a thing! He had come to walk home with him after his shift.

Finally, after what seems like hours, they have the blood and pain abated enough to transport him to Doc's office. Louis and I help load him onto Doc's buggy and follow to help.

Hours of surgery are needed to remove one leg and stitch up the other. It has been a long night indeed.

We watch dawn creep slowly over the horizon. The three of us sit exhausted on Doc's front porch drinking coffee, smoking cigars and talking quietly.

Louis is telling Doc that he has decided to become an M.D., just like him, and has been accepted at the South Carolina Medical College in Charleston, South Carolina. "I will be leaving sometime within the next two weeks and plan to study straight through, including summers," he says. "Mother and sister Julia will remain here, of course, as Mother has the boardinghouse to run. As for the drugstore, it will run just fine with the employees on hand and I will return periodically to check in on things."

I see the excitement in his eyes and hear it in his voice as he talks about his plans. I leave him and Doc to the medical talk, and head home to catch a couple hours of sleep and a bath before starting my workday.

Upon arriving at work I am reminded by my boss, Mr. Wood, of the council meeting this evening, and hurriedly write a note to be sent around to Pauline to postpone our meeting to Friday night, since council meetings tend to be long, drawn-out affairs.

Another long night is in store for me; I will be ready for a good night's sleep, for sure, I muse. Looking up, to my surprise, in marches Pauline with a look of doom on her pretty face.

It is a rare occasion for her to visit my office. Fearing something is amiss I hurriedly stand to greet her, but she gives me no chance to offer her a seat before dropping down in a very unladylike manner on the horsehair sofa facing my desk.

"Mama is home packing trunks right this minute, readying us to depart on the *State of Texas* on Sunday!" She is shouting loud enough for everyone in the building to hear. "Three days from today I will be gone! I just can't believe it! I won't do it, I won't!"

She now sobs uncontrollably and, as if struck by lightning, I can only stare dumfounded at her.

I offer her my handkerchief and make a space to sit beside her. Finally her sobs subside enough to tell me—between hiccups and wiping tears away—the morning's events. Seems the *State of Texas* arrived early this morning and will unload its cargo, restock cargo and essentials for passengers and set sail again on Sunday for New York. The passenger list will include Pauline, Sophie, and Mrs. Meddaugh, as well as Mrs. Sweeney.

Pauline has confronted her parents but her pleas went unheeded.

"Listen, sweetheart, I don't like this any more than you do, but temper tantrums won't get us anywhere. We must show maturity in the face of our despair. It is now the end of September. You will be back home for the holidays in just a few months, and before you know it the spring break and then summer will come around. Don't you see how quickly this will pass?"

Rising, I pace back and forth trying to think of what to say to ease her fear of our impending separation that looms so soon it gives neither of us a chance of a clear thought.

Kneeling down beside her, I say, "Louis Horsey is leaving in a week or two to study in Charleston at South Carolina Medical College. If I can arrange things, I will go with him when he leaves. I have never been to Charleston. Then if it is permissible with your parents, I will journey on to New York for a quick visit to see how you have settled in. What do you say? Does that make you feel better?"

She tilts her tear-streaked face up and I see a slight smile begin to form at the corners of her mouth.

"My darling John, would you really come all the way to New York to see me?" She quivers, throwing her arms around my neck and at the same time throwing all decorum to the wind. She plants a sweet-salty kiss on my lips.

"I would not say it if I did not mean it, Pauline, my love. Of course I will. Now go home and help your mother pack. I will call on you tomorrow night as planned. Remember, I love you no matter the distance between us. Time and distance will only serve to make our love stronger."

After she departs, I lower my head onto the stack of invoices awaiting attention for tonight's council meeting. I feel exhausted from lack of sleep and the emotional pain due to our upcoming separation.

Slowly I begin the tedious job of listing items neatly in the ledger. Salaries for November for approval to be paid for the police officers, for city marshal, for Acting Mayor Suhrer; coffin and burial for a pauper provided by Mr. R. M. Henderson; and other sundry items of business to be covered during the meeting. Setting the report aside for the ink to dry, I decide to head home for one of Miss Annie's delicious dinners and a quick afternoon nap to refresh myself, or I won't make it through the evening.

Miss Annie's eleven-year-old daughter, Gracie, is helping serve the noonday meal. She is a vivacious and friendly child and I always enjoy her company. Her topic of conversation today is the upcoming opening of the new school year, her new pair of shoes bought this morning at J. H. Prescott's, a new dress and books for the event.

I calm her fears about the new principal, my friend C. A. Key. She already adores Miss Helen Dozier, who will be his assistant. Gracie chatters on about other things as she serves food and refills our coffee. The meal passes by in a soothing family atmosphere that I miss so acutely at times.

I have been invited on numerous occasions to the house of Miss Annie's sister, Marie, on West Ash Street, for family celebrations of one sort or another. Soon it will be to Gracie's Holy Communion. Plans are already in the making as her twelfth birthday nears.

Marie's husband, Joseph Higgins, is a blacksmith by trade. Strong and muscular, he always wins at arm wrestling and lager drinking. I can attest to that!

They have an unspoken Irish-Catholic family code of love and honor that binds them and their friends together through the storms of life as well as the calm seas.

Chapter 4

1883

The Year Ends

Sunday is here all too soon. I have been invited to afternoon tea after church. The whole family, friends and neighbors are gathering to bid farewell to Mrs. Meddaugh, Pauline and Sophie.

It is a festive affair. Dainty pastries provided by Frank Waas Bakery are on hand as well as several kinds of sandwiches, champagne, tea and punch.

Everything tastes like sawdust in my mouth as I nod and talk to first one person, then another. In only four hours the ship will sail and Pauline will be gone for months.

Putting a smile on my face, I reach for her empty plate, set it on the buffet table and hurry her out the back door.

"What do you think you're doing?" She laughs at me, obviously having had too much champagne for teatime.

"You know full well what I'm doing," I say as I lead her behind the kitchen building, which stands a safe distance from the house. "Stockpiling kisses and hugs until we see each other again. I can't get enough of the way you feel in my arms."

"Didn't you get enough last night in the gazebo?" she asks while wrapping her slender arms around my waist, pulling me too close for comfort in broad daylight.

"Pauline," I groan, "stop before I lose my sanity."

"Well, I'm not the one who drug you out here and started kissing you and touching you, now am I?" She steps back, straightening her hair, looking all innocent like a cat licking cream.

"Come," I say, "let's sit on the back porch for a while and talk about our plans for the holidays. Your father says you will not be coming home for Thanksgiving; he will be going up there instead. That means it will be two and a half months before you return for Christmas. If I go with Louis to Charleston in two weeks, spend a week there and journey on to New York, it will be approximately three weeks before we see each other again. Also, I will not be able to stay very long due to my work here."

We are so deeply involved with each other and our plans that we don't hear the door open or realize the presence of a third party until Mr. Meddaugh clears his throat loudly.

"Go inside, Pauline, I need to have a word or two with this young man." The stern tone of his voice leaves no room for argument from either of us.

"There will be no visit from you to New York in three weeks' time. Don't you see that will only make her more miserable and the adjustment harder?" His voice is just under a shout, barely within a controlled rage. I have never seen him like this before.

"If you love my daughter as much as you say you do, then you will abide by my wishes." Turning on his heel he leaves me standing there, mouth agape, as he firmly closes the door behind him.

This leaves me no alternative but to saunter off in the direction of the shipyard to await Pauline's arrival for boarding the *State of Texas*.

My mind is in a quandary as to Mr. Meddaugh's change in attitude toward the relationship ... or is it me he has the problem with?

Backtracking, I stop to pick an exquisite *Camellia japonica* from the heavily-laden bush in Naylor Thompson's garden on Seventh Street, and as soon as I spy the carriage carrying the Meddaugh women I rush over to help them alight, and put the flower in Pauline's hair. Her tearstained face brightens up at the sight of the flower and me.

"I knew you would be here!" she exclaims, throwing her arms around my neck and not caring who is looking.

"Papa is being so mean and Mama is not speaking to me. The way they're acting, you would think I have committed a criminal act or disgraced the family beyond repair, when all I have done is show my bloomers and ankles at the beach and gone fishing without a chaperone. Oh, I am so mad I could just spit!"

Her temper is soaring to the point of an erupting volcano, eyes narrowing to steely slits, face as red as the tomatoes in Doc's summer garden. She can hardly get the words out without actually spitting.

"Hold on now, Pauline, we'll get this all ironed out. I plan to have a man-to-man with your father. There has to be a reasonable explanation for all this. I understand your parents wanting us to wait a couple of years, but I don't understand sending you away to school and not allowing me to visit New York, with the exception, of course, of allowing you time to settle in. Christmas will be here before you know it and I have a very nice surprise for you to come home to. Write every day and I will also." I whisper in her ear, "Remember the gazebo," which makes her face flush.

Giving her a hug and a kiss, totally disregarding her disapproving, glowering and tut-tutting mother, I usher Pauline onto the gangplank of the *State of Texas*.

"Mrs. Meddaugh," I say as I also escort her and Sophie onto the gangplank, "I wish to make my apologies for whatever it is I may have done to have caused you and your husband any concern or distress over my and Pauline's relationship."

Pauline's mother turns slowly toward me and I am surprised to see a tear in her eye.

Placing her hand on my shoulder, tilting her parasol back to better see my face, she imparts these words: "When I was a young girl growing up in the Bahamas, I was very much like Pauline. Running all over the island with my native friends, boating and fishing until I was as brown as they were. It was hard for my mother to even get me to wear shoes. ..." She laughs at the remembrance. "I also remember how difficult it was for me when my parents sent me away to school. This has nothing to do with you. These next two years will make Pauline a more refined young woman and in turn a better wife. You will see."

A more refined young woman ... hmm ... I don't know about that. I just hope this supposed refinement does not dim Pauline's spirit that I love so much.

These thoughts are on my mind as I stand waving to Pauline as long as I can see the ship sail out onto the horizon.

Louis is waiting for me at the drugstore as we had agreed. He is dressed as usual, in his white linen suit, with Panama hat on his head. At the ripe old age of twenty-seven, Louis is one of Fernandina's most eligible bachelors. There is not a female of marriageable age within two hundred miles who has not been brought into Louis's company by her mother via some scheme or another. But alas, Louis still finds sole comfort in his family business, Horsey & Company Drug Store, and now his interest in becoming a doctor.

"If your face gets any longer you will be walking all over it with your boots," he says to me as I enter the store.

But seeing as how I'm not amused at his attempt to cheer me up, he comes around the counter, throws an arm around my shoulder and gives me a pat on the back.

"Come on, let's get out of here. I was ready to lock up as soon you came in, hat on and all. Let's go down to the saloon and have a drink, make plans for the trip to Charleston. We have a lot to do in only a few days. You aren't going to have much time to think of anything else."

He pulls a handkerchief from his pants pocket and wipes his brow, saying, "I can't believe how hot it has been for this time of year. The thermometer at the drugstore read eighty-two yesterday and eighty-eight today! Still, that's cooler than last week's ninety-degree weather and we really can't complain. I heard from a good source that out in Arizona Territory the thermometer ran up to 118 in the shade last week!"

On and on he talks about first one thing and then another, trying to take my mind off Pauline as we make our way to the saloon.

After we enter through the swinging doors, it takes a few moments for our eyes to adjust to the dim interior. The music and laughter are loud as usual. The crowd also is the normal mix of tourists lingering on at the hotels, locals and sailors. A card game is going on in the back corner and one of the players does not look particularly happy. Trouble could be forthcoming, but Bart the bouncer appears to have an eye on the situation.

Threading our way among the crowd we reach the bar, order two lagers and then head to a table in the front corner where we can talk and watch the action, one of our favorite pastimes.

We have spent many an evening at this very table. It is our private ringside seat to fights over women, cards and booze. We have seen barmaids catfighting over men, cursing like sailors, hair pulling, dresses flying.

Now, don't get me wrong. The saloon is not as bad as it sounds, but it can get that way and when it does, it's best to be out of the way watching, not in the middle of the action.

Dispensing of the first lager in our usual quick manner, we order another to nurse along as we sit companionably making plans for our trip.

"Come, let's go to my house for some cold supper," Louis offers. He rises and stretches after an hour of sitting. There has been no untoward action in the saloon this night. "Mother and Julia promised to prepare something for us before leaving for evening church services."

The thought of Mrs. Horsey's southern cooking makes my stomach grumble in anticipation and I readily agree to the invitation.

After enjoying a repast of palate-pleasing delight, and excited about our plans, I bid Louis good night and head home for some much-needed sleep.

The days roll by in a rush of work and personal matters to be taken care of. An incident of extreme sadness affecting all of us took place on Thursday morning with the sudden death of Julian Acosta.

Today's *Florida Mirror* (October 6) writes this about our friend:

Julian J. Acosta

SUDDEN DEATH OF ONE OF
FERNANDINA'S OLD CITIZENS

Mr. J. J. Acosta died suddenly at his residence on Third Street, on Thursday morning last, of congestion of the lungs. He had not been feeling well for several days, but was not considered dangerously ill either by his family or by the physician who had been called in to attend to him. In fact, on the morning of his death he felt so well that he proposed to go to his office, but yielded to the solicitations of his wife and remained at home. He died suddenly, with little warning, at about half-past ten o'clock.

Julian J. Acosta was born at Old Town, on this island on February 15, 1834, and was consequently one of the oldest resident citizens. He was engaged here in merchandizing when the war broke out. Joining Company I of the Eighth Regiment of Florida Volunteers, Confederate Army, he was made first lieutenant, and during the greater part of the hostilities was in command of the company, and frequently acted as adjutant of the regiment. His gallant conduct and genial ways won for him the love and esteem of his comrades. He was never known to be missing at his post, especially in a fight. Mr. Acosta went through numerous engagements, notably the battles of the Second Manassas, Sharpsburg, First Fredericksburg (where he was slightly wounded), Chancellorsville and Gettysburg, and participated in all the fights around Petersburg, surrendering with the army. After the close of the war he returned to his native city, where he has resided ever since. He was appointed by the Governor to be inspector of lumber and timber for this county, which position he has creditably filled up to the time of his death. In performance of the duties pertaining to this office, he was necessarily compelled to expose himself to all kinds of weather, and it is believed that the exposure, recently to the hot rays of the sun, was the primeval cause of his death. He was as good a citizen as he had proved himself a soldier. Generous to a fault, genial and social, he made hosts of friends. He was elected to fill several responsible positions in the city government, but of late years he had confined himself solely to his business.

Mr. Acosta was a devout adherent to the Catholic faith, and a loving and affectionate husband and father. His death in the prime of life will not only prove a sad and irreparable loss to his bereaved family but will be felt by the entire community. He leaves a wife and five children.

The funeral took place last night at half-past five o'clock from the Catholic church, and was largely attended by numerous friends of the deceased.

Louis and I set sail under a cloud of sadness for the loss of our friend and mentor. Julian had never been too busy to take time out to help with a problem or just to pass the time of day.

Standing on deck looking back at the receding harbor of Fernandina, I feel an unusual mixture of emotions. This is the first time I have actually left on a trip, other than to Jekyll or Cumberland islands, since I moved here after the war.

Louis's description of the city of his birth and the sorrows due to the destruction from the bombardment of war, as well as praises to the belle of the South for her rapid rise from the ashes, are overwhelming. I can hardly wait to arrive.

Soon the coastline is lost from sight and the gentle swells of the ocean along with a slight northerly breeze push us rapidly toward our destination. One of our stops is Savannah, Georgia, where we disembark for a quick tour and repast at an Irish tavern while the ship takes on new passengers and cargo. The cobblestone streets along the waterfront remind Louis of Charleston's Battery, and he is even more excited to get there to show me the sights.

Arriving in Charleston on a crisp, bright morning, we hurriedly unload our baggage and Louis's trunk of books. After negotiating with a strong young Negro to carry the trunk, we head off in the direction of the college.

"I have obtained board downtown near the college for a mere four dollars per week, and a room for you as well for your stay," Louis says as we walk the narrow streets, getting our land legs back. Not an easy task after days at sea, for landlubbers like us.

Looking around me I am truly amazed at the beauty of the city, the size and style of the homes and the obvious absence of immediate telltale signs of the recent war.

But as we walk along, Louis points out the signs an ordinary person would overlook, such as indentations caused by mortar fire to chimneys and brick structures. He says, "Along the Battery wall there are still cannon and mortar shells left in the wall!" He looks over his shoulder at our young fellow walking a safe distance behind. So he does not overhear our conversation, Louis whispers, "Did you know that the first Union troops in Charleston were black? It was a terrible time for Charleston, what with the fires and looting by draft dodgers and deserters. Why, the mayor was actually glad for the Union Army to take over to put an end to it all."

Our conversation comes to a halt when we reach our destination, a charming row house, which we enter through an ornate iron gate and side garden complete with manicured beds and fountain.

Responding to our knock on a brass knocker of pineapple design is a rotund black maid outfitted in a gray dress and stiffly starched white apron and cap. Her demeanor is that of all southerners whether they are servant or master, warm and friendly from beginning to end—you can bet your mama's Bible on it.

Wiping her hands on the dishcloth she is holding, she directs us into the front parlor to await the proprietor while our paid lackey is ordered to the back servants' stairs to dispense of our baggage and Louis's books.

Seating myself in a comfortable chair facing an ornate marble fireplace, I cannot help but speak highly to Louis for his temporary quarters during his next three years at school. "I am impressed, old man," I say with a groan of pleasure as I sink deeper into the chair. The walk from the harbor was a little farther than I had anticipated and my new boots have my feet aching to be released.

"Please, stay seated," we are instructed as Louis's landlady enters carrying a tray of assorted biscuits, followed by the maid with a tray of hot tea.

"This should hold you over until supper at six o'clock." Smiling, she passes around the tea and biscuits. Diminutive in height, with gray hair piled high on her head in the current fashion, she is a pleasant woman of approximately sixty or so years of age. Widowed in the war and the mother of three daughters, she was forced to take in boarders in order to maintain her home.

"My boarders are mainly medical students at the Medical College of South Carolina or interns at City Hospital. I delight in their intelligence and drive. Somehow I feel like I am contributing in some small way by providing a decent home and meals while they are studying so hard." She speaks with a twinkle in her kind eyes. "The majority of my boarders keep in touch with me long after they have gone on to their medical or pharmacy practices."

Standing, she walks around the room pointing with pride to several photographs arranged on tables and on the fireplace of individuals and families. "These are all former boarders of mine and I must say I am mighty proud of each and every one of them.

"Now, I know you gentlemen are in want of a nice hot bath, some rest and change of clothes before supper. Maum Hannah, who has been with me since I was a newlywed bride to the late Major, has the bath ready and will see you to your rooms. Anything you need, just ask her and she will see to it."

Right on cue, the same servant who answered the door appears to show us to our rooms upstairs, which we find to be very light and airy and more than adequate.

The bath down the hall is equipped with a large claw-foot tub, shaving mirror and clothes tree. A young maid is adding the last bucket of steaming water, and she then lays out white fluffy towels for our use. Heaven, simply heaven, I think as I slide into the almost scalding water. My aching calves and feet sing praises for their slow loosening of tight tendons and sore arches.

As I shave and Louis bathes, we make plans for the next day's tour of the city. Tonight we will relax with a smoke and a toddy after supper, on our hostess' side porch which overlooks her delightful garden, and call it an early night.

Which is exactly all we are able to do after a gargantuan meal of fish chowder, shrimp and grits, fried chicken, collard greens, apple pie and coffee.

"Louis, my friend, if you eat like this for the next three years you will be double your size by the time you return to Fernandina," I chide him.

We sit with our feet propped up on the porch rail, enjoying our cigars.

"Don't worry," he says, laughing, "with walking to school and back every day and all the long hours of studying, there's not a chance of my putting on any weight. If anything, I will lose weight. The courses are arduous and long, such as Surgery, Anatomy, Gynaecology, Obstetrics, Hygiene, Chemistry, and so on. I will be burning the midnight oil as a rule, but it is what I have chosen to do."

Rising, Louis walks to the far end of the porch and stares out at the clear, star-laden sky. He says, "Working in the family pharmacy has been great, but watching Doc Palmer and Doc Starbuck heal people, deliver babies and perform virtual miracles of medicine has inspired me to become a doctor."

He speaks with such a serious, deep conviction that I am quite taken aback.

He turns to face me and says, "I want to do these things also. I want to be a healer. Do you understand?"

Looking at my friend, seeing the earnestness on his face, hearing the passion in his voice, I can only be sure of one thing. Louis Horsey will graduate in three years, return to Fernandina and be a truly great physician.

The next morning after another hearty meal, we head out for our tour of Charleston in a rented horse and buggy, for reason of a huge blister on my right heel caused by new boots and the long walk from the wharf yesterday.

Louis explains that Fort Sumter was an engineering marvel created by the federal government and started in 1828 in a plan to develop a string of forts to protect our country's harbors. It was built by piling tons of rock on top of a sandbar to create the base. The fort wasn't complete when Major Robert Anderson occupied it in 1861 and the Confederates damaged Sumter's three original stories. The Federals bombarded Sumter in 1863 and 1864, bringing down the two top stories. Looking through a spyglass provided by Louis, I am able to see the fort as we ride along the Battery.

Pointing to No. 5 East Battery Street he tells me this was the home of Dr. St. Julien Ravenel, a physician who was also an inventor of the "David," a boat much like the *Hunley*, with the exception that it did not fully submerge. There were several "Davids" in use during the Civil War and on October 5, 1863, the CS *David* severely damaged the armored frigate USS *New Ironsides* by ramming her and setting off a torpedo seven feet below the Federal ship's waterline.

"Dr. Ravenel was a brilliant man who also developed fertilizers and the theory of plowing under crops in order to return nutrients to the soil. He passed away last year at the age of sixty-three."

I am amazed at the diversity of Dr. Ravenel's inventions; from products of war to products of life.

"During the war the retreating Confederates blew up a huge cannon located in front of the doctor's house in order to keep it out of Federal hands. The house escaped damage due to its thirty-two-inch-thick walls, but a five-hundred-pound piece of the cannon crashed through the roof of No. 9 East Battery, two houses up the street, landed on the beams in the attic above the master bedroom and is still there to this day!"

Louis and I both shake our heads in amusement at the thought of attempting to remove such a thing, and more so the thought of trying to get a good night's sleep with it balancing on the beams over our heads!

"The tallest house is No. 13 East Battery Street, where many Charlestonians watched the bombardment of Fort Sumter in 1861. Further on is the Edmonston-Alston House at No. 21, which was occupied by Robert E. Lee after the December 1861 fire."

I am impressed at the varying architectures of the grande dames that have withstood the test of war, standing stoically facing the enemy, enduring pounding after pounding and occupation by Yankee soldiers, to stand even prouder today, a testament to us all.

We are now back to the intersection of East Bay Street and the wharves on the Cooper River where we docked yesterday, and also where, during the Civil War, blockade runners and packet boats also docked.

Heading down into the city along narrow, tree-lined streets, Louis takes me to the square where City Hospital, Roper Hospital and the Medical College of South Carolina are all situated and bordered by Queen, Franklin, Magazine and Mazyck streets.

Louis hops down from the buggy, waters the horse and ties him to an available hitching post of black cast iron. He then turns to me, saying, "After my appointed meeting with Dean Prioleau at the college, we will have dinner, call it a day and continue our tour tomorrow. You are welcome to look around. The grounds are nicely laid out and the buildings are open to the public. The scheduled interview is only for an hour."

At that he turns quickly in the direction of the medical college, leaving me to some sightseeing on my own.

I decide to head in the direction of Roper Hospital in order to give Doc Palmer a report, as promised, upon my return to Fernandina. On entering I am lucky to find a second-year medical student who is willing to give me a tour of the city hospital, which is also a teaching hospital for MCSC.

As we walk the hallways, looking into surgeries, patient rooms, and even the morgue, he informs me that the hospital was completed in 1852 and was used briefly in 1854 during a yellow fever epidemic.

"In 1861 Colcock Hall was built as a foundry by the Confederate States of America government on the site of the U.S. Arsenal. Also, just this year the School of Nursing of City Hospital was opened in conjunction with MCSC," he tells me with obvious pride.

I am very impressed with the hospital, and having taken a lot of notes for Doc as well as asking the hospital administrator to forward some requested medical information to him, I thank my guide and return to the buggy to await Louis's return, which isn't long in coming.

Spying Louis across the lawn, I note that he is almost dancing with excitement. The lightness in his step foretells the outcome of his meeting.

Grabbing me by the hand, throwing his hat in the air and dancing a little jig right there on the streets of Charleston, he then swings me around—frightening the horse!

"Everything is going much better than anticipated!" he exclaims. "The dean and I hit it off quite amicably. He is a very intelligent physician and forthright individual. I am looking forward to studying with him these next three years."

The fever of his excitement takes hold of me and I throw my hat in the air as well, whoop out loud in joy and spin him around—to the amazement of passersby.

"Well, I don't know about you," Louis says, "but I'm starving. Let's go to town to a tavern I know that serves up a thick steak and a pitcher of lager fit for a king. The entertainment is not bad either." He winks at me. He unhitches the horse and jumps in the buggy in one fluid movement.

Off we go at a fast trot, down narrow streets turning this way and that, past homes nestled side by side like charming little ladies sitting prettily in a row.

Soon we are at our destination, a noisy waterfront tavern full of patrons trying to outtalk each other over the guy banging out a lively tune on the piano in the corner and the scantily clad, buxom beauty sitting on top of it belting out a raucous ditty of a song.

The bouncer gives us the once-over when we enter, and motions toward a table barely visible in the smoke-crowded room, to the right of the piano.

"At least our backs will be against the wall," I mutter to myself as we settle in.

We order our food and drink and sit back to listen to the music.

"Relax, old pal," Louis says, and laughs at me. "It's as safe here as our own saloon back home, only the food and entertainment are much better!"

He barely gets these words out of his mouth when the piano player switches to a livelier tune and the girl hops off the piano and onto the top of the bar, where she is joined by four others clad in scanty sailor suits.

The skirts barely cover their long, sleek legs. They dance and twirl to the music, raising the skirts higher and higher as the song goes faster and faster, and I am shocked and excited to see they are not wearing the usual bloomers! Kicking their heels up and swinging each other arm in arm in time to the music, they suddenly turn their backs to the audience, and to our utmost delight, flip their skirts over their heads, giving us a view of almost bare bottoms.

"Whew," I gasp at Louis, "you sure were right about the entertainment!"

The crowd roars for more, more, more!

"It is a different sort of place and not one I will be patronizing while in school, since I won't have the time nor the inclination. I just thought it would be a fun experience for you while visiting the big city," he said, punching me in the arm.

We observe the barmaid coming our way with a huge steaming platter.

"Anyway," Louis says, "the food is soon to be served, and you'll see I'm as true to my word about it as the entertainment."

Later that evening, sitting on the balcony, watching people stroll past Louis's temporary home, I am still so stuffed from dinner I can hardly move. Never have I had a steak cooked to such perfection … and the potatoes and vegetables were equally delicious.

Joining me for his nightly Havana, Louis drops into the rocker next to mine with a slight groan, rubbing his stomach. Puffing lazily on our cigars, we reminisce about our day and make plans for the next.

Early the next morning Louis and I tour The Citadel, which opened in 1842. At the outbreak of the Civil War there were 224 Citadel alumni and of those, 209 joined the Confederate army. Almost all served as officers, with the exception of four generals and 19 who headed regiments.

After touring The Citadel we take a ride into the countryside with a picnic graciously packed by Maum Hannah. We look forward to a lunch of ham between thick slices of homemade bread, a jar of sweet tea, and Charleston cookies called Benne Seed Wafers.

As we ride along tree-dappled roads, he points out stately plantations with names such as Middleton Place and Drayton Hall, still standing proudly along the rivers that once helped grow cotton. Southern planters grew little food; in fact, they planted almost every available acre in cotton and imported millions of dollars in food supplies from Western farmers.

"That is why, in 1858, South Carolina senator James H. Hammond declared to Northern senators: "You do not dare make war on cotton! No power on earth dares make war upon it! Cotton is King!"

But declare war they did, only three years later, in 1861, against the very heart of the land that supplied the Northern textile industry with the steady supply of cotton fibers on which it depended.

"None of it makes any sense, if you ask me," I muse out loud. "Seems like the system was working for all, until the politicians got concerned about the slaves."

"Or was it about slavery at all?" Louis asks in turn.

"Well, thank God it's behind us, and for whatever the reason. Enough blood has been shed amongst our own, on our own soil, by our own hands. And by the grace of God, may it never happen again."

"Amen to that," Louis affirms.

Arriving back at our domicile we are met by Maum Hannah's husband, Jube, who is waiting patiently to return the horse and buggy to the livery stable. Jube is a descendant of the Sierra Leone tribe of western Africa and speaks in a language called Gullah, which is difficult for me to understand. I enjoy listening to him and Maum Hannah conversing in the lyrical, almost Caribbean-sounding words, but Lord help me if I can make sense of but a few words of their conversations.

He, Maum Hannah and Little Sue were once slaves, and are now paid servants to their former mistress. According to them, they would stay even if they were not paid.

As Maum Hannah stated to me, "We all is family, we is all de Mistress has got since de Major done got kilt in de war. De Major done gib me to her on dere weddin' day fo' her personal maid and I be here ever since and I plans to be here till de Lawd calls me home."

Maum Hannah is one of those former Southern house slaves who served in a unique capacity of lady's maid and wet nurse when the babies came along and, in doing so, developed a strong, almost familial bond not only with her mistress but also with the master of the house and the children. A bond that traverses color, race and even religion in some instances.

During the war the three of them remained with their mistress, helping tend the small vegetable garden behind the house where roses once grew, milking the goat she kept hidden from sight of Yankee soldiers and deserters, and trading with neighbors for eggs. These neighbors now raised chickens instead of attending tea parties.

Tonight the mistress of the house has laid out a splendid meal. Tomorrow I will set sail back to Fernandina, leaving Louis to his studies and, alas, I will be without one of my best friends for a short while and in the doldrums without my sweetheart as well.

But my philosophy in life has always been to never allow a bad moment make a bad day, so I shall venture forward tomorrow, making new beginnings, as Louis will do, and fill the days with work and enjoyment of my other friends until we are all together again.

So, with a cheery wave of my hat I bid Louis adieu the next morning, and Jube and I trot off in the same horse and buggy from the day before.

With the exception that the weather has taken a seasonal turn for the worse, everything is as when I arrived. The wind is blowing and I am assured a northeaster will give my stomach a churn when we head out to sea. The *State of Texas* is tossing and tugging at her moorings as if in a hurry to get away before the storm heightens. Boarding the hardy vessel, I can hardly keep my balance on the gangway and I can tell by the worried look on the captain's face that he is as anxious to heave the lines as the ship is to set sail.

Not being much of a sailor, I have my qualms about leaving dry land for the uncertainty of such a tumultuous sea, but the captain assures me once we are out to sea and away from land, it will be better—but we must hurry.

When we cast off, the rigging snaps to attention and we are immediately flying away, out to sea at a high rate of speed. I have no choice but to hunker down in my cabin, miserable in my own world of first rocking in one direction, then rolling in another.

Crawling into my bunk I lie here, hands clasped behind my head in a pose of seeming indifference while knowing I am at the mercy and skill of the captain and his crew.

Soon this indifference is taken over by a rolling in my stomach which refuses to go away and I am assaulted by my first ever case of sea sickness. I pray it will be my last, for I am forced out of my bunk in search of the chamber pot and a wet cloth. Before long I begin to wish the ship would sink and put me out of my misery.

But after what seems like endless hours, the seas calm and I glimpse blue skies shining through the porthole. Weakened by the vomiting, I crawl out of my bunk on trembling legs, wash up in the minute amount of water left in the water bowl, change clothes and venture out on deck to peruse the damage.

One of the smaller masts has snapped, bringing down with it sails and rigging, and leaving the captain with no choice but to make an emergency stopover in Beaufort, South Carolina, a small town just south of Charleston.

"Had I any idea the storm was this strong, I would have ridden it out in Charleston," he says, shaking his head as he surveys the damage.

"This storm almost had the strength of a hurricane. Luck was on our side to have only minor damage. We should be on our way by tomorrow morning."

Eager to feel mother earth under our feet, two other passengers, a fellow from Georgia named Joshua and his cousin Franklin, and I go into town while the crew starts their labors of repairing the ailing craft.

Beaufort is a charming town with dozens of two- and three-story homes that outdo many of those I saw during my visit to Charleston. These homes, I learn, belonged to rich cotton and indigo plantation owners who would move to the coast, away from the sixty marshy islands that fan out from the town, during the "fever season."

Many of these homes were sold during and after the war to pay "war taxes," even though South Carolina had seceded from the Union that was imposing the tax to pay for the conflict. But that is why these beautiful homes were spared destruction; the city was captured before "total war" and became part of the Federal government's strategy.

One of the most interesting stories I am told is about Congressman Robert Smalls. His home is located at 511 Prince Street, and was built by his former master, Henry McKee, when Smalls was a slave in Charleston.

In May of 1862, Smalls, a twenty-three-year-old slave, made Civil War history when he stole the *Planter*, a 147-foot boat armed with heavy cannons. Disguised as a white man, and accompanied by his wife, children and other slaves, he slipped past guards at Fort Sumter and delivered the *Planter* to Union troops. For the duration of the war he served the Federal forces as pilot of the ship.

After the war, Smalls used the $1,500 prize money he was paid for delivering the *Planter* to the Union, to purchase his former master's home in Beaufort, and settled down to the full life of river pilot, trading agent and congressman.

"It don't sit right with me," Joshua says, staring at the stately home of Robert Smalls. "It just ain't right for some uppity nigger to be livin' in this here house while the rightful owner's family done lost everything in the war. It just ain't right!"

Spitting on the lawn in front of the house, he turns and stalks away in the direction of the ship, his shoulders thrust forward in an attitude of anger.

I have a bad feeling, like "someone walking over your grave," as the old saying goes. I recognized the look of hatred in Joshua's cold, hard eyes. The wounds are still fresh and deep from the war. The healing process will go on for generations, and some things I am sure will never completely heal. There will forever be scars and reminders, things that will never be forgiven, such as Sherman's march through the South burning homes, libraries, crops, and the stealing of livestock. Taking away the genteel way of life that had become the very essence of the South. But little did he know that the South would rise again, stronger and better for having to endure these things. It will take time and forgiveness.

But not for men like Joshua, who fought the battles and suffered the agony of seeing the head of his best friend blown off right beside him. Who returned home to find his only child dead from starvation. His wife gone who knows where. And his farm auctioned off to a Yankee carpetbagger. He sees what he sees here today and passes the hatred on to the next generation, which will cause the healing process to stall and falter.

A young mulatto servant, who looks to be in his early twenties, had ceased his chore of sweeping the front porch during our heated exchange. Venturing down the stairs toward me he introduces himself to me as David and asks in a subdued voice if I have business with Mr. Smalls.

Without prompting, he adds, "Missus Smalls done pass away in July and de Captain, he keeps real busy up in Columbia passin' laws and stuff, or on de river. He misses her real bad, he does. Yes sir, he does. I heard what dat other man said. He was wrong cause he don't know dat Mr. Smalls's daddy was his momma's Massa McKee dat built dis here house."

According to young David, Robert Smalls was born to Lydia in the backyard of the McKee house. She was descended of slaves from Guinea. He was a house slave until the age of twelve, when he was sent to Charleston to hire himself out for pay. He worked as a waiter, lamplighter, ship rigger and sailor, and was allowed to keep only one dollar per month of his pay until age eighteen, when he was allowed to keep fifteen dollars per month.

While living in the McKee home, Smalls had tutors and was taught to read and write.

"Well, David, you must understand that it has been only a few short years since the war ended. Our country is still recovering and rebuilding. Some things will take a lifetime or two, maybe even more, to change. You and I will not see these changes. Our children more than likely will not see these changes. It is men like Mr. Smalls, who are making political changes, and even men like you and me, who on a daily basis make small changes as we go about our daily lives, that will cause changes to occur."

Holding out my hand I shake his firmly, ask that he give my regards to his boss and then I head toward town again.

Checking in on Joshua, I find that he has gotten himself falling-down drunk, and to my relief, passed out in his cabin. Not eager to board the ship again until the last possible minute, I decide to go in search of a tavern or inn, for all this walking has created quite an appetite and thirst.

After stowing my camera equipment I walk in the direction of the nearest tavern, as suggested by the captain, and to my delight, find it to my liking in quantity and quality of food and service. After the meal is cleared away I linger over a lager, take out my quill, ink and journal, and while the day's events are fresh in my mind, put them to paper.

Perhaps someday, I muse, my thoughts and travels will be of interest to my children and future generations.

A scant hour later the captain has sent a sailor seeking me out. The *State of Texas* is shipshape and ready to continue. Finding myself now eager to return home, I gather my things, tip the barmaid and hasten aboard.

Staying up top as we clear the harbor, I commence to tell the captain the story of Robert Smalls, and to my surprise it is a story familiar to him.

"I was a blockade runner for the Confederate army during the war," the captain says without turning his gaze from the waterway, "and Smalls was well known to me. Smalls was as much a prize, maybe more so to the Union Army as the *Planter* was. Having been taught to read charts he could navigate all the creeks and rivers near Charleston, even in the dark. He was the pilot of the ironclad *Keokuk* during a failed Union attack on Fort Sumter in 1863, during which the *Keokuk* sank. The Union made him a war hero.

"Since the war, he has helped found the first public school system in South Carolina, and has served in the house of representatives as well as the state senate. He also participated in drafting the state constitution."

The captain turns to see my reaction, and adds, "I feel sure he has been involved in other things, both politically and personally since the war, that I am not aware of, because that is his nature. During the war he was sent to New York on a speaking tour to help raise support for the Union cause, and was presented an engraved medal by 'the colored citizens of New York' for heroism, his love of liberty and his patriotism."

Seeing my eyebrows raise in surprise at this bit of information, he holds his hand up before I can speak.

"Even though Robert Smalls fought for the Union during the war, he is a Southerner from birth and at heart. He was caught in a situation many men were. A situation that split not only the nation apart but also families, where brother fought brother for the cause."

Such a long speech from Captain Risk is rare, and even though he and Robert Smalls championed opposing sides during the war, he holds the man in the utmost esteem and respect.

We enter open seas and the ship turns smoothly due south. The sails fill themselves fully with the evening breezes and we are soon clipping along at a fast pace toward home.

The captain and I grin at each other, having just digested a conversation that would not sit well with many men such as Joshua. But we have been friends for quite a while, having spent many an evening with Doc, Louis, J. J. Acosta, and C. A. Key at the Idle Hour or one or another's parlor discussing and arguing politics and life in general. Such talk would not affect us in any other way.

Also, our fair city of Fernandina is the proverbial melting pot of Southerners, Northerners and foreigners. The true natives, the Timucuans, have long since been vanquished by the early settlers. To hold which side of the war any of our friends fought on against them would severely limit the number of our friends!

Finding myself a comfortable spot at the bow to enjoy the clear night, I am soon joined by Wilhelm Wellge, an artist hailing from Milwaukee, Wisconsin. On Amelia Island he plans to make a perspective sketch of the town for a publishing company in Milwaukee.

"I was born in Wurtemburg and studied at the Polytechnic School in Stuttgart, Germany," he informs me in a deeply accented voice. "My job for the publishing company takes me to many interesting places. Tell me about your Amelia Island."

We have quite an interesting conversation, discussing not only Amelia Island but also his homeland. Before turning in for the night I ask where he would be lodging and it turns out he will be at the Mansion House managed by my friend, Ferdinand Suhrer, and also where my friend Professor C. A. Key lodges. I promise to direct him to the hotel and introduce him to both men upon arrival.

*

Ah, home at last! What a beautiful sight Amelia Island is. I indicate points of interest to Wilhelm and he is sketching away as fast as his pen can fly across his pad. I did not realize how homesick one could get in such a short period of time. I cannot wait for some of Miss Annie's home cooking and my own bed again.

Looking around for my young friend, Moses, I easily spy him with a group of older men, one being his father who so recently lost his leg. Motioning him over, I give him charge of my camera equipment and trunk.

"Take these over to Miss Leddy's for me," I tell him while slipping a coin into his hand.

Once he is on his way, Wilhelm and I strike out in the direction of the Mansion House, carrying his trunk and artist supplies.

Along the way I give him an abbreviated tour of the town and some of the island's history.

"The first known white man to step foot on the island was the Frenchman Jean Ribault in May of 1562. He named the island 'Ile de Mai.' In 1565 the Spanish defeated the French and founded St. Augustine, and during their dominion concentrated on converting the Timucuan Indians, and the island was then renamed Santa Maria. Amelia Island was so named for the daughter of George II, after the English destroyed the Spanish mission and settlement here, in 1702. From 1763 to 1783, the island became known as 'Egmont,' from the Earl of Egmont's large indigo plantation. Revolutionary forces invaded in 1777 and 1778.

"After the Revolution, Britain ceded Florida back to Spain. Jefferson's Embargo Act of 1807, which closed U.S. ports to foreign shipping, made the border town of Fernandina a center of smuggling and piracy. The most famous pirate was Luis Aury, born in Paris around 1788. Aury actually gained control of the island under the Mexican Republic in 1817, along with 130 mulattoes known as 'Aury's blacks.' Of course, this did not last long, due to racism among the whites who were forced to garrison with the mulattoes. The mulattoes were headed by Ruggles Hubbard of the American Party. Forced to make concessions, Hubbard soon died, and Aury saw an opportunity to declare himself supreme civil ruler and military authority. Little did Aury know that President Monroe had invoked a secret act passed by Congress in 1811 as a preliminary to the War of 1812. The act empowered the President to expel by force any foreign power occupying Spanish Florida. At Monroe's direction, the U.S. War and Navy Department were issued orders to occupy Amelia Island.

"Meanwhile, Aury's privateering continued and in November, Lloyds of London received a report that prize goods valued at half a million dollars had been sold in Fernandina.

"Aury knew that some sort of a resemblance to a legitimate government must be created; therefore he called a meeting of his officers and proposed an election, one where every free inhabitant of fifteen days' residence could vote after subscribing an allegiance. Aury's constitution never became operative because it became known that the U.S. intended to occupy Amelia Island.

"At this point Aury drafted a document of protest with his 'legislators,' to be delivered to President Monroe, but on giving this considerable thought, decided to surrender to U.S. forces led by Captain J. D. Henley and Major James Bankhead on December 23, 1817. The American flag now replaced the Mexican flag and the U.S. controlled Amelia Island in trust for Spain. Bankhead loaded all of Aury's mulattoes aboard one of his ships and sent them off, probably to Santo Domingo.

"Aury remained behind for over two months as an unwelcome guest, until he left for New Granada, where he spent the next three and a half years attempting to free his adopted country from Spain. He died there, at the age of 33, as a result of being thrown from a horse. That was in 1817. In 1821, Spain ceded Florida to the United States and in 1850 Fernandina moved from Old Town to where it is now. I will take you to

Old Town while you are here, and also to Fort Clinch, built in 1847, if you wish to see it."

Nodding his head in acceptance, Wilhelm looks at me in amazement. "You know so much history of the town you were not born in. Why is that?"

"It is my nature to be curious in regards to history. I should have been a teacher of the subject instead of a town clerk tediously copying down numbers all day long. But alas, my family did not have the means for a college education—and then of course the war came along."

He asks, "What of the photography equipment? Is that a hobby? Did you go to school to learn?" Sweat beads his brow and he stops to catch his breath, indicating a few minutes' break in our ramble.

Wilhelm sits down on his trunk on the walkway in front of J. H. Prescott's store, his left hand shielding his eyes from the sun as he wipes his brow with his shaking right. I did not realize he was not of physical strength or I would have hired a wagon for the short ride to the hotel. Looking around for a familiar face but finding none, I decide to seek assistance in Prescott's.

Entering the cool, dark interior that smells richly of shoe and boot leather, I am quickly greeted by a clerk who, upon hearing of our plight, hurries to Mr. Prescott's office and soon returns with him in tow.

"Well, well, it's good to see you again," he says, shaking my hand. "Let's see what we can do to get your friend safely to the Mansion House. My horse and buggy are ready behind the store. I was just leaving for home and the noonday meal. It is opportune that you should come along at this precise moment."

Introductions are made, luggage and supplies loaded and we are off to the hotel in no time. Along the way I am saddened to learn that my friend, John Ferreira, passed away on Thursday while I was gone. He was sixty-nine years old, having been born in St. Augustine on November 14, 1813. He had been a resident of Fernandina since 1858, and leaves behind to mourn him a wife and four grown sons.

There is an old saying that bad things happen in threes; this makes two, and I shudder to wonder what the third will be.

A Negro servant hurries to gather Wilhelm's belongings, taking them inside while we both thank Mr. Prescott profusely for the transportation.

The Mansion House is swarming with the usual number of new and returning guests arriving, as well as Wilhelm checking in at the desk. Looking around, I note among them are Captain John Brewster of the schooner *De Mory Gray*, having arrived from New York with rock for the jetties on the St. Johns bar, and I also see A. P. Williams, of the *Times-Democrat* in New Orleans.

Coming across the lobby, hand outstretched in greeting, is my friend and manager of the hotel, Ferdinand Suhrer.

Ferdinand is one of those men who exudes a certain charisma and charm that immediately puts one at ease regardless of one's station in life or gender. I personally believe it comes from being a leader of men in battle, having mustered out as a major in 1865, and then government. Presently serving as temporary mayor, he also is president of the city council.

He poses a striking figure: dark, wavy hair combed back from his forehead, slightly taller than average in height and broader in build and, as always, impeccably dressed in a suit with high collar and tie.

Ferdinand was born in the Grand Duchy of Baden, in southern Germany in the village of Hochhausen, in 1837. Both parents died when he was young, his mother when he was five and his father when the boy was eleven. He gained permission from the French police to leave the country on the ship *Toulon* at age eighteen, and landed alone in New York on August 12, 1856.

He made his way to Elyria, Ohio, where he was employed as a licensed pharmacist when the war broke out. He fought in such battles as Chancellorsville and Gettysburg, and finally, toward the end of the war, was garrisoned at Fort Clinch outside Fernandina.

Shortly after the war he returned to Elyria, married Eva Rosa Plotts, and returned to Fernandina with his bride. They are raising six children: George, Mary Elizabeth, Ferdie, Rosa, Frank, and Mark Joseph.

Eva Rosa Suhrer *Ferdinand Suhrer*

Ferdinand and I have become well acquainted over the years, not only in our daily work but also as friends. I have spent many an evening by his fireside with one or the other of his children dangling on my knee. I listened to his many stories of the old country while drinking mulled wine and eating Eva Rosa's romptoff, a German cake of fruit and nuts. Devoted Catholics, they never miss Mass at St. Michael's Church. Eva Rosa brought from Germany a prayer chair belonging to her mother. I had never seen one before. Its front legs are slightly shorter than the back, giving the person using it comfort as you kneel on the padded bottom, facing the back of the chair and resting your hands on the padded top of what appears to one's untrained eye, a headrest. This chair holds a place of honor in a corner of the master bedroom, along with statues of patron saints and candles, which are lit at prayer time. This is where the family gathers every evening prior to bedtime, to pray and recite the rosary.

"Ferdinand, my friend, may I introduce my new acquaintance, Mr. Wellge. Recently of Milwaukee, but born and raised in your mother country of Germany, in the city of Wurtemburg. He is on assignment to produce an artist's sketch of our fair city."

Looking less weary than he had a few moments ago, Wilhelm holds out his hand in greeting and is immediately given the old country hug and hearty slap on the back in greeting.

Ferdinand says, "I have been looking forward to meeting you ever since we were given notice of your impending arrival. I have booked you into one of our newly refurbished rooms. We have recently installed new carpeting in all the guest suites, plastered, painted and ordered new bedroom suites of cherry with marble tops. I am sure you will be very comfortable."

Ferdinand personally gathers up Wellge's belongings and indicates with a nod of his head the direction of the stairs they are to take as they continue their conversation.

"My wife, Eva Rosa, and I would enjoy the pleasure of your company for supper tonight if you are not too tired from your journey."

Wilhelm replies, "After a light repast, bath and nap, I will be fine."

"In that case, we shall see you in the hotel dining room at seven this evening," Ferdinand says with a big smile, turning to include me as well.

However, I decline, wanting nothing more than a good hearty meal at Miss Annie's and an early night in my bed.

But alas, this will have to wait until after I make my call to the widow Ferreira to offer my condolences and support.

Bidding my companions good day, I turn with a heavy heart and equally leaden feet in the direction of the Ferreira home. Thoughts of John and his family run like a dark river crashing through my mind. Not like J. J. Acosta, who died unexpectedly, John has been in declining health for some two years. But still, the loss of another pillar of the community and friend is deeply felt.

John and Lauriana moved from St. Augustine, Florida, with their young family in 1858, just prior to the Civil War, and up until a few months before his death, he was actively employed as an engineer for the railroad and involved in city affairs.

In the darkened parlor, family and friends are gathered around Lauriana. I am ushered in by Manna, John's youngest son who at age twenty-eight, has continued to live in the family home in order to take care of his aging parents.

"Come, sit by me," she bids in her husky Portuguese voice. The matriarch of the family sits straight and tall. Not a tear mars her porcelain, unlined face that is framed by perfectly coiffed, jet-black hair with traces of silver.

"They wanted me to cover his portrait in black and also all the mirrors in the house, as is the custom, but I would not allow it. I want to see his face. We were married for forty-six years and had four sons and a daughter together. There are many grandchildren who survive to carry on his name. I miss him greatly, but he leaves me with many happy memories to comfort me on lonely nights."

George Bender, Maria Josepha's son by her marriage to John Bender, is now eighteen years of age and also lives in the parental home. He hovers close by, ready to do any bidding needed by his grandmother. I spy him near the parlor entrance, assisting the guests in his usual friendly, outgoing manner. I never have had the courage to ask the circumstances of the situation, as no one knows what became of John Bender. John and Lauriana have raised George as their own child since the death of his mother, when he was but a babe of five.

Everyone accepts it and goes about his or her own business.

I came to offer her peace and consolation and instead I receive from her a sense of the happiness she shared with John. She recounts stories of their life together. I can visualize the young couple as they marry in

St. Augustine, the joy at the birth of each of their children, the adventure and excitement of the journey to Fernandina and the good life they created in their home with family and friends.

Blinking as I step out into the bright sunlight, I cannot help but marvel at how lucky the Ferreiras were to have found each other. I suddenly realize that the lead in my feet and heaviness in my heart have disappeared.

Chapter 5

Goodbye, Friends

Today being Saturday and the high tides prevailing, a plan has been laid out for several of us to go shooting marsh hens for Miss Annie to cook for supper. It's a wonder what a good night's sleep in one's own bed will do after a long journey. Also, the weather is still hovering in the upper 70s and low 80s, making it a perfect day to be outdoors rather than in.

Doc, C.A., George and I head out after a hearty breakfast at the Idle Hour. We are loaded with rifles, sandwiches and the ever-present flasks, to the inlet just after daybreak for a morning of companionable hunting and catching up on local happenings, including my recent travel adventures.

The hunting is good; after only two hours we have bagged more than enough marsh hens for Miss Annie and George, so we find a shady spot on the bank of the river to relax.

Reaching into the bag of sandwiches, George says, "The missus left for New York on Friday, hoping the cooler weather and rest will bring her back to good health. The boys miss her already, but with school starting they have to stay here with me. Also, I need the help at the Idle

Hour. Even though we have but a few tourists right now, it will pick up during the holidays."

Taking a big bite of his sandwich, all of a sudden a look of pain flashes over his usually friendly, smiling face. Dropping the sandwich on the grass, he grasps the sides of his head with both hands, rocking back and forth on his heels, squeezing his head hard and grimacing.

"What's wrong?" Doc demands, trying to pull his hands away from his head. "Let me look in your eyes!"

But the pain is so severe it keeps George's eyes closed tight until it diminishes, some thirty seconds to a minute later.

"Jesus, Mary and Joseph, that one was bad!" he exclaims. "It has been a while since I have had a headache like that!"

"That was no headache," counters Doc. "You need to come into my office for a complete checkup as soon as possible."

After Doc extracts a promise from George to come in the next day, we settle back for lunch. But I can tell Doc is keeping a wary eye on George.

Conversation turns to the opening of the roller skating club at the end of the month at Main Beach, a place Pauline and I enjoy. I will write her this evening, making plans to skate during the holidays. I had several letters waiting from her on my arrival home, and I have so much to write in return. That will take care of my afternoon, after dressing the marsh hens.

On the trek back to the Hour it seems to me George is not quite himself. After bidding him farewell, I mention this to Doc and C.A. as the three of us continue on into town. With a worried look on his face, Doc agrees.

"Did you notice he was favoring his left arm and leg after his supposed headache? And his speech was a little slurred," he says as we near his house. "I will go back later when I make my evening rounds to make sure he is okay."

*

The next week flies by and I am so swamped with work and correspondence to catch up on that before I know it, the first meeting of the Fernandina Roller Skating Club has come and gone, with an agreement to open the rink in time for a Halloween costume party.

The club will be offering tickets to their entertainments at the rate of twelve for $1.00 and twelve skating tickets for $1.00. Also, ladies and children will be given the opportunity to learn to skate at a Monday matinee, to which gentlemen will not be admitted. Members of the club will be in attendance to teach beginners.

George is at the meeting with his two sons. He looks none the worse for his episode during our hunting trip. This makes me feel better and eases my conscience for not having taken time to call on him during the past week.

The two of us catch up as we watch the boys romp up and down the beach, playing with first one, then another treasure washed onshore.

*

"George Sweeney is dead," announces Miss Annie when I enter the kitchen for breakfast the next morning. "Died of cerebral apoplexy during the night, according to Doc's housekeeper."

Stopping abruptly, coffeepot midway in the process of pouring himself a second cup, William Young, our resident lawyer and also close friend of George, seems frozen in time.

As for myself, I drop into the nearest chair in a state of shock and disbelief. It has happened, the old wives' tale: bad things come in threes. First J. J. Acosta, then John Ferreira and now another of my friends, George Sweeney. It is almost more than my mind can comprehend and my heart can bear.

Pulling myself together with a start, I jump up and head out the door without breakfast, coat or hat. My only thought is of George's sons, left bereft of father, alone until word can reach their poor mother and her untimely return from New York.

Reaching the Hour, I find numerous friends have gathered and the housekeeper is in full command of the situation. Doc summoned the undertaker, Robert Henderson, who has already removed the body for burial preparation. George will be returned home for the Irish wake he always said he would have.

Both boys almost bowl me over when I enter the family parlor; the hotel guests have naturally departed to other quarters in town due to the circumstances, not wanting to intrude on the family's grief.

Taking the boys outside, away from the hushed talk of "I'm so sorry about your father" and so on, we huddle together on a sand dune and look out at the sea George loved so much. We talk about happier times. I hug them close to me and they cry like they would not do inside, in front of so many people. They are trying so hard to be the men of the house, but at ages twelve and eight it's an impossible task for ones so young.

It will take at least a week for their mother to receive the telegraph message sent by William Reynolds of her husband's death, and her return home. In the meantime it has been agreed that the boys shall remain in their home under the care of the housekeeper, with friends and neighbors looking in on them.

Scooping up a handful of fine white sand, I let it flow back upon the beach. A gentle breeze blows some of it away in a swirl, like a fairy maiden dancing out to sea. How similar to our lives is this handful of sand: here one minute, gone the next, with the exception of the impression we impart on the lives of those left behind.

*

I have never before attended an Irish wake and, to say the least, it is quite an experience. Upon the arrival of Mrs. Sweeney, George's body has been returned home to rest in the parlor. Sheets surround three sides of his casket, lit candles in candlesticks keep vigil and someone is always in attendance, day and night. He is dressed in a robe called a habit, with a crucifix upon his chest and rosary beads placed in his hands.

Upon entering the house each mourner goes directly to the casket to kneel in prayer, and then spends several hours with the family. The weather is nice, so the men tend to congregate outside on the porch and lawn while the ladies help in the kitchen and keep up with the young folk.

Snuff is offered on a plate, as well as tobacco and pipes, wine, port and beer. The mourners are offered food and drink and all spend their time speaking kindly of George. The visitation lasts until midnight, at which time a rosary is said and all mourners go home with the exception of those few who stay with him until morning. Another rosary is then said. We sit around quietly, drink tea and whiskey and tell anecdotes until it is time for the funeral at the Catholic church. Then on to the cemetery.

Mrs. Sweeney intends to keep the Idle Hour on Amelia Beach open during the season. I feel she will be well supported by the local community and the patronage of previous clientele. Of course the boys love the sea as their father did, and share with me their lack of desire to move to New York—or anywhere else for that matter.

Returning home from the funeral Mass, George's friends bring out the bagpipes and other musical instruments and play the music he so loved. Well into the night the whiskey and lager flow, along with remembrances of our friend.

Chapter 6

Holiday Cheer

Life goes on and we are moving forward into the holiday season with the annual Skating Masquerade Carnival held at Lyceum Hall.

My only wish is that Pauline were here to enjoy the fun! My boss, William Wood, is dressed as a schoolboy while his wife is an Italian tambourine girl, Katie Stark is Red Riding Hood and we have two Goddess of Liberty, Mrs. C. V. Hillyer and Miss Simpson, a niece of Mrs. Dr. Snyder, who is on a visit. Gracie Leddy, Lula Pope, Emma Maxwell and many others are sporting charming masks.

The most original and best-sustained character of the gentlemen is Sammie Swann, as the "girl of the period," while Charlie Stark has folk roaring with laughter in his costume personifying the poem *The Heathen Chinee*.

The dancing will be starting soon but I decide not to join in, not wanting to cause talk to reach the tender ears of Pauline. I enjoy the show from the sidelines, watching the others.

Not so with Katie Eppes! There is no mistaking that figure and long black hair, no matter the costume. Dressed as a shepherd girl, she is dancing with an Indian chief I am sure is not her husband. I know for a fact that he left town yesterday on railway business.

I smell trouble brewing, big trouble. I should stay the hell out of it, I tell myself. It is none of my business. Let T.J. take care of his wife. But I'm afraid that is exactly what he will do, with the gentleman bearing the brunt of T.J.'s wrath.

Sauntering over to the dancing couple, I tap the gentleman on the shoulder, cut in and dance Katie immediately over to the chairs against the wall. I sit her down none too gently.

"Just what do you think you're doing?" I ask her sharply. "Didn't you learn your lesson at the Harvest Ball?"

"I deserve to have fun like everyone else!" she fumes back at me. "T.J. promised to attend the carnival with me and then he leaves town. Why can't you understand how I feel!"

Exasperated, I look her straight in her beautiful, coal-black eyes and patiently explain: "Katie, it's not that we don't want you to enjoy life. That's not the issue. The issue is you are a married woman and in being so, you have obligations and rules governing your actions that reflect not only on you but on your husband. Come, let's get you out of here before anyone else recognizes you, before any harm is done." I hold out my hand in an offer of friendship.

"Oh well, I can see you're not going to take no for an answer, so I might as well leave!"

She rises in a huff, ignoring my offer, and hurries to the door almost faster than I can keep up.

"You can stay here and enjoy your silly ol' carnival," she says. "My carriage and servant are waiting outside." And with a toss of her hair she is gone.

Whew, what a woman. Makes me glad Pauline is so gentle and ladylike! Not saying Katie isn't a lady, don't get me wrong. It's just that she is ahead of her time. Yes, that's a better way of putting it. A woman ahead of her time: demanding equal rights with men, going about unchaperoned and doing as she pleases when she pleases, regardless of the consequences.

*

The suspense is killing me. I pace up and down the docks, squinting into the bright sunlight as it sparkles and dances on the incoming tide. I wish that the ship bringing Pauline home for the holidays would hurry.

It should have docked over an hour ago. The youngest captain, John Risk, recently hired by the Mallory Line and the steamship *State of Texas*, prides himself on being punctual, if not ahead of schedule. Why, two weeks ago he made the trip from New York in a remarkably fast four days, having made a stop in Port Royal—a mere seventy-four hours from dock to dock. Darn it, why does he have to be behind schedule today of all days!

There it is, I can see the smoke billowing from her stacks as she rounds the last curve in the river. What a glorious sight!

As soon as the ship docks I am rushing up the gangway. I grab Pauline in my arms and not giving a thought in the world to who is looking, I hug and kiss her with all my might.

"Set me down, set me down!" she squeals in feigned horror and sheer delight. "You are mussing my clothes and all of Fernandina are watching us!"

"Yes ma'am, your wish is my command." I set her down with a kiss on each cheek, and still holding her by both arms, look her over from head to toe. "Well, lookee here at how the flower has blossomed in the cold north. I do believe the climate has agreed with you. And all this time I thought you were wilting on the vine as you pined your little heart away for me night after lonely night."

Pauline is more beautiful than when she left, if that's possible. Laughing up into my face, her eyes sparkle with pleasure at my comments. She slips an arm through mine for the short walk to her house and the family gathered awaiting us there.

"Come," she says, "let's get this welcome home over. Then we can have our time together to catch up." The little minx winks at me from under long lashes, making my heart skip a beat.

I honestly believe the temperature has just risen at least ten degrees, and here it is only a week until Thanksgiving.

On the way, I fill her in on all the sad news and such, so that later we can speak of only happy occurrences.

"I'm surprised your father relented and allowed you to come home for Thanksgiving. Why the change of heart?" I ask.

"It has nothing to do with me, but rather with mother's health at the moment," Pauline replies, a frown appearing on her face. Her eyes cloud over. "She is not up to a trip, so I came home instead."

Stopping in front of the house I attempt to smooth the worry lines from her forehead as I search deeply into her misting eyes.

Pauline adds, "Father wrote that I am not to fret, it isn't anything serious. It's just best this way."

On entering the Meddaugh house I am greeted with a firm handshake by Mr. Meddaugh and an almost-smile. I can see that I must be at my best behavior and so must Pauline. Taking her aside I impress upon her the need for proper decorum if we want to make the most of her holiday visit.

I whisper softly in her ear, making sure not to be overheard: "Your father will have us under constant watch this evening. Bide your time until you can slip out later tonight, after everyone is asleep."

A sudden hush falls over the room as Katie Eppes enters, followed by none other than her usually absent husband, T.J.

With a flash of bright red lips and cheeks that are in stark contrast to her creamy white skin and black velvet gown, she rushes over to Pauline to welcome her home.

The room is charged with electricity, alive and glowing. Women twitter, men preen their feathers. It is always the same when Katie enters a room. It isn't anything she does; it is what Katie naturally is.

Flicking out an ostrich fan of black and white plumes and fanning furiously, Katie talks as rapidly as she fans. "Why Pauline darling, you look ravishing! Doesn't she, Jeff?"

Not giving T.J. a chance to answer, she is off to another subject, and Pauline and I look at each other, helplessly wondering what is going on.

Giving T.J. the old raised eyebrow and head gesture, I make our excuses and we leave the ladies alone. Glancing back over my shoulder I see Pauline is none too happy with me.

T.J. and I join others in the dining room, where the majority of the men have gathered to smoke, drink and discuss current politics. After pouring Jeff and myself a whiskey from the sideboard, we settle into two chairs next to the windows overlooking the gardens of the neighboring Prescott house.

Talk drifts amicably from the unanimous call from the congregation of the First Presbyterian Church for Pastor Yerger to remain another year, to the commencement of the new brick buildings being built on Centre Street, replacing those destroyed by the fire. James McGiffin, the contractor, will supervise this, as well as work on the Stark buildings being built by Mr. Scott, who also built the new convent of the Sisters of St. Joseph.

No more wooden structures will be allowed, per city code.

Col. Frank Papy, of the Transit Railroad, who recently leased the home of David Yulee on Third Street, is in attendance, regaling us with stories of his time served during the war.

There are rumblings and discontent in the letting go of two of our policemen in order to pay for the reduced cost of day scavenger work. Mr. Avery patiently explains the reasoning for the adjustment in manpower to cover the cost and still be able to hire extra police service for special events. We would still have the best streets and sanitary conditions for the least amount of money of only $ 2.50 per day. Better, he maintains, than we have had in the last ten years and still be able to provide adequate police protection. He further explains that the cost also includes the drayman's horse, harness and cart. We cannot complain of the reasoning of the finance committee's decision.

Combined with the late hour and the roaring fire in Mrs. Meddaugh's cozy dining room, I begin to feel the effect of the two whiskeys and excuse myself for a breath of fresh air. Exiting out the nearest door into the backyard I stumble over Katie Eppes crumpled into a heap of black velvet.

She is sobbing uncontrollably on the back stoop. "Those old biddies are so mean to me," she wails, hiccupping at the same time. "I came here to welcome Pauline home, the same as them, and all they do is snicker behind their hands, roll their eyes and drag their husbands away like they think I want their dried-up old excuses of manhood."

Not tonight, of all nights! is the first thought to pop into my head. Why can't things ever be without social infractions when Katie is around, and why do I have to be caught in the vortex?

If anyone were to come along, this scene would appear anything but innocent. Here she is crying, and it would appear I am the culprit. What to do, what to do?

"Listen, Katie, you must dry your tears, hold your head up and go back inside before you're missed. Show those ladies you are Mrs. T. J. Eppes and deserve respect. And while you're at it, please remove all that rouge from your face and lips. You don't need it and ladies don't wear it. When you realize your actions are causing these problems, this type of thing will stop. Now come on," I say, handing her my handkerchief, "do as I say before T.J. comes looking for you."

No longer needing sobering up I head back into the house in search of Pauline. I find her at the piano in the parlor, surrounded by family and friends playing and singing Christmas music.

Leaning on the piano I join in, my smooth baritone harmonizing well with her sweet soprano. Song after song we sing, the holiday spirit enveloping us like a warm cloak.

Stopping to catch our breath, we amble toward the punch bowl to quench our parched mouths and run smack into Katie, now laughing and giggling on Jeff's arm, having obviously taken my advice.

"What say we go down to Glaiber's Restaurant for some sauerkraut with pigs' feet?" Jeff asks us. "Pauline, I am sure your parents will not be averse to your being chaperoned by a married couple at dinner in public. This new place is run by Germans and the food is plentiful and good."

Pauline rolls her eyes and wrinkles her nose at the mere mention of pigs' feet. "Do they offer any other menu items?" she asks, obviously not adventuresome enough to try such a dish nor particularly eager for Katie's company. But as an afterthought that this is a good excuse for an escape for the evening, Pauline seeks permission from her father and it is granted, providing Jeff and Katie chaperone us to and from the restaurant.

Oh well, an escape is an escape, so off we go in the direction of Glaiber's. Upon entering we find it to be quite a surprise and to our liking. We are met at the door by Albert Glaiber's wife, Matilda, a short, rosy-cheeked, friendly woman who promptly ushers us to a table neatly laid with a starched, crisp white linen cloth and shining silver. Perusing the menu, we discover that even though it is not large it is indeed varied, and we each quickly find something to our liking. Only Jeff orders the pigs' feet and sauerkraut.

We settle down to a companionable silence, enjoying our meal with only an occasional comment. Soon we have satiated our hunger, and order after-dinner drinks from the Glaibers' young daughter, Helena, while she removes the destruction we have made of the delicious meal.

"You know," Jeff is saying, "I respect Sam Swann highly, but this business of him requesting the city council to have George Wilson remove his house, outbuilding, fence and other improvements he built on the lot on Sixth Street in front of Sam's property while he was away on business, doesn't sit right with me, and I'm not the only one it doesn't sit right with. How in the name of God do you ask a man to tear down his house because you find it objectionable?"

"Well," I reply, "according to Sam, George built on property that Sam cleared in order to improve the appearance of the neighborhood."

"But Sam does not own that property and even though he cleared it at his own expense, he had no authority," Jeff retorts.

"Also," I answer, "there is the issue of there not being a suitable chimney, which endangers the adjacent properties from fire."

Jeff replies heatedly, "Then allow the man to build a chimney, do not require him to destroy his home just because you find it objectionable!"

"Whoa, hold on, fellow. I'm just giving you the facts that were reported to city council, not what I believe. Between the two of us, I think Sam is acting a bit of the snob and doesn't think the house fits, if you know what I mean."

"Permission was given George to build his home on his lot and he should not be required to remove it simply because someone doesn't like it. I doubt seriously that city council will require him to do so."

Pauline and Katie have not joined in this conversation, but instead have their heads together discussing the new winter fashions and are looking at a fashion-plate book Pauline brought along from her recent stay in New York.

Katie begs to borrow the book as we rise to take our leave. Pauline is at first hesitant but relents at the longing in Katie's eyes.

I say, "Come, let's walk down to King's Bazaar on Centre Street. I feel the need to walk off this heavy meal and enjoy the sights of the wondrous Christmas displays in the store. There is a velocipede like I have never seen before, the horse's mane and tail are of real horsehair and his saddle and all details are beautifully painted."

Rising, Jeff and I assist the ladies with their cloaks.

"Also," I continue, "I wish for you to see a doll I have in mind for Sophie, and I need your advice on my decision of either a glove box or handkerchief box for your mother for Christmas. I have already purchased a cigar cutter and selection of cigars for your father."

Jeff and Katie are in a holiday mood as well, and the four of us stroll leisurely down Centre Street window-shopping with the ladies. We also dart first into one store and then another, oohing and aahing until we reach King's Bazaar.

The store is in abundance of all kinds of toys for girls, from dolls to parlor and kitchen furniture, as well as for boys, including rocking horses, toolboxes and express wagons. Every space is taken by a large variety of games and too many other toys to mention.

With me in tow, Pauline is off like a child in Santa's workshop, the excitement showing in her rosy cheeks.

"Look at all these pretty dolls!" she exclaims. She picks up one after another to examine it closely. "There are so many to choose from, it makes me want to be a little girl again!"

Turning to me with a Bébé Teteur, a nursing doll from France held lovingly in her arms, I involuntarily catch my breath at the sight of her standing there, for the doll seems so lifelike as to depict a scene of mother and child. I can only stare speechless at her. Oblivious to my thoughts she turns back to the shelf, replaces the doll and selects a Poupée de Modes, also from the same manufacturer in France. This one is a fashion doll dressed in the most recent style of clothing offered to the ladies. She is exquisite, measuring approximately eighteen inches tall, with a bisque head, painted eyes, human wig, pierced ears and a slightly smiling mouth as if she has a secret to tell. A somewhat smaller doll from Germany is the next to catch Pauline's attention; a Max Arnold made in Neustadt, also with a bisque head and wig, but with glass eyes and painted lashes.

The one I have chosen is the fashion doll, and I wait to see if it is the same one Pauline chooses. After a few moments of holding first one, then the other, she turns to me with the fashion doll in her arms.

"This is the one Sophie will like because she is growing into a young lady and does not play with baby dolls any longer," she states, handing the doll over to me.

I watch Pauline closely to see what catches her eye, for I am at a loss as to what gift to purchase her for Christmas that also is appropriate.

She keeps wandering over to an elegant toilet set and also a jewelry stand. I will have to ask her mother's advice. If it were up to me, I would purchase both, but I know that would not be wise. Decorum always, I remind myself.

I purchase the doll for Sophie and a glove box for Pauline's mother. With these two gifts neatly wrapped and tucked under my arm, we are off again in the direction of the Mansion House Hotel for a game of cards—a suggestion from Katie—before ending our evening with a stroll back to Pauline's.

Ferdinand Suhrer, the German artist Wilhelm Wellge, C. A. Key and Willie Jeffreys are in the main parlor upon our arrival. A card game of their own is in progress. All four men rise at our entrance in deference to the ladies and Ferdinand sets a table for our use.

Refreshments ordered consist of mulled cider for the women, and whiskey for Jeff and me. The game begins, ladies against gentlemen.

The game of Quiz we are playing is fairly new and is one in which the players race to determine whether they hold the card containing an announced quotation. It is called the professor card. The game is intellectual and fun, as well as more suitable for the ladies than the game of poker being played at the adjoining table.

After an hour of much laughter and complete annihilation by the ladies, we decide it's time to call it a night while we can still keep our dignity. It's obvious to Jeff and me that our opponents have had practice at this new game!

Helping Pauline with her cloak, I turn to Jeff and say, with a wink, "You know, it's only a few blocks back to Pauline's. We really don't need chaperones to walk us. We promise to be good, don't we, Pauline?"

Both of us know full well that as soon as we are out of sight of our friendly watchdogs we will be in each other's arms catching up on missed kisses.

But Jeff, regardless of his friendship with me, takes his role of chaperone and orders from Mr. Meddaugh seriously and won't hear of it. "Come now, ol' man, you know he'll be watching for her return. Don't mess things up on the first night."

And sure enough, the glow of his cigar is evident on the front porch where he sits with his feet up on the rail when the four of us approach the house a few minutes later. Saved by the bell—or should I say the watchdogs!

After polite pleasantries and small talk, the three of us bid good night to Pauline and her father. We continue our stroll, parting at Centre Street. Frustrated and lonely, I shuffle in the direction of Second Street and a tall lager. Jeff and Katie, holding hands as any newly wedded couple should do, promenade back toward the Mansion House, their temporary home until their house on Tenth Street is complete.

*

Halfway to the saloon I change my mind. My heart is not in an evening of revelry, but rather in holding my darling Pauline, so I turn toward home and a night of tossing and turning until daybreak.

My room in the Florida House Hotel is unique in that it has a private entrance on the front balcony which overlooks Third Street and the carriage house across the street. In order to reach it you must enter the hotel from the main entrance, go up the main stairs, past Miss Annie and Gracie's room, then go out the exit door onto the front balcony. My room, to the left, is the only room with a front balcony entrance. A large room with a fireplace and well-appointed furnishings, it is situated over the main dining room downstairs.

Miss Annie offered to move me to the new addition when it was finished last year and even though it is nice indeed, I prefer the feeling of solitude in my present quarters.

Many mornings such as this I go down early, usually observing servants and children of guests who have an earlier mealtime than the adults. I bring up a cup of coffee, sit in one of the many rockers on the balcony and watch the town come to life.

John Ellerman, sheriff of Nassau County and also justice of the peace, is out and about early as usual on his morning rounds, soon followed by Cuban cigar manufacturer Andrew Bonitel and his sons, who make the most wonderful cigars I have had the pleasure to smoke—outside of a true Havana—and work long, hard hours in their business.

The dairyman and iceman have long since delivered to Miss Annie, who is in the kitchen with her morning help. They prepare breakfast not only for her permanent residents such as myself and seven others, but also the tourists who fill the other of the total of twenty-five rooms.

My hat goes off to Miss Annie. She oversees the kitchen with a dinner menu that changes daily and also a staff who clean the rooms and maintain the grounds and buildings. She handles it all with her Irish eye for cleanliness, comfort and a jolly personality.

With reluctance I give up my comfortable spot, head down to breakfast and another day at work, with the bright ending being an evening with Pauline.

*

Thanksgiving eve services at the Presbyterian church have begun. I quietly slip into the pew beside Pauline while nodding to a scowling Mr. Meddaugh. What I will have to explain later is my tardiness due to an unexpected need to assist a friend in trouble.

Late this afternoon I sat engrossed in the never-ending columns of figures when my attention was interrupted by the unexpected entrance of young Moses. He stood there, eyes downcast, nervously twisting his hat in his small, grimy hands.

He stuttered so hard he could hardly speak, but when I came around the desk and knelt beside him, the words came so fast I was at a loss to keep up.

"Please Massa John, we needs yo' help," he pleaded. "Dey done took our house 'cause de railroad ain't pay since Papa done got hurt."

I was so shocked and distraught by his plight that I grabbed his hand, practically dragging the poor child with me, headed straight for the railroad office.

After a lengthy meeting with Col. Frank Papy of the Transit Railroad, the situation is resolved, back pay issued, home restored and food on the table in time for Thanksgiving.

It pains me that Moses had to experience this, but I feel honored he felt he could come to me for assistance in his time of need and I was able to do something for him and his father. Their future is now assured, with a small pension from the railroad and a part-time job for Moses after school and in the summer months.

Looking around at the well-dressed, well-fed congregation as we rise to sing the songs of Thanksgiving, the holiday has a different meaning to me. No longer will I sit at a table laden with food, eating and drinking with family and friends, and not think of those who are less fortunate, nor do something for at least one family.

Today's meal will be enjoyed at the home of Josiah and Mary Prescott, neighbors of the Meddaughs. Their daughter Clara is a close friend of Pauline's, being the exact same age of sweet sixteen. Clara attends Notre Dame Convent in Baltimore, and it is a treat to also have her home for the holidays.

Upon arrival I am pleased to find Dr. Starbuck and his family are guests. He will be able to give me an accounting of my friend Louis Horsey. Dr. Starbuck receives regular reports from South Carolina

Medical College since he is the preceptor for Louis's attendance and stays in close touch with him for counseling.

The children are entertaining themselves with the fairly new game of Parcheesi, while the ladies put the finishing touch to a table fit for a king in the formal dining room.

At the head of the table, Josiah proceeds to attempt carving the turkey amongst good-humored jibes from the rest of the menfolk blaming the unworthy, dull knife blade on the annihilation of the proud bird. Finally the task is assumed by the cook at the sideboard while sweet potatoes, turnips, onions and potatoes, dumplings, squash pie, cranberries and coleslaw are passed around.

After this is enjoyed and cleared, we partake of mince pie, nuts and candies along with coffee and mulled cider.

Politics are not allowed on this joyous occasion. Instead, laughter prevails, and memories of past Thanksgiving meals with family members absent and present are the topics passed round with the delicious food.

We men push back our chairs, excusing ourselves and adjourning to the side porch to smoke. The menfolk make haste to relieve ourselves of our tight neckwear, and loosen our jackets with a sigh of satisfaction, as I am sure men all over town are also doing.

An omnibus from McGinnis & Rawson has been secured to drive us all to Amelia Beach for an outing after dinner, and the younger children can hardly contain their excitement. Their energy is evident in the cartwheels and games of chase being performed while they wait in the side yard. Little James Starbuck has been designated the lookout and is hopping from foot to foot in front of the house, watching for the bus to arrive at the corner of Centre and Sixth streets.

"It's here!" he shouts in his high-pitched six-year-old voice. He runs onto the side porch and grabs his father's coat sleeve in his haste to be first to board.

But alas, he must wait. The ladies are handed up first, as is protocol. Then he, being youngest, is allowed to sit directly behind the driver, which we know is his fervent desire.

Normally the omnibus would stop along the way to pick up passengers for a low fare. Those who want to get on wave their hands, and to get off they signal by tugging on a little leather strap that is connected to another leather strap around the driver's ankle. But today they will have to take one of the other two omnibuses owned by McGinnis & Rawson; this one is filled to the brim with family and friends.

What a sight we must seem to the citizens of Fernandina: we speed along at four miles an hour hanging out the windows, waving and wishing everyone happy holiday, the season's mood having come upon us all!

Arriving at Amelia Beach, Pauline and Clara immediately run to the water's edge in their bathing costumes of dark flannel, which cover them from neck to ankles and wrists. Throwing off their overcoats and caution to the wind, they decide to brave the icy November waters and the later chastisement from their mothers. They stoop to roll up their costume legs, kick off slippers and dance among the ebbing waves.

Amelia Beach

I would not expect less from my Pauline, but the look of horror on Mrs. Prescott's face tells a different story of expectations of Clara.

It is obvious neither girl wants to nor can be heard over the roar of the surf and wind. They cavort down the beach laughing merrily. Seagulls swoop down to join them in hopes of a treat, wings holding them aloft in motionless flight as they float just above the young ladies' heads.

What a contrast they make to the older women dressed in tight corsets and bustles, with cane hats covered in straw, called "uglies," to protect their faces from the sun.

The younger children are making use of the low tide to build sand castles and fill the moats with water. They scurry like fiddler crabs as fast as their little legs will carry them to fill them up, but it is a never-ending affair; it seeps out as fast as they fill them.

Soon tired of this activity, a game of King of the Hill ensues among the boys, who have found sticks for swords. The girls have joined their mothers for a promenade along the beach with other ladies, Mrs. Sweeney from the Idle Hour, and Mrs. Ferreira. Both are dressed in mourning crape and have come to the beach for an outing with their families.

The Strathmore Hotel is our destination for a light evening repast and ultimate return home on the omnibus. We gather the children, and upon arriving at the hotel, find the rest of our party waiting on the verandah in polite company of friends and neighbors.

Pauline and Clara have made a change of costume and seem demure, obviously having been chastised by their mothers. Clara's eyes are downcast but Pauline has that look of defiance in hers that I know so well, and a twinkle when she first sees me.

I offer my hand. She rises without a look toward her mother for permission and we walk to the other end of the verandah.

"Well, looks like you did it again, my girl," I say, gazing into her radiant, sun-kissed face. "I hope you found it all worthwhile, for I am sure the punishment will be strong and extended, seeing as how you will be blamed for leading Miss Clara astray."

"Oh, phooey!" she retorts, stomping a delicate foot. "Clara was the one who suggested it! And yes, it was worth every glorious minute. Did you see the birds? Hear the sound of the ocean and wind? The feel of the water and the shifting sand under our feet is without description! One should not go through life without experiencing these pleasures because one is female, for God's sake!"

Shaking my head, I can't help but laugh at her words and actions.

"First, Daddy wants us girls to be educated like our brothers, to be able to think like men, to be able to take care of ourselves. I can balance his ledger books, order his supplies. Then on the other hand, Mother wants us to be proper Victorian ladies, to be a fragile, delicate flower incapable of making a decision beyond selecting the menu or teaching our children moral values. They send us to school to learn French, sewing and etiquette so that our households run smoothly and comfortably so our husbands can concentrate solely on earning money and not be bothered with anything else."

Seeing the serious look on her face, I stop laughing and draw her near to me in the shaded corner of the verandah.

"Do they not understand the difficulty I have with this upbringing?" Pauline gazes at me with tears in her eyes and an expression of anguish.

Without a care who is looking, I tilt her head up, wipe away the tears with my handkerchief and lightly kiss her trembling lips. Then I offer this advice: "Be yourself. That is all that matters."

She returns my kiss with sweet, salty kisses of her own.

"Both your father and mother have good intentions and be it as it may, all in all, I like the way you have turned out." I punctuate my statement with a hug. "Now let's join the others. I see they have gone inside and your father has graciously allowed us to remain here alone. But he will come looking for us if we tarry any longer."

The Strathmore was designed by Robert Schyler and built in 1882 by the Florida Transit Railroad, the same year the expansion was completed at the Florida House. The hotel is a center of activities not only for tourists but also for locals such as us.

Upon entering, we are immediately seized by George Bender and Katie Eppes, who are flushed by excitement of the three-piece band playing in the front hall. They hurry us forward and we have no choice but to join in the square dance in progress. Looking around I am relieved to see T.J. is in attendance, and I heave a huge sigh of relief as he and George good-naturedly change partners in the middle of the dance.

Afternoon fades into evening and an exhausted, sleepy troop of youngsters is loaded into the omnibus for the short ride home. Night has brought a pleasant chill to the air, though the stars are peeking out of an occasional cloud in an otherwise clear sky.

After tucking quilts provided by the driver over the ladies and children seated in the front, the men light cigars and seat themselves in the rear of the coach, finally given a chance to discuss business and politics.

Mr. Meddaugh broaches the subject of the approaching presidential election of 1884.

"According to telegraphic advices," he says, "there seems to be no doubt that the entire Democratic ticket has been elected in Ohio, with a probable majority in the legislature on the joint ballot. In Iowa it was hardly to be expected, as was reported in the *Florida Mirror*, that the Republicans would be defeated. And the *New York Sun* reports 'the Republican Party must go'! We remain a Democratic majority who are better skilled and experienced than the Republicans, not only in my opinion but also that of most politicians."

"But," I interject, "the Democrats continue to spend money building public buildings in Washington at a high rate of speed. Did you not see the list in the *Florida Mirror* some time back, listing the enormous sums spent on the White House, Capitol Building, Treasury Department, National Monument, Washington Monument, Naval Observatory, United States Jail, and the list goes on and on. Millions upon millions of taxpayer dollars, our dollars, yours and mine! Of course they try to appease us by stating that any American who has obtained the age of twenty-one years is an equal shareholder in these properties, but this does nothing to appease me!"

Back and forth we continue to spar, he becoming red around the collar as he expounds the virtues of the Democratic Party as I do the same in defense of the Republican Party to which I have most recently become affiliated.

It seems not only do we disagree on certain aspects of Pauline's and my relationship, but also our political views. Will we never agree on anything?

Pauline will remain through Christmas, and is planning her costume for the masquerade carnival at the skating club, along with mine. She has informed me we are to be an Arabian sheik and his slave girl. I have learned to do as Miss Pauline bids in these affairs and go along with the fun, since everyone else usually comes up with interesting costumes also. How well we remember past carnivals, with costumes ranging from hilariously funny, such as the beautiful woman who really was a man (guess who that was), to the Statue of Liberty. Great fun is always had by all—and anticipated—as great secrecy is placed upon the wearers' costumes and unveiling comes later in the dance.

Sad news is sent via William Reynolds, the telegraph operator, to Louis, and he soon arrives home to attend the funeral arrangements of his mother, Louisa, who has passed away of consumption. Yet another death in the circle of my close friends that leaves us saddened this holiday season. Louis will remain until after Christmas with his sister, Julia, and settle the details to allow Mrs. George Davis to continue running the boardinghouse and for his sister to remain living there.

But through the holidays he has taken rooms for himself and Julia at the Strathmore Hotel at Main Beach, for poor, grief-stricken Julia has a need of change of abode to relieve her distress.

Having lost both my parents, my mother when I was but nine years old and my father during the war, I can relate to Julia's grief. I can see the dreadful pain in her eyes and the way she tries to carry her body, but her shoulders slump nevertheless. I want to console her, say the right things ... but only time will heal the gaping, raw wound and the scar will remain. Her mother was her compatriot, best friend and mentor, and with Louis away at school, Julia will need the companionship and guidance of her friends to pull her through these next two years until he returns home for good.

Julia has no need to work and, other than social affairs, has no need to venture outside the home, so we will have to make a concentrated effort to assure that she socializes.

"You know Julia is fragile, and I will worry about her," Louis confides to me.

We sit on Miss Annie's back porch smoking, rocking and staring at the huge old oak tree. We have been contemplating his return to college, and left Julia behind to fend for herself.

"I don't think you give Julia enough credit," I respond, turning to him. I stand up, stretching and yawning; it has been a long day. "She will surprise you, take my word on it. She may appear fragile, but she is stronger in spirit than you give her credit for, and intelligent to boot. You don't have all the brains in the family, ol' man!" I make this good-humored jab at him as he also rises.

"Not only that, but she is pretty as well, and has caught many a man's eye. I would not be surprised if she does not marry before long. She is twenty-three, you know." I grin. "I would contemplate her myself if not for my love of Pauline."

I am surprised by the startled look on Louis's face, at the thought of his sister with a husband. She has never even had a beau.

"You don't want her to be an old maid, do you? Hanging around your house in corners in dark clothing, trying to tell your wife what to do, how you like things done?" I ask him in earnest.

Old maid. The words seem to have an unsettling effect on Louis, for he stops and cocks his head to stare at me.

"Julia deserves to lead her own life," I say. "I guess you haven't noticed that up until now she has done your mother's and your bidding. All things social centered around you two, not Julia. She has given freely—of course that is her nature—but now it is her turn. Her friends will stand guard without her knowing, but mark my words, fragile little Julia will prove to be strong and do just fine." I assure him of this with a shake of his hand and pat on his back.

Walking Louis across the street to the carriage house where Joseph Higgins is waiting to give him a ride back to the Strathmore Hotel, we make arrangements to meet again tomorrow after church. We are to take George Sweeney's boys and little Moses surf fishing. It's something I have been doing since George died and I believe I get as much pleasure from it as they do. There is peacefulness about the constant waves upon the shore, fish or no fish. Of course the excitement of the boys as they bring in "the big one" holds no bounds!

Standing there, hands in my pockets, I am overcome with a desire to turn toward my favorite brothel, the night air having refreshed me; all tiredness has vanished with the thought of caressing the lithe young body of sweet Mary. It has been a long time and the mere thought has my heart racing, palms sweating and limbs tingling. I have no control over this yearning desire and make no effort to do so.

Soon, a new doorman, huge as a mountain and black as soot, answers my knock on the door. Standing with arms crossed over his impossibly larger-than-life chest, he bellows at me as to my intention. Answering his query I am soon ushered in to see Miss Lizzie, who—will wonders never cease—is wearing an even tighter dress and more greasy makeup than I can recall. The place looks seedier and has an unusual smell. I begin to have a feeling of unease; the tingling in my lower region is quickly abating.

Fanning herself with the same bedraggled ostrich fan, she calls for the girls to parade forward and down as usual. She knows good and well the one I am seeking. Laughing her cackling laugh out loud in glee at her own sick humor, she calls for Mary to come to the head of the stairs.

With eyes downcast she appears, dressed in a long, flowing diaphanous gown of pure white virgin silk. Her nipples protrude through like succulent, juicy plums and the dark blonde V between her thighs is visible, making the tingle between mine return in full force.

I want my hands and mouth on her so badly that I can hardly wait and start up the stairs, but am halted by the sharp voice of Miss Lizzie and the iron grip of the doorman on my forearm.

"Hold on, young stallion, that will be triple the pay in advance, not double as before," she states, holding out her wrinkled hand for payment. Sweat pouring down her greasy face has made deep tunnels between her eyes and on her cheeks.

Startled by her announcement I pause with one foot in the air, hand on the railing. I look up at Mary, who is gazing down at me with a look of joy at seeing me again.

"Of course, madam," I say, bowing to Miss Lizzie. I reach into my pocket, drawing out the money and placing it in the doorman's hand. I then bound up the stairs, not looking back at either of them.

We rush down the hall and into Mary's room. We can hardly wait to close the door, discarding the ugliness below. Mary's room is cleaner, the air is sweeter and of course the girl is more beautiful than any of the others.

Pulling her to me I do not rush like before. I abate my hunger, I savor the feel of her body, the taste of her lips and skin as I pull her gown over her head, revealing all her glorious nakedness. Her skin is white as new snow, without blemish, her ripe nipples are my strawberries, and in the valley of her thighs lies the silky, dark blonde patch I so love to stroke first with my fingers, then with my tongue before we part her long legs for my entrance.

She is so beautiful it is difficult for me to imagine her in a place like this and not in some mansion. The world has not treated Mary fairly, I think as I pull her down on my lap and begin to stroke her breasts and kiss her lips slowly, softly. The passion rises, rises and rises between us. Her nipples harden under my insistent stroking and tweaking, her breathing quickens and she gently pushes me away.

Standing, she straddles me as I sit on the one chair in the room and she gently, slowly lowers herself until I am deep inside. Up and down she slides, hands on my shoulders, stopping each time she senses I am about to come inside her. She repositions herself, with her back to me, my hands on her breasts. I am again inside and she slides up and down. I can hardly stand the pleasure and exquisite pain of non-release.

Finally I can stand no more. We rise, still together, I position her on the bed on her knees and drive home. It is over in three short strokes, both of us moaning in pure pleasure.

"Jesus, Mary, how can you drive a man so wild!" I ask, gasping for breath and holding her close to me, unable to move.

Murmuring my name, she reaches between us and her long fingers begin stroking me back to life. We rock back and forth in the age-old rhythm. Stroking her blonde wetness as we move, I feel her shudder again and again while we make up for lost time.

*

"I do not think I will be here next time you come," she says while slowly washing me with her special lavender water. Her eyes hold sadness and yet there is a spark of hope glimmering deep inside.

Sitting up abruptly and knocking over the water basin, I hold her by both arms as I question her statement. "Where are you going?" I demand. "Is she selling you to another brothel?" No, not possible, I think. "Are you running away?"

My firing questions at her, not giving her a chance to answer, has visibly upset Mary and she has a worried look on her face.

"Please do not say anything to Miss Lizzie," she implores me. "Yes, I am running away! With a very nice sea captain from the Spice Islands who is gentle and kind. He will be good to me and promises to marry me. You are the only one I have told because I trust you and care for you and I did not want to just up and disappear, leaving you wondering what happened to me." She tells me tearfully, "I cannot stand it here any longer. It is impossible to tell you how I feel having to let any man, old, young, fat, dirty, bad teeth or drunk who can pay Miss Lizzie, do unimaginable things to my body. She takes the money I earn to pay for this horrid room, my meals, clothing, laundry, food, medicine and so many other things, that I have very little left."

The visions conjured in my head by what she is saying anger me so badly I want to lash out at Miss Lizzie and kill her! I have never had such feelings before.

"What little money I have saved was stolen from me by the other girls who are jealous of me, so I have no other alternative." Her voice breaks as she speaks, and she cries softly.

Pulling her gently to me, I cradle her in my arms as I would a small, wounded child, rocking her now in a different way, wiping away her tears until they slowly abate.

I wonder what will become of Mary. Will her sea captain truly be her savior, or her worse nightmare? I look around her tiny room in this squalid whorehouse and I know it would be selfish of me to try to detain her for my own pleasure. I can only wish her happiness and good fortune.

*

After church, little Moses is waiting for me, fishing cane in hand, beside the buckboard we have rented from Joseph. Eager for his fishing trip and afternoon with the boys, he is hopping from one dust-covered bare foot to the other, eager go.

"Whoa there, slow down, Moses. I have to change clothes and grab the picnic basket Miss Annie has prepared for us. Then we'll be off to pick up Mr. Louis and gather up the rest of the boys."

I laugh at his enthusiasm as I pat his dark, curly head, and bound up the stairs of the Florida House.

Though it must seem like hours to Moses, we are soon loading up Louis and his gear at the Strathmore, then off to the Idle Hour for the Sweeney boys nearby.

Mrs. Sweeney has also packed a picnic basket emanating smells that make my mouth water. I determine to drop a hook and grab a bite as soon as possible.

Arriving at our favorite fishing spot on the north end of the island, the boys eagerly hop down and we set up our fishing camp for the afternoon. Hooks are soon baited and in the water, quilts spread under a cluster of trees and a jug of lemonade opened to quench our thirst, for the weather has been unusually hot for December and a drought continues with no sign of letting up.

"The wells and cisterns are dangerously low," I relay to Louis as I unhook yet another fish. I bait up and walk into the surf, casting past the incoming waves. "We should look into drilling an artesian well, such as the ones at Daytona and Volusia counties. I understand St. Augustine is to undergo boring another one, only on a much larger scale this time. Reeds Mill has already obtained water in this manner, and normally a depth of 250 feet is all that is required."

"I should ask your boss, Mr. Wood, to take it up with the city commissioners at next week's meeting if I were you, and I will also look into it myself," he responds as he hauls in a huge drum fish, and backing up when the fighting fish chases him onto shore.

Looking down at my scarred hands, I shiver in the bright sun at the thought of another fire without sufficient water with which to fight it. It's a disaster in the making.

Talk drifts to the refrigerator storage house, built and located at Centre Street dock by the Egmont Hotel Company, for the hotel's use. But now Mr. Way has decided to branch out and allow storage by the Mallory Steamship Line of products for hotels statewide.

I say, "A very wise business decision on his part." I explain to Louis that Mr. Way represents William Ottman of Fulton Market, New York, the largest butcher of that city. "The Mallory and Savannah lines will arrive with shipments of beef two to three times a week."

Casting his line into the foamy surf, Louis settles down beside me as we continue our catching up on local news while waiting for the big one to bite.

"Also, a new route on the St. Johns River connecting Fernandina with Savannah via Darien and Brunswick has been proposed, that will connect the steamers with the Florida Railroad. So thus continues the growth of our little island. It is amazing how much industry and new businesses are attracted to this area," I say while pulling in a ridiculously small fish.

The boys laugh, pointing with glee as they struggle to hold up their string of fish.

"Well, I can see the boys have caught their share, and ours too, while we have been catching up on local happenings. Let's enjoy our picnic and then head back while they are still wiggling and fresh. Miss Sweeney promised to cook some up for our dinner if we had any luck today."

Calling the boys to join us, we head over to the cluster of trees and settle down to enjoy the treasures found in the picnic baskets.

"I sure do miss my dad when we are together like this," George Jr. says, his eyes watering as he tries to hold back tears and not choke on a mouth full of Miss Annie's famous fried chicken at the same time. "Remember how he would tell us stories about his sailing days before he settled down with Mama? The famous people he met on the ships, the places he went, the storms and what a great life it was?"

George stands up and I can see the startling resemblance of his father in the set of his jaw when he turns to stare at the horizon.

"I think I shall become a ship's captain and go to sea. But when I mention it, it upsets Mama. I know it is a long time off. I am only twelve years old, but I can apprentice as a mate when I turn fifteen. She tells me how she needs me at the Idle Hour and to be the man of the house for my little brother."

To change the subject he falls onto the quilt, grabbing Moses in a bear hug, and the three boys are soon wrestling the way they used to do with George, at the end of an afternoon's fishing excursion.

"Twelve is too young to bear his burden," I say quietly to Louis. "Do you think I should talk to his mother or leave it alone?"

"Leave it alone," he advises me. "Sometimes manhood comes far too early to some of us. Look at me. My father died, leaving me alone to support Mother and Julia, and it has done me no harm. Sure I missed out on some things, but on the whole I think I'm stronger and a better man in the long run." Louis shakes his head. "Don't coddle him. It's not what he needs. You're doing the right thing mentoring him, taking him hunting and fishing, and just being with him and his brother."

Watching the boys wrestling like young pups, I nod in agreement at his words. "Besides, you never know. Mrs. Sweeney may find a good man and marry again. She is only thirty-two, after all, and a very attractive woman."

Shucking down to his skivvies, Louis issues the challenge of a race to the ocean and we are off for a refreshing swim in the cool blue sea. The boys swim like young porpoises, laughing and splashing without a care in the world, young George joining in, a boy again if only for the moment.

*

I lather the soap to wash the sea salt from my body in the comfort of a much-needed bath. The day has been well spent in the company of friends, I think, and the perfectly-cooked fish at the end topped it off.

Closing my eyes I soon drift off in the warmth of the water. Confusing dreams of two women intertwine, weaving erotically through my mind when, with a jerk, I am brought back to reality by the banging on my door and the now cold bath water.

John Clay, resident druggist, is on the other side demanding entrance in his usual boisterous voice. "Come on, open up, John. Clinton and I need a fourth for a game of cards in the parlor and you are the only one available tonight."

In my rush to answer the door, he is still yelling when I slip and almost fall in the soapy water splashed on the shiny hardwood floor.

"Damn, John, you almost made me break my neck!"

I yank open the door and drag him in while wrapping a towel around my waist. Peering out to see if the others are close behind, I say, "Besides, you know Reverend Thackara and all the rest of the holy Fathers view it a cardinal sin to play cards on any day—and especially Sunday!"

He laughs at my attempt at a serious countenance, which I could hold only for a few seconds and soon we are both laughing.

"Right," he retorts, "it is also a sin to go fishing on Sunday but I did not see that stopping you now, did it?"

John is an easygoing, likeable kind of fellow in his early thirties. Born and raised in Virginia, he is the epitome of the Southern gentleman. Always impeccably dressed from his hair kept neatly trimmed at J. C. Rutishauser's Barber Shop to his shiny new boots purchased from Prescott's store, he is always ready if needed, to go in at a moment's notice and concoct drugs for some poor, sick soul.

"We will be waiting, so get dressed and come on down." Without pausing for an answer he is gone, so I have no recourse but to do as requested.

Downstairs, the table is set for poker, cards ready to be dealt, bottles of lager at each man's seat.

"Boys," I say when entering the parlor, "you are living dangerously. Miss Annie will have our hides if she catches us."

"She has gone to late Mass with her sister, Marie, and Joseph, and then they are having supper at the Lucy Cottage afterwards. We will be finished and all put away long before she and Gracie return," Clinton smugly replies while dealing the first hand. "Besides, we will not be smoking inside. That's what gave us away before."

The time passes pleasantly, the grandfather clock strikes the hours as games are played and bottles drunk. William Young, our resident lawyer who hails from Alabama, is winning the majority. Clinton Haley, who works as a clerk in town, good-naturedly pokes fun at him, swearing he is somehow cheating as all shyster lawyers do.

Finally winning a hand, I give a startled look at the clock and push my chair back, leaping quickly out of it. "Hurry, Miss Annie will be here any minute!"

We scurry around like little boys about to be caught with our hands in the cookie jar, cleaning up, putting things in order for the imminent arrival of the innkeeper.

We find ourselves rockers and cigars on the back porch without a minute to spare before she arrives. We grin at each other like Cheshire cats, bidding her good evening, blowing smoke rings at the moon and bursting out laughing when she is out of earshot. We continue to rock for awhile, not believing our luck at getting away with it.

Next morning at breakfast, sitting directly in front of each one of our places is an empty lager bottle, but not a word from Miss Annie when she makes the rounds pouring coffee and humming an Irish ditty. She smiles and chats merrily as she pauses to pass the day with the other boarders.

It goes to show, there is just something about the Irish. They have this extra sense about them. One thing I know for certain, you can't get anything past Miss Annie!

*

The week flies by and Friday night arrives, with it the long-awaited Skating Carnival. A servant of Pauline's has delivered my costume. I can't help but laugh in amusement at the image in Miss Annie's pier mirror of the Arabian sheik peering back at me. I puff up my chest, trying to look more the role, to my and Miss Annie's amusement. For no matter how I try, the image does not change; my height falls well short and my chest refuses to stay inflated. Surely my beautiful slave girl will make up for the laughs I am about to incur.

Entering the already overcrowded hall I am relieved to see that my costume is no more ridiculous or amusing than many of the others in attendance. Pauline and I are immediately swallowed up by the crowd, which consists of Mrs. R. W. Southwick and Miss Willie Harn as nuns, Mr. A. H. Crippen as an Indian chief and George Hubby as Oscar Wilde, among others.

We work our way toward the refreshment table. I spy Miss Voorhees, very prettily turned out as Flora, with Gracie Leddy, Bessie Swann, and Emma Maxwell in costumes and masks, standing alongside the wall, for there are no seats to be had.

Removal of masks and dancing will start at ten o'clock. Until then, skaters are trying to avoid being recognized by skating in ways different to their usual style, which causes unabashed laughter, for few are successful.

Twirling Pauline lightly around the floor, I am amazed at her grace on the rink floor. She is so graceful, even in the awkward costume she is wearing. We skate to the waltz now being played.

I whisper in her ear as I catch her by the waist, "You are the most beautiful slave I have ever owned."

"I am your only slave, sir," she whispers back, "and besides, you don't own me. I only allow you to think you do. Now you know my secret." She laughs coyly and spins away from me with a "catch me if you can" look on her face.

Taking up the challenge I skate after her, weaving through the crowd none too fast until I spy her at last stepping out the door into the night air.

On the verandah I sit beside her, where we quietly enjoy the coolness, and the comings and goings of other members as they parade in and out. We comment on their costumes, complimenting some, and laughing as if our sides would burst at others—as soon as they are out of earshot.

Mary and George Dewson, dressed as peasants, come out looking for T.J. and Katie.

"I know they were coming tonight," Mary says, looking around the verandah. "I helped Katie design and sew their costumes. We worked on them for weeks."

"Probably waiting to make a grand entrance," Pauline whispers under her breath to me as they return to the carnival.

"You should be ashamed of yourself! I thought you and Katie were getting along better these days, or rather it seemed that way the other night when we were out to dinner and cards."

Turning toward me with her best Miss Prim and Proper look on her face, Pauline begins a litany of the most recent gossip learned since her return from school.

"Now, Pauline, gossip is a mean, ugly and nasty habit, and one I did not think you had and I sure hope you are not about to acquire."

I stand and hold a hand out to assist her to her feet. The unmasking is about to commence.

"You know I would not repeat anything I hear to anyone but you," she responds in her usual reticent manner while holding on to me for balance. "Besides, you are quite right. The more I am around Katie, I can see how things can get misconstrued about her."

Inside the hall an air of excitement is at fever pitch; the announcement is called to unmask at the stroke of ten. To our surprise, standing almost within arm's reach are T.J. and Katie. They laugh at our shock to see them unveiled as plantation master and ragged little slave girl. So artfully are the costumes done, we can see how even Katie's sister did not recognize them even though she helped with the costumes!

The band strikes up and dancing commences.

Just before midnight, Mr. Meddaugh collects the ladies of his house and I return home as I had arrived, dropping Louis and Julia off along the way.

All had a smashing evening and are in agreement that the next carnival to be held in January is looked forward to. It is sure to be an even greater success. In the meantime a reception and hop will be held on Christmas night for members and friends.

I think I shall suggest to Pauline that I prefer not to be an Arabian sheik ever again. A pirate for me, or maybe Romeo and Juliet for the two of us, would be nice, I muse as I allow the horse to trot along toward home to the livery stable across from the Florida House.

On arrival I am surprised to find John Clay sitting on the front porch, rocking in deep thought.

"What keeps you up so late?" I ask, settling in the adjacent rocker. "Something bothering you?"

"Not really what you would call bothering," he replies, staring at the moonlit night. "Just decisions needing to be made that I have been putting off because I enjoy this town and my friends here so much that I hate to contemplate leaving."

"Leaving?" I ask in shock. "Why would you do that?"

"Well," he says with a sigh, and stops rocking, "I miss my wife dearly and I want her with me. There is not sufficient room in town for another pharmacy, so I have been looking around and found a good situation on the St. Johns River. Therefore lies the dilemma. I must resign my position, tell my friends and the good town of Fernandina goodbye and start over in a new town, albeit with my wife."

Of course we all knew John was married and that he was working to earn enough to bring his wife here, but none of us had any idea it would come to this.

"You will be sorely missed, my friend," I tell him, "but family always comes first and you will be a happier man, as I am sure you already know."

We sit in companionable silence, soaking in the feel of Fernandina at the witching hour. ... The sounds of trains uncoupling down at the yards, ships bumping against the wharf, two drunks yelling obscenities at each other as they stumble their way home and the gentle whisper of the night breeze wafting in across the river.

Yes, John will miss this town and the town will miss him.

*

Christmas Day is closing in on me and I have yet to select a gift for Pauline. Arising from my bed with that purpose in mind, I set off in the direction of King's Bazaar for another look at the jewelry stand and toilet set she had an eye on.

My dilemma is apparent to Mrs. King who, knowing Pauline well, leads me to a beautiful china tea set that is more appropriate for me to give and she knows Pauline has her heart set on.

With that taken care of, I am finally in the Christmas spirit! I begin looking around for items: foodstuff, toys and such to make a gift basket for Moses and his father, and one for Mrs. Sweeney and the boys. Then there's little Gracie ... a doll? No, not for our Gracie. A book is what she would prefer. And for Miss Annie, who puts up with my misdemeanors, a new apron, all white and starched so stiff.

Finally, after two hours of shopping and wrapping of gifts by helpful clerks, I have exhausted myself and my wallet. Messengers will deliver the gifts.

Stepping out onto Centre Street into the bright sunshine of a cold, clear December day, I am suddenly reminded that only two weeks ago it was unseasonably warm and now the temperature has dropped to a record cold of thirty-two degrees!

Thankfully, no harm has been done to the orange or castor bean trees here due to the freeze, or at Gainesville, Waldo, Tampa or Orange Lake, where temperatures dropped below the freezing mark. In fact, some very large oranges measuring twelve to fourteen inches in circumference and weighing eleven ponds, from the Higginbotham place two miles from the ferry, were brought to town this very week.

I clutch my coat tighter around me and pull on gloves. I walk in the direction of the harbor in search of fresh seafood, hot coffee and, I hope, a warm fire to sit by for lunch. All this shopping has worked up my appetite.

The street is teeming with holiday shoppers laden with bags and parcels. They merrily call to each other as they rush from store to store, eager to see what prize is offered at each.

J. T. Kydd, Mode Brothers, King's Bazaar, Hoyt & Company, Prescott's, Meddaugh's, Lake's Jewelry and all the others have gotten in the best selection seen in years of gifts, candies and fancy groceries to choose from. Every man, woman and child is sure to open their eyes on Christmas morning to something wonderful that will fulfill their heart's desire.

I note with pleasure as I walk, the progress of rebuilding the business district and the multitude of bricks on vacant lots ready for the bricklayers and carpenters. Fine new buildings will replace the wooden ones destroyed by the fire.

The New Year should see this rebuilding well under way and completed shortly thereafter, and the town will be better off in appearance and safety because of the brick.

A disturbance has drawn a crowd outside Prescott's store. Hurrying over, I see Andrew Boitel, the Cuban cigar maker and his wife, Carmen. Some tramps who have been loitering around have pushed them off the sidewalk, and their parcels have fallen to the ground in every direction.

Yelling at the unkempt bunch as I rush over to assist, they scatter down Second Street, Andrew chasing after them toward Old Town.

"Here, Carmen." I offer my hand to steady her as she shakes the hem of her dress. "Are you okay?"

"Si, senor, muchas gracias," she replies in her sultry but now unsteady Spanish voice.

"Those tramps are getting to be more and more of a problem," I tell a worried Andrew upon his return.

Seeing that Carmen is still rattled by the episode, I invite them to lunch with me. The three of us continue the short distance to the restaurant, where we find a nice, quiet corner to relax in. After a while amongst the company of friends and good food the episode is all but forgotten.

Between bites of succulent shrimp fresh off the boat, I say, "The growth and affluence of the town is attracting some unwelcome tenants who are camping out in the woods by Old Town and must be summarily dealt with."

Andrew nods in agreement, patting Carmen's hand, still trying to soothe her frayed nerves.

Entering with a swirl of cold air, John McKenzie, his wife, Augustina, and their three daughters, Luella, Mabel and Bertha, enter and are ushered to the table adjoining ours.

Carmen and the ladies compare Christmas lists, leaving us gentlemen to discuss the ridiculous situation of having a mayor and vice-mayor, due to the mayor having interests on a steamer and being gone for long periods of time.

"Whether or not he collects a salary while he is absent is not the issue," expounds John, "it is the fact that he cannot duly perform his duties with all these comings and goings. He is either mayor or needs to step down, is my opinion."

He has punctuated each of the last words firmly and finally with a fist on the table, startling the ladies, who turn their heads as one to look at him quizzically.

"It would be the same as me trying to hold a political office while traveling as often as I do, tending my business as sewing machine agent. Sometimes I am gone for days or even weeks at a time. It would be impossible."

"Mayor Haley is a good mayor," I agree, "but he does not have the best interests of the city in mind as far as this is concerned. At almost every council meeting there is a request for payment of monies for Acting Mayor Suhrer and a separate request for payment for Mayor Haley. It is an ongoing bookkeeping nightmare."

Changing the subject to a different note after seeing the look on the ladies' faces—you know how they hate politics at the table—I ask if any present are attending the Oyster Supper and Sociable on New Year's Eve at Lyceum Hall.

To our pleasure, all have plans on attending and the conversation becomes a lively one about who else is and is not going, and the music planned for the occasion.

We finish lunch on this pleasant note, the earlier troubles overshadowed by holiday cheer. Bidding each other "Merry Christmas," we go our separate ways.

Back at the Florida House I relax on the back porch while enjoying the rich Cuban cigar made by Andrew in his factory. He gave it to me in a parting gesture of thanks for my assistance and friendship.

Miss Annie's cats watch me from a distance while they laze in the late afternoon sunshine. The old tabby practically sprawls on top of the newest member of the lot, a sleek black male with white paws that Gracie has appropriately named Socks.

Gracie always seems to have a litter of kittens to tend to in the back toolshed, near the privies. Under Miss Annie's guidance, Gracie watches over them like a little mother, taking particular care of the runts, nursing them to health and crying as if her heart will break at their funerals when everything fails to ensure their survival.

Gracie is a tenderhearted and loving child, full of grace, so her name fits her well. She was born in 1873 in the front upstairs room, over the dining room of the Florida House, soon after her parents purchased it from the railroad. This is the only home she has known.

As an only child she was very close to her father, and she was bereft when he passed away—inconsolable to the point that her mother became extremely worried about her decline and grief.

Her aunt Marie Higgins gave them their first kitten, the now toothless old tabby that rules his silent kingdom. Thus began the climb out of her dark misery, and the many cats and kittens followed.

I myself enjoy the cats, as well as do the guests, especially the children. Aloof and indifferent one minute while the next they are in your lap purring, their little motors run to your satisfaction while you stroke away.

Lost in thought, I do not hear the approaching sound of boots until I am startled out of my reverie by the sudden sight of a very drunk Joseph Higgins on the side of the porch.

"Oh no, Joseph, Marie will have your hide!" I yell at him, and jump up so fast I knock over the rocker.

"Here, have a drink," he slurs, holding up a whiskey bottle and taking two steps backward at the same time, almost falling over the rail.

Grabbing him under both arms I hoist him up and over my shoulders—no easy feat—for as a blacksmith he is a brawny man, and I half carry, half drag him across the porch, across the street and into the livery stable.

After I extract the whiskey bottle from him, I lay him down in one of the stalls. He turns over and immediately begins snoring. He is passed out for the night.

Damn the Irish and their whiskey, is all I can say. Joseph is a good man, hard-working at the stable and at the Florida House. In fact, he helped build the new addition last year. He just loves his whiskey too much.

Marie will be looking for him, but I will not be the one to tell her that he was in the bottle again. I will leave that up to him when he sobers up.

*

Tomorrow is Sunday, December 21; just four more days until Christmas. My darling and I will attend church and Sunday dinner together, and an afternoon tea at Mrs. Duryee's home.

The office is closed until the day after Christmas, so I will have more time with Pauline. Then there is the reception and hop at the skating club—no costumes, thank goodness!

The year is rapidly coming to a close. I wonder what the New Year will bring. So much has happened this past year, what with the fire and deaths of friends, but let's not forget the good things. New businesses opened, bringing progress to our little island, my love for Pauline and hers for me, new beginnings in the marriages of friends and family, and births of babies.

Yes, I remind myself and smile while turning in for a good night's sleep, the old year has been pretty good after all, and the New Year has a lot to look forward to.

Chapter 7

1884

A New Year Begins

The whole town is talking about Wellge's "Bird's-eye View" lithographic map of the town. It is the most amazing pen drawing ever seen. It is small enough to picture the entire town, including not only the houses but also steamboats and small crafts in the harbor—with a grand view of the Atlantic Ocean. The "bird" is half a mile in the air!

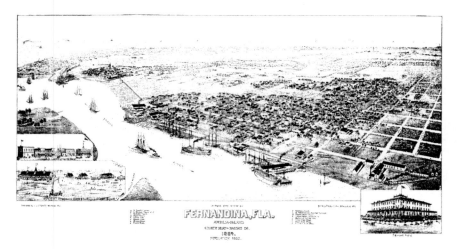

Bird's Eye View

121

Subscriptions are available in the amount of $4.50, no small sum for sure, but well worth the price. Mr. J. D. Trimmer, agent for the publishing house of J. J. Stoner of Madison, is making this truly a bargain for any business or household, and a valuable relic for our children for years to come.

I myself will be one of the first to purchase one, having met Mr. Wellge personally and having introduced him to our fair city. He is an artist like none I have ever known.

Shaking the ice—yes, I did say ice—from my coat before entering the council meeting tonight, I wonder the significance of such foul weather in Florida. It has been up and down for the last month or so to the extent no one knows how to dress from one day till the next. The thermometer outside Horsey's Drug Store is hovering around the thirty-degree mark and the constant rain of the day has turned this to ice.

I hope the meeting won't take long but am afraid that is wishful thinking on my part, for this is the first session of the New Year and there was no session last week.

Surprisingly, the agenda flows along smoothly, with the petitions for Mr. Lakes's two-story concrete building on Centre Street with a tin roof, and Braddock & Company's 10 x 18 shed for fish packing readily granted.

Then the following bills for salaries for December are ordered paid:

R. F. Smith, Marshal	$ 40.00
J. Hippart, Police	$ 25.00
N. Bradley, Police	$ 35.00
S. Cook, Police	$ 35.00
H. Clay, Contractor for scavenger work, etc.	$ 33.00
W. F. Wood Jr., salary from Aug. 1, 1883, to Jan. 1, 1884	$ 208.30

Also a bill from H. E. Dotterer of $3.80 for merchandise.

The fixation of the 1883 tax rate passes, and nominations are received as follows for a fire chief: James McGiffin, C. J. Kimball and W. S. Rawson.

Aldermen Robinson and King beg to be excused from voting on the question, and the election is postponed until the next meeting.

Alderman Kelly introduces a resolution, which is adopted, making it obligatory upon the marshal to notify storekeepers to put waste paper, garbage, etc., of their premises into barrels or boxes, in order that the scavenger cart can remove it.

Next, the ongoing issue of reducing the police force arises, followed by a lengthy filibuster by the opposers; Aldermen Robinson and King continue for some time until at last they withdraw from the chamber, leaving the council without a quorum.

The council has no choice but to adjourn.

After wearily blotting the ink on the final page of notes, I arrange the other pages in precise order for tomorrow morning's report to Mr. Wood. He likes to have it ready prior to his arrival at eight o'clock.

I pull my pocket watch out of my waistcoat and am surprised at the lateness of the hour, half past ten. No wonder my stomach has been making embarrassing noises for the past hour! I hope Miss Annie has some cold meat or cheese and bread I can filch from the kitchen to stave off this hunger until the morning meal.

Hurrying along in the bracing cold air I am acutely aware of the stillness of the night. The whole town is covered in a thin, white layer of ice that crunches underfoot and announces my approach. It is the only sound in the slumbering town.

*

I am astonished to find Miss Annie sitting at the kitchen table, hands wrapped around a steaming cup of coffee, as if in wait for the tardy boarder. Rising, she pours a cup for me, strong and black just the way I like it, and we sit facing each other quietly, two kindred spirits passing a few moments without need of words.

I know how hard it must be for her raising Gracie and running the hotel without the Major, in a day and age when few women work outside the home and rarely are the proprietress of such a large endeavor. Even though she blessedly has the help and support of her sister, Marie, and Joseph, the daily workload is monumental. I have seen Miss Annie work from before dawn to way after midnight on many occasions. She changes the supper menu on a daily basis and may the saints protect the cook who wavers from it or prepares a dish that is unsatisfactory in any way. The bed linens are always freshly laundered, white and crisp; the furniture and floors polished to a high shine and fresh flowers placed in every room.

All these things taken for granted are exacting a toll on her, as can be seen by the fine lines around her mouth and forehead that I can swear were not there yesterday.

The sudden rumblings of my furiously hungry stomach, announcing its need to be fed, break our companionable silence. Laughing out loud at the startling noise in the quiet kitchen, we both are soon searching the icebox, bringing out platters of cold ham, chicken, cheese and tongue to add to the fresh bread and butter already on the table.

After we settle down to our late-night repast, I ask Miss Annie to tell me about her husband, Major Leddy. This causes her face to light up and her eyes to sparkle like a young girl's.

"I wish you could have known him," she softly replies. "We met in Hancock, New York, just after the war. My papa thought he was too old for me, he being fourteen years my senior, but I finally won Papa over to my side. Papa could never say no to me very long, anyway."

The room has grown chilly, so I rise and put more wood in the stove while listening to Miss Annie's wonderful love story.

"Thomas was the second oldest son to John and Bridget Leddy, in a family of six children, Mary and Margaret being twins. They were your typical hard-working, fun-loving Irish family. The farm was their life; from sunup to sundown they worked the land, remembering the potato famine that had driven them from Ireland in 1848, along with John's brother, Thomas. Those were horrible years for my family, as well as for countless others who lost their loved ones to starvation and loss of property.

"There were many Irish-owned farms in the area, like one big family when planting and harvesting time rolled around, everyone helping each other. It was a big move for us to come here after the war, but Thomas had fallen in love with Fernandina during the war and with his new position as justice of the peace, it was a big step for him from the farm, an opportunity not to be passed up. So I put on my bravest face, hugged my papa goodbye and set out on the adventure of my life, not knowing that Thomas would give me a beautiful daughter and soon leave me a widow and all this to tend to alone." She motions with a sweep of her hand.

"I miss his handsome, smiling face across from me at the dinner table and the squeals of laughter as he tossed Gracie in the air. … But most of all, he was my first and only love. I hope you will experience the lasting kind of relationship with Pauline as I did with Thomas. Even though it was for a short time, it was enough to suffice a lifetime. I will never remarry, for no man could ever make me feel the way he did. So special, so loved, so truly fulfilled."

Miss Annie shakes her head as if to bring herself back to the present, and rises, gathering her wrapper close around her. She comes around the table and gives me the first hug she has ever bestowed upon me and bids me good night. She departs, leaving me to savor the feeling of love not lost but locked away, as a treasure one keeps to be brought out at special moments to be shared, or in times of crisis to get one through the difficulties.

Next morning the cold persists, bringing with its icy breath word of yet another death of our babes. Daisy Busby has succumbed to bronchitis at the tender age of four. Just before Christmas, the winter hiatus caused the loss of Leopold Barr on December 11 at only nine months, of cholera infantum, and Priscilla Denefield, three years of age, of ulcerated sore throat on December 23. It grieves Doc not to be able to save these little ones from disease brought on by poor sanitary conditions coupled with changing winter weather.

"More the reason for drilling an artesian well and increasing garbage collection," John Clay, resident druggist, states over his second cup of coffee. "We surely don't want another epidemic on our hands from drinking foul well water."

He turns to Miss Annie. She is passing around another pot of steaming coffee and a plate of golden-brown biscuits. "You are boiling your water used for cooking and drinking, as I suggested?"

"Of course I am, you need not have asked," she retorts with an exasperated frown and hand on her hip as she turns toward the formal dining room. Located on the other side of the ice room, it was added on after the Leddys purchased the inn from the Florida Railroad.

The hotel is, as are all the hotels in town, booked solid with guests and have been since the holidays. We, the permanent boarders, prefer to eat in the everyday coziness of the kitchen, leaving the formal dining room to the "here today, gone tomorrow" guests. Not that we don't care to acquaint ourselves or mingle with them; we do so on occasion. It's just that we prefer to not have to stand on our P's & Q's or entertain the travelers as we go about our daily schedules.

"The Carnegies are in residence at the Egmont along with two of their children and servants," prattles little Gracie upon entering the kitchen with an empty platter. From the cook, she reaches for another one loaded with ham, destined for the dining room.

"Mrs. Carnegie is giving a tea Saturday afternoon for the ladies, and Lizzie Gunn, Lula Pope and I are invited as well. It will be such fun!"

Without giving us a chance to respond she is out the door, hurrying about her chores, helping her mother as she usually does when school is out on holiday.

The lack of sleep last night coupled with the kitchen's warmth causes me to linger longer than usual over my third and final cup of coffee, which in turn is the reason I, for the first time ever, am late for work.

Upon my arrival, however, the lateness goes unnoticed; to my surprise the office is empty.

After I add wood to the banked fire it is soon roaring to life. With the chill off the room I can comfortably start my report of last night's commission meeting. The hours tick by and still no Mr. Wood. I begin to wonder if I have missed a required meeting elsewhere. But there is no notation on my calendar to that effect. Finally, at the approach of the noon hour he arrives looking harried and worn. He explains that his child was grievously ill during the night and morning but the fever has now broken.

"Please make note for next week's commission meeting, the importance of the city council giving attention to improvement of the drainage and sewer system before summer." He is adamant on the subject. "Those pipes have been laid down for many years and some are stopped up or broken, causing leakage into nearby wells. I know Doc will agree with me as to the cause of these fevers and sickness. Something must be done and soon, before we have an epidemic on our hands."

"This subject is cause for concern among the citizens and was discussed at breakfast this very morning," I inform him.

"Next on the agenda is the need of more street lamps on the main avenue into town. Seventh Street, being the prominent thoroughfare, has a great need, especially at the corners of Date and Cedar streets."

We continue working on items for next week's meeting without realizing we have worked well past our dinner break. William makes an early day of it, first to stop by his stationery store to check on things there and then home to be with his wife and child. I conclude my paperwork and then go home to freshen up prior to dinner with Pauline and her family.

The holidays have sped by and she will be leaving for school on Sunday. She will return at semester's end in May and will remain home for the summer. Needless to say, we're looking forward to the long months of summer and have made a multitude of plans to fill them.

The usual family members are in attendance this evening as well as a variety of neighbors for the "sending-off feast," as Pauline calls it.

"You should be happy to have such a large and close family and caring friends," I tell her later as we walk down Centre Street. "My parents are gone, and I was an only child. But I am making new friends here, which I am grateful for, and I am looking forward to becoming a part of your family."

We stroll past stores quiet after the hustle and bustle of the day, empty lots piled high with bricks and lumber ready to rebuild from the terrible fire, and homes glowing with the light of cheery fires within.

"I'm surprised your father allowed us to walk alone tonight without a chaperone," I say, looking at her with a smile at our good luck.

"That was Mama's doing," she replies with a twinkle in her eyes. "She told him I am maturing into a proper young lady and have shown so during the holidays, and should be given the opportunity to prove myself to him. So what do you think, fine sir?" At that, she takes off at a run down Fourth Street in the direction of the gazebo, skirts held high and slippers singing a wild, erratic song as they hit the street. Laughing gleefully over her shoulder, she calls out "Catch me if you can" and zigzags through the churchyard. Reaching her destination, she drops down on the bench.

Breathlessly I sit down beside her. I don't have a chance to admonish her for taking such a chance to be seen because she turns to me with trembling lips, parted to be kissed, and I lose myself in them like a drowning man floundering to be rescued.

Finally surfacing for a breath of air I am shaking from head to foot. My body is as warm as a summer day in the midst of this winter ice. I look at her in wonder, not believing that I have reached another level of feeling that goes beyond anything I ever thought possible between a man and a woman. Holding her at arm's length, I see the look of wonder in her eyes as well. Gone is the girlish prankster of a few moments ago, replaced by this glorious, almost holy, too wondrous female who blessedly chooses me.

Before I can speak, she touches my lips with her fingers in understanding. She rises, takes my hand and in companionable silence we walk in the direction of Sixth Street. The chill in the air does nothing to dissipate the warmth surrounding us.

No father sitting on the porch awaiting her return is further proof of his willingness to allow his next to youngest the opportunity to follow her own path as he himself has taught her.

On my walk home, thoughts are whirling, spinning out of control, wishing the next two years away. I gaze longingly at houses with smoke curling from chimneys and imagine the sounds of laughter, the smells of food … and ache to be snuggled up by our own cozy fire.

Remembering my words to Pauline of how quickly the time will pass, it is now difficult to accept my own counsel.

"Lord, please, please make the time go quickly," I pray as I drop off to sleep.

*

I cannot help but be a little jealous of Pauline's excitement as she chatters away at the prospect of returning to school and her studies. No, I am not like other men of our time, wanting our women to be only wives and mothers. She is too intelligent a woman to waste her mind. But she could at least wait until the ship has sailed to be so excited to be gone!

Oh, I know, I'm feeling sorry for myself on this last day. I want her to cling to me and weep and wail as before, so I can hold her tight, dry her eyes and kiss the tears away. But that's not happening today. Our Pauline is truly maturing, as her mother said yesterday, and to be honest with myself, it is for the best. So I must dry my own eyes before she sees. Smile and wish her bon voyage with all the rest, and get on with it until May.

T.J. and Katie are at the docks as well this morning. Katie has been more subdued of late, which was the high topic on my walk with Pauline to the dock earlier today. And lo and behold, here they are. For the last two weeks there have been no incidences of going out while T.J. was out of town working, and her attire has improved also. No more low-cut bosoms—maybe because of the cold weather? Probably not, to Pauline's thinking, but Katie gets my vote on that one.

"When do you plan to return?" Katie is asking Pauline as we wait until the very last minute for her to board.

"Well, my friend Effie Mae Wilson's wedding is on May 7, and even though it is to be a small family affair, I have been invited to attend and will be able to arrive in time to do so."

My eyebrows shoot up in surprise at the word "wedding," but she eases my worry by mouthing back "small" to me, and I smile at the hidden laughter in her eyes. She knows how I dislike these affairs and only attend the ones society most demands.

"Mama and Sophie will book passage to New York in late April in order for us to visit with family and do some spring shopping. Then we will return together on May 4. It's always so much fun shopping for the new fashions in New York with Mama. You should see the department stores there! They are so big, it takes days. And the restaurants are fabulous! We stay in the hotel and have all our purchases delivered to us. You should come with Mama and Sophie. You would be one of the first in Fernandina to wear the newest fashions."

With the invitation still on her lips and excited by her idea, Katie turns to Jeff. Pauline is surprised by the looks that flash between husband and wife and the slight negative shake of Jeff's head. The conversation comes to an embarrassed halt.

Clearing my throat I try to think of what to say, and am thankfully saved by the loud blast of the ship's horn signaling all aboard.

After T.J. and Katie leave, I walk Pauline up the gangplank for my private goodbye, with our usual promises to write, and a hug and kiss.

"What do you think that was all about?" she muses, obviously as curious as I about the scene played out between Katie and Jeff.

"Katie seemed so happy one minute and the next she looked on the verge of tears, like there was something she wanted to tell me but Jeff was warning her not to. Did you see that dark look on his face when he shook his head at her? I wonder what's going on. See what you can find out and write me as soon as you can. I just can't stand it with me leaving and not knowing, especially with the change in her the last couple of weeks."

"I don't plan to interfere between a husband and wife," I respond, "but if I hear anything I will write you post-haste. Now how about my kiss?"

*

The weather is beginning to warm up a bit; actually, a southeasterly breeze is blowing today and the high this afternoon, according to the thermometer at Horsey's Drug Store, reads seventy-two degrees. Doc and I have decided to take a leisurely stroll to walk off our supper after dining at Beard's Restaurant on Second Street.

2nd Street, North

"I don't know when I have eaten a better steak," Doc declares. He grins, rubbing his rotund belly in proof of its fullness.

Equally as satisfied, I reply, "Lately they have been buying their beef from the Fulton Market branch at the ice house on the Centre Street dock, and the freshness and quality speak for themselves."

Mr. Beard has been serving huge portions in his restaurant to the black and white populace for a number of years with the help of his mulatto cook, John Dufour, who in his own right out-cooks some of the finest chefs in our local hotels. He has been sought out to do so, but has not been persuaded. His allegiance is to Henry, with whom he and his wife, Jane, also board.

"Well, I and my stomach hope he continues on for a long time to come," Doc says happily as we near our destination of the Mansion House and our appointed card game with Ferdinand and Senator Farrell of Rochester, New York. The senator is a guest there for an undetermined length of time while he looks into the possibility of purchasing some orange grove properties in Florida.

"You would do better to look farther south and inland around Lochloosa Lake, as David Yulee has done," I advise Senator Farrell after our first round of cards has passed in my favor.

He shuffles the deck while giving me his full attention.

"Even though we have some very nice orange groves in the county and some fine trees right here in town, they are nothing compared to the grove owned by Yulee and, better yet, it is located near the Peninsular Railway tracks for ease of shipment. He presently is building a residence on the property for his manager, Mr. King, and also for the other employees, as well as surveying, fencing and building a residence for himself nearby."

Dealing out cards for the next hand, with his cigar smoking on a tray beside him, the senator stops long enough to reach in his suit pocket and hand me the *Florida Mirror*, dated October 13, 1883, with an ad circled:

For Sale: Three hundred acres of
land within two miles of King's
Ferry, Fla.; eighteen Acres improved.
Good dwelling, kitchen, etc. and 75
young orange trees, on the place. For
particulars, address R. W.
Swearingen, King's Ferry, Fla.

"This is what brought me here," he says, "as well as an ad placed by George Fairbanks for twenty-acre parcels located on Orange Lake suitable for orange growing and truck farming, conveniently located for shipping by water or rail. So, you can see I have researched well my subject, but as to whether or not I will invest is another matter."

At that moment Katie Eppes approaches Ferdinand and lays her hand upon his shoulder, which I think a little odd and unusual for a married woman to do, but since she and Jeff live at the Mansion House and are friends with Ferdinand, surely I am putting too much into it.

She says, "Please pardon my interruption, gentlemen. I know your game is important to you and the hour is late, but I have an unusually bad headache and my husband is out of town on business."

She removes her hand from Ferdinand's shoulder and touches her brow. She turns to Doc with a beseeching look. Her usually bright dark eyes look dull and are smudged with rings of black beneath. Her skin glistens with a moist, pale, unhealthy sheen. There is something else I can't quite figure out, but don't have time to before she suddenly drops to the floor in a dead faint.

Never without his satchel, Doc scrambles to open it in search of smelling salts while Ferdinand lays her on the nearest parlor settee.

Doc sends me to the kitchen for a cold cloth for her brow and Ferdinand for a quilt, and Doc continues trying to revive her, testing her pulse and checking her eyes.

Finally coming around with a cough, choking from the salts, Katie is embarrassed to be lying on her back surrounded by four men.

"Oh my," she exclaims, "what has happened to me!" She struggles to sit up but cannot; she is as weak as a newborn kitten.

"Don't try to sit up yet." Doc pushes her back gently on the pillows. "You fainted outright and your pulse is still weak. I will have Ferdinand put you in a buggy and take you to my infirmary for the night for observation. We still have your headache to consider as well. My wife will tend to you when we arrive." Seeing a look of resistance on her face, he admonishes her with a look of his own.

*

After gently placing Katie in the buggy, I assist Doc in transporting and settling her in for the night. Rousing Sarah, Doc explains what is needed and she goes about putting Katie to bed as good as any nurse or better. Ever the doctor's wife, Sarah never complains of late-night calls and circumstances, nor questions ailments.

After returning the buggy to Ferdinand, we decide to call it a night, as it has become quite late. Senator Farrell has retired, and Eva Rosa surely awaits Ferdinand, to spend a few quiet moments alone with him after their brood of six have been tucked in bed.

The night air is chilly, lingering in the forties. Ferdinand and I walk in the same direction, he to arrive at his house sooner than I am to reach mine, and both of us wonder out loud at the reason for Katie's malaise.

"She has been looking very hearty and lovely as of late," he remarks as we walk, hands in pockets, heads lowered to ward off the cold.

I interject, "Of course, she tends to pout and seek attention whenever Jeff is out of town for more than a day or two." I turn toward him to catch his reaction, but see none to amount to anything.

What am I looking for, I muse, what am I thinking? A hand on a shoulder, a remark about her looks surely must be innocent. Ferdinand has never given me reason to suspect he would sully his marriage vows.

And as for Katie, in my opinion, she is an innocent flirt at best. Give up the bad thoughts, I counsel myself. I bid my friend good night and turn toward home, down a sleeping Centre Street where a darting shadow catches my attention.

Freezing at a standstill I stare at the point where the shadow crossed the street. I stare very hard up and down the street for a few moments. Nothing moves across my point of vision again until old James Lang, our mulatto policeman and night patrol officer, taps me on the shoulder.

Jumping backward and almost falling into the street, I yell, "Oh, James, you scared the life out of me!"

Widowed for many years, James prefers to work the night shift, allowing the married men with families, time at home.

"What yo' staring at up yonder?" he asks, looking up the street and back at me.

I explain what I thought I had seen and he looks back and forth, seeing nothing either.

"You go on home and I be check'n it out." In his official policeman's tone of voice he instructs me, "It probably some of dat riffraff dat been camping out down to Old Town lately. Up to no good at dis time of night, fo' sure."

He runs his fingers through his kinky gray hair and hitches up his uniform pants before he heads west, away from the harbor, seeking the night prowlers. His hand rests on his billy club, ready to take action if need be.

Next morning the town is abuzz with the news of burglars who struck Dr. Starbuck's house. Several articles of clothing, the doctor's watch, gun and hypodermic syringe were stolen.

The thief entered at a rear window where good guidance was given by a lamp, which is always left burning all night by Mrs. Starbuck. It appears the thief very coolly entered the doctor's bedroom, removed every article of clothing and then proceeded to the parlor, where he spread them on the floor and evidently proceeded to take an inventory, as many of the articles were found piled up near an open satchel in the parlor.

Mrs. Starbuck's slumber was disturbed by the crying of her small child and, on awakening, she noticed the lamp was out. Hearing a noise downstairs, she arose and inquired, "Who is there?"

She received a reply, evidently from the front hall, of "John."

Before the doctor was aroused, the burglar escaped, carrying the above-mentioned stolen articles with him.

Also during the night, Steil's New York Sample Room was broken into, where the intruders sat down and helped themselves to an abundance of wine and delicacies.

Lake's Jewelers and Mr. Linville's residence were also attempted to be burglarized but unsuccessfully due to the barking of a little terrier at Lake's Store and by the presence of Mr. Linville at his residence.

Around the breakfast table we all agree this has to be the work of strangers, that we have not had a burglary in over two years, and the locking of windows and doors and a loud, barking dog are not bad ideas.

I myself wonder how our night policeman missed all this nocturnal action.

This week's meeting of the Amelia Lodge, No. 47, F. & A. M., will not be held in the Duryee Building as usual, since the annual meeting for the Grand Lodge of Free and Accepted Masons of the State of Florida is being held today in Jacksonville for the election of officers for the ensuing year.

Reverend Yerger, Warren Scott, William O. Jeffreys and I are meeting at the train depot at 4:30 p.m. for the trip to Jacksonville to attend the meeting and installation of officers.

Warren expects to be nominated to Deputy Grand High Priest, to which he will accept, I am sure. He presently holds the office of Deputy Grand Master of the Seventh District, comprising the counties of Nassau, Duval, St. Johns and Clay.

The train ride takes under two hours, arriving at 6:15 p.m., and is a comfortable one, given the new passenger cars recently added by the Florida Transit & Peninsular Railroad, the good company and the flasks in our pockets.

As you can imagine, the meeting is long, due to the election not only of statewide officers but also officers of the Grand Chapter. It finalizes at 10:30 p.m.

The Order of Freemasons was established sometime during the 1600s and is a secret society ... or is it a society of secrets? Depends on how you view it, I imagine. There are certain rites of passage a man must take in order to join, as well as secret handshakes and passwords and, above all, he must believe in a Supreme Being.

Masons are upstanding citizens of their communities, going about the business of ensuring that decisions made during meetings are carried out, and quietly keeping their word to each other. I guess you can say they can keep a secret.

The last train to Fernandina departs from Jacksonville at nine o'clock, leaving us to find accommodations for the night. I have my thoughts (unspoken, of course) on this, but due to Reverend Yerger being with us, they are soon and at once quashed.

Reverend Weller of Jacksonville graciously offers accommodations in his home, to which William Wood and I are transported by his servant, a young mulatto named Josh, who has been patiently waiting outside during the meeting. He clicks softly to the matched pair of bays hitched to the carriage and it is but a short ride to the Reverend's large, well-turned-out home near the St. Johns River on Market Street.

Caroline, Reverend Weller's wife of over twenty-five years and mother to his nine children, gracefully shows William and me to our rooms for the night. She confides to us, as we navigate the stairs, that it is not unusual to have houseguests at all hours of the day or night, immediately putting us at ease.

The next morning dawns bright but a bit breezy and cool. We partake of an early breakfast with the Reverend, his wife, their son Reginald Jr. who is also a clergyman, and a number of younger Wellers who are readying themselves for school.

"I met and wed Caroline when she was but seventeen," he says while patting her hand gently, "and I was a relatively older man of twenty-nine. But as they say, it was love at first sight and still is to this day."

She blushes and laughs like the girl she was those many years ago. Her eyes crinkling at the corners and belying the years, Caroline answers, "I have followed you from South Carolina to Missouri, to Kentucky, to Florida, having babies every step of the way and would do it all over again."

She reaches across little Cordelia's highchair to give her husband a hug. There is not a doubt as to the validity of his words by the look in her eyes.

Thanking our host and hostess, William and I make haste to reach the train station in time to catch the nine o'clock train that will transport us to Fernandina by 10:45 a.m. There is still much left to be desired as far as schedules are concerned, but all in all it is better than traveling by horseback or buggy down dusty roads and across the river by ferry—as well as the tremendous amount of time saved.

T. J. Eppes happens to be the conductor this morning. He stops by to take our tickets and pass the time of day for a while, since the train has few passengers during the middle of the week.

"I should have gone into law, followed in my father's footsteps as he wanted me to," he laments. "I would of course rather be home every night with Katie than be gone two to three nights a week. I come home tired from these trips and she is bored from being cooped up at the Mansion House Hotel and wants to accept every party invitation and all I want to do is stay home with her. We have been arguing a lot lately," he admits with a glum face as he slumps down in the seat across from me.

Listening to what he is saying, I remember the look between them on the dock the day Pauline left for school. Now things are falling into place. Yet something else is left untold. I feel it.

Jeff comes from very wealthy families. His mother is Theodosia Burr Bellamy Eppes of Monticello, Florida, and the daughter of one of the most prosperous planters in Jefferson County. She married Thomas Jefferson Eppes (great-grandson of Thomas Jefferson) in 1858 and to that union they had six children, with Jeff being the eldest.

When Jeff arrived in Fernandina as a single man in 1880, he confided to me that his father had passed away in 1869, leaving him with quite a large inheritance. Also that his grandfather was Judge Eppes of Monticello, but his desire was to "make it on his own."

We sit on the train watching the barren winter fields and pastures fly by.

In a lowered voice I suggest to him, "You know, Jeff, I think you should take some time to spend with your bride. Consider attending law school. Use some of your inheritance."

"Maybe so, maybe so," he agrees, rising to continue his ticketing.

"What was that all about?" William asks, rejoining me a few moments later. "Jeff should be all smiles with a beautiful wife like Katie waiting for him at the door. I know I would be. She's about the best-looking woman to hit our town in many a year—not meaning any offense to your Pauline. I would think twice about leaving such a beautiful, tender young thing all alone if I were him, yes sir, I would." He grins with a teasing, lecherous look on his face.

"And I would be careful of my tongue if I were you," I caution him while glancing around for Jeff.

*

Miss Annie is full of herself at supper tonight, what with the report of the purchase, through Mr. Greenleaf's store in Jacksonville, of new and elegant flatware and cutlery by Eva Rosa for the Mansion House.

"She invited all the hotel owners for tea today just to show it off," she tells us in her Irish brogue that tends to get stronger when she is excited or angry. "It is supposed to be a facsimile of the ones used in the Hotel St. Denis in New York."

"Was it as nice as all that?" I ask, looking down at the much-used sterling silver knife with which I am about to carve my ham.

Her gaze follows mine and then around the table at the other settings … knives, forks and spoons, apparently comparing them against the fine new ones at the Mansion House.

The Florida House and the Mansion House hotels are not rivals, per se, as they are not with the other hotels in town, but I can see the thoughts turning over in Miss Annie's head when it comes to setting a nicer table.

I'm thinking, I bet you a gold piece she will be ordering new silverware before the month is out and maybe new linens and lace as well just to be one-up, if you know what I mean.

Especially since the Mansion House recently purchased new cherry, marble-topped furniture and completed a lot of refurbishing including new carpets.

She and Marie have their heads together at one end of the table, making notes on a piece of paper as they talk. I can already see shiny new flatware in my hand before Valentine's Day.

The conversation at our end swings to the hectic routine of the new year that has us all to the point of exhaustion.

As city tax collector, Mr. Meddaugh is duly collecting taxes for 1883, and Warren Scott is county tax collector doing the same. Any properties with taxes remaining unpaid as of February 1 will be advertised for sale. They sure don't let moss grow under their feet here when it comes to paying and collecting taxes.

Ferdinand Suhrer, city council president, requested and was granted to have Alderman Hoyt assume his duties again as chairman of the Finance Committee.

City council is engaged at this time clearing up old business for 1883 and establishing new business for 1884; therefore I have been working late hours and have not had much time to write Pauline, as she reminds me regularly in her letters to me.

I have had to decline a number of social invitations due to my workload, such as the Manse Fund held at the Mansion House with Miss Emma Adams, the distinguished elocutionist from Massachusetts, along with vocal and instrumental music.

I hope to be able to join my friends next week on an excursion train to the state fair in Jacksonville, for which the Fernandina and Jacksonville Railroad has put on a special fare.

*

Here I am again working late tonight. I am freezing; the small fireplace does nothing to alleviate the draftiness of the room's high ceilings. Unable to bear it any longer, I am in the process of moving my desk closer to the fire when in walks William with another stack of paperwork needing attention by tomorrow's meeting.

He had left at five o'clock for home and a warm supper, and I thought not to be back until the morning.

"Whatever are you doing?" he asks, stopping midway through the doorway with papers held at arm's length. He notes aloud that I am wearing my overcoat and scarf with no apparent intention of leaving.

Of course William would not know how cold it can get since he never works this late, even though I have requested on more than one occasion that he install one of those wood-burning Franklin Fireplace stoves I saw in a catalog that are said to put out enormous heat and vent right up the chimney.

"It is so cold in here my fingers cannot hold a pen to write in the ledgers," I reply in exasperation while eyeing the additional stack he has placed on the desk. He must know there is at least another two hours' work to be done before I can leave.

Hearing the tone in my voice and seeing the weary look in my eyes and being the kind and generous man he is, he helps me push the desk back, picks up the work to be done, and orders me to bring along the necessary writing supplies. We head for his stationery store, which he says "is warmer, brighter and more conducive to getting the job done in a better environment."

The sandwich and lager ordered for my supper from Beard's Restaurant along the way arrives as the hour approaches nine o'clock and we are nearing the halfway mark to finishing.

"This situation of cattle roaming down Centre Street must be addressed at tomorrow's meeting," William adds to his notes as a finale to the agenda. "It's bad enough the streets are a quagmire when it rains, that we also have to contend with livestock roaming through the town."

I say, "I would suggest owners of all livestock within the city should be responsible for fencing their property in and also be fined for livestock found loose." Looking to him for his approval before making these notes, I find him nodding his head.

He looks up at me and says, "If it were up to me, I would not allow livestock within the city proper, but I have suggested that in the past and gotten nowhere. Your landlady is a fine example with her laying hens, but mark my words, there will come a day when this will come to pass."

"You're right," I reply. "Why, just two houses farther north on Sixth Street from Mr. Meddaugh there are pigs and a horse, and the stench can be unbearable at times."

The mantle clock strikes the hour and we wind down the final sorting of paperwork for tomorrow's meeting. It is done in record time with William's help, to which I express my gratitude.

Standing at last with a groan, he stretches his long limbs and calls it a night for the both of us. "The meeting tomorrow proves to be long in itself, what with the regular agenda and the items we have added: sanitary measures, drainage and now the livestock issue. It will be a long night. We best be going home and get what rest we can with what is left of this night."

We walk out into the cold air. He turns in one direction and I in the other, both bundled up against the light rain that has started to fall. The town is tranquil at this time of night. Only the sound of a train coupling and uncoupling boxcars down at the depot and a lone ship's horn disturb the peace as I find my way to my corner of Third Street and turn toward home and a nice warm bed.

Thankfully, no surprises await me tonight. I insert the key and quietly let myself in the double front doors. I slip my shoes off and pad softly into the kitchen to prepare a warm cup of milk, leaving Miss Annie ten cents and a note to please wake me early.

With shoes and milk in hand I tiptoe up the stairs to the second floor and out onto the front balcony in order to reach my room. The rain has stopped and the air has that sweet, fresh scent I so often associate with the sensation of the earth at the moment of creation; as pure and new as if the rain has cleansed everything. I take a moment to breathe it in before entering my room for the night.

A room of good proportion, furnished with a bed of mahogany, a matching night table with a reading lamp, a desk and chair on the far wall and a fireplace. There is also a table with a man's shaving mirror, washbowl and pitcher, as well as an armoire and dresser. The hardwood floor is partly covered with a thick wool rug in a deep red and blue pattern matching the quilt on the bed.

The morning sun enters my red velvet- and lace-covered windows each day to awaken me and makes the upstairs front porch a comfortable spot to drink my coffee and a cool, shady place to relax in the evenings.

During the tourist season, other guests, too, enjoy the porch with its long row of rocking chairs. I don't mind that much, but I have to say I like the off-season when it becomes my private place again. The other regulars seem to prefer the downstairs front porch where they can speak to neighbors as they pass by.

*

February 8 is the skating club's Calico Ball, to which I have agreed to escort Pauline's younger sister Sophie, much to her delight. She has demanded my presence tomorrow afternoon at J. H. Prescott's on Centre Street to select our costume materials. At twelve years old, she is taking this all in a serious, grown-up manner. How many different colors of calico can there be? I only have to be concerned about a shirt. She is having a dress and parasol made, and I understand the programs are also to be made of calico.

Tomorrow will be a busy day, but regardless of the hot milk and my bone-tiredness, sleep won't come. I toss and turn, kick the quilt off, pull it back again and pummel the feather pillows nearly to death.

Finally giving up in disgust I throw back the covers, yank on my robe, light the lamp and settle down at my desk to the half-finished letter to Pauline. Soon I am startled by the rattling of something being thrown against my window.

Peering out the rain-streaked glass, I can barely make out the figure of a woman but not who she is. I dress hurriedly and find the rain-drenched, shivering creature on the front porch is, to my surprise, of all people, Mary!

The street and porch are still and dark. She is alone. I have never seen her or known her ever to be outside Miss Lizzie's establishment. None of the girls are allowed to step foot outside. They are watched closely by the huge black bodyguards at the door day and night.

Looking nervously around her and clutching my hands, she speaks hurriedly, barely catching a breath: "I tied my sheets together and climbed out my window after everyone was sleeping, I have my money and Mama and Papa's wedding picture sewn into the hem of my cloak and I am off to meet my sea captain, but first I wanted to tell you goodbye. I watched your window and saw the light come on. I am sorry you could not sleep but happy to be able to see you one more time."

Her eyes sparkle as she speaks. The hood of her cloak has fallen, revealing her long golden hair. It cascades around her shoulders and frames her face, which is radiant and flushed with the promise of a bright future.

Tucking a lock of hair tenderly behind her left ear, I stroke her soft cheek. Then, covering her head once more, I whisper these words of encouragement: "Do not allow anyone ever again to take from you what you are not willing to give."

Smiling at me, she stands on tiptoe, kisses me softly and is gone into the night.

I stand on the porch for what seems like an eternity but for only a few moments I stare into the misty rain where she has disappeared from my life forever. An emptiness fills my heart, which I know is selfish on my part, but cannot be helped.

The soft glow of a cigar suddenly brightens at the far end of the porch, lighting up the thin lips and pockmarked face attached to it, nearly scaring the wits out of me.

"Well, well, what a touching little scenario," he says, rising while knocking the ash off on the heel of his boot. "Seems we have a runaway and I just might get me a reward if I hurry down to Miss Lizzie's place before she sails with the tide."

"I would not do any such thing if I were you." I threaten him with fists curled, ready to fight, backing him into the farthest corner.

We stand toe to toe and I can smell the rancid stench of whiskey and cigars on his breath. He is not one of the hotel guests, as far as I can recall, nor is he the type Miss Annie would allow in her establishment, so what is he doing here? All I know is I must keep him away from Miss Lizzie's long enough for Mary to make good her escape.

Darting his shifty eyes around for a means of breaking away and finding none, he proceeds to try to shake me down. I will do whatever to help Mary, but blackmail from a creature such as this makes my blood boil. Before the thought even enters my head, my right fist comes up, hitting him squarely between the eyes, knocking him out cold and into a heap at my feet.

Now the question is, "What to do with him?" I can't leave him here all night, and when he wakes up he is bound to tell his story to all who will listen. But of course, who will they believe, him or me?

The jail is just down the street so I run as fast as I can in the now pouring rain and, after much banging and yelling, wake our jailer, David McHaffie, with a concocted story that I found a vagrant on the porch snooping around, scuffled with him and knocked him out.

David hitches a mule to the buckboard and we are back in minutes, to find the man still out cold. We load him up and haul him off to a night's stay with the rest of the derelicts.

In my room again, I stoke the fire back to life by adding more wood. I then peel my sodden clothing from my shivering body and dry my hair as best I can. I add another quilt and crawl into bed, exhausted enough to fall into a deep, albeit short, sleep.

Too soon, the housemaid is knocking on my door as requested. I answer and roll out of bed with a groan. I am happy at least to find the rain has abated and the sun is making an attempt to dry the street that was last night's muddy river.

The kitchen is already packed with other early risers and they all stand and cheer me when I enter. It takes me a minute to realize they have heard the rumor of my lie as Miss Annie gives me a hug and a peck on the cheek.

"David McHaffie was just here to tell me about last night's happenings." She continues proudly: "Seems the vagrant you caught is a thief wanted in Camden County, Georgia, and was shipped out this morning."

Suddenly, my need to rush to the harbor has passed. I had wanted to insure that the Spanish-registered brigantine *Salve Virgin Maria*, owned by Llorca from Cienfuegos, Cuba, had cleared port last night. So I settle down to an enormous and leisurely breakfast, with time to spare.

At the office, William has arrived ahead of me and is accompanied by Telfair Stockton, a civil engineer from Jacksonville who is presently staying at the Egmont Hotel. William introduces us.

"Telfair has graciously offered to look over our drainage system and offer some advice before the council meeting." William motions to the unrolled charts lying across my desk.

Scratching his head periodically as he peruses sheet after sheet, Telfair makes notes in a ledger book. When he finally finishes, he rolls them together again.

He says, "It appears that your sanitation and drainage system is, for the most part, well planned and should need very few changes." Rising, he puts on his coat and tucks the rolls under his arm. "Shall we take a walk to examine the present physical condition of the system?"

Without waiting for an answer he is out the door, with us following at a trot close behind.

After last night's heavy rain, it proves to be an easy task. Drains are overrunning in several places and the odor of raw sewage is evident in others as well, and all are noted.

The worse areas are Front Street near the docks, Second Street, Seventh Street and right down our main street, Centre.

"This is due to the heavy amount of traffic traveled in these areas," Telfair explains.

We spend the rest of the morning and into the early afternoon checking out the rest of the town toward the beach and farther north, spotting only a few minor problems.

"My stomach tells me it's past time for a lunch break," William says as we near the entrance to Glaiber's Restaurant. He looks to each of us for approval before reaching for the door handle.

Selecting a table, Telfair rolls out the charts, pencils in some notes to correspond to items in the ledger he brought along and in a few moments he has finished.

"The state of disrepair is not bad," he says, "but new and larger sewer pipes need to be installed due to the increase in population, keeping in mind future development."

Smiling, rosy-cheeked Matilda sets our steaming plates of red cabbage, veal and potatoes in front of us, and words are few as we consume the delicious food.

Finally slowing down enough to talk, Telfair tells us a little about himself and his visit to Fernandina. "I recently moved to Jacksonville, having given up my job of twelve years with Southern Express Company, and along with two of my brothers, have begun two newspapers. I also am looking into property development. As to my trip here, I was curious to see the place my sister Mary's husband, Bishop John Freeman Young, has spoken of so often. Shortly after his consecration he purchased the former home of Confederate general Joseph Finegan, turning it into an exclusive girls' school known as St. Mary's Priory, which since has been moved to Jacksonville."

"Ah, yes. St. Mary's Priory. Miss Annie told me something tragic about it. Isn't that the school that caught fire back in 1871 in which Major Call's daughter, Mary, died?" I ask.

"Yes, what a grievous time that was for everyone," Telfair says, shaking his head sadly.

"The poor girl had stayed up late to study and when turning the lamp down, instead turned it up and in trying to douse the flames by covering the top of the lamp with her book, the sleeve of her nightgown caught fire and in no time she was running down the hall and out the door, rolling on the lawn, a living torch. Nothing could be done for the child and there was considerable damage to the school as well."

Seeing his sorrow at remembering and telling the event, I change the subject back to that of Bishop Young.

Telfair proudly responds, "You may or may not know that my brother-in-law is the famed Bishop Young who is the translator of the Austrian hymn 'Stille Nacht! Heilige Nacht!' which is now the Christmas song 'Silent Night, Holy Night.' "

After hearing this, Matilda stops clearing the table and immediately starts singing the song in its original version, much to our pleasure. Her beautiful voice brings tears to our eyes.

"What a delightful ending to a wonderful meal," Telfair tells her, smiling broadly. "I will be sure to bring my wife and children here in the future. We have a two-year-old and a newborn, and Willie was not up to traveling with them this trip."

Walking Telfair to the Egmont, I beg my leave at the corner to meet Sophie for our appointed calico selection, before heading back to the office to finish up the council meeting agenda.

Entering the cool interior, I find her with several bolts of material laid out for inspection.

"What do you think of this pink one?" she asks with an impish little grin, knowing full well my answer.

"I have agreed to escort you and will do so most delightfully and in any color you desire, but with one exception—pink!"

Looking at my stern face she bursts out laughing so loud, other shoppers turn to stare at us.

Putting her hand over her mouth to try to stop laughing, she only succeeds in hiccupping and turns red in embarrassment. "I was only teasing," she says. "I knew you would not want the pink one. You are not adventuresome like Sammie Swann or Charley Stark."

"Oh really," I banter back. "Let's see that pink material after all." Walking over to the pier mirror in the gentlemen's section, I hold it against my chest, looking this way and that while making funny noises for her benefit.

"Yes, I do believe it suits me after all," I tell Mr. Prescott. "We will take enough for a gentleman's shirt and this young lady's dress and whatever else she needs for the Calico Ball."

The stunned look on her face will be worth every tortuous minute I have to wear the darned thing. Not adventuresome, am I?

Leaving Sophie to her fitting, I head back to the office and several hours' work before the council meeting. I hope I won't fall asleep at my desk; with hardly any sleep last night, the long day is fast catching up with me.

I stop by Beard's Restaurant for a cup of strong black coffee to wake me up and keep me going.

Henry is drying dishes when I walk in. Pouring the rich coffee, he leans toward me and whispers, "Have you heard about Miss Lizzie's girl dat done run away last night?"

Startled by his words, I lean back and nonchalantly take a sip of the hot coffee to give me a minute to gather my thoughts before answering. "No, I haven't, Henry. I've been working since early this morning and haven't heard a word. So tell me what happened."

"Well, from what dat big major drumo guard seys dis morning at breakfast, de best gal she got up there done slipped out de window in de night. Done tied her bed sheets together and is long gone!" He smiles at passing on this bit of important news as he continues to dry his dishes, and looks at me with a knowing sideways look on his face. Or am I imagining it? Did Miss Lizzie's man tell him I was Mary's best customer and are they thinking I had something to do with her disappearance?

Gulping down the coffee so fast I burn the roof of my mouth and tongue, it causes me to spew coffee everywhere. Henry gives me a questioning look as he grabs a cloth for me to clean off my suit.

"Damn, Henry! You should warn people your coffee is hotter than hell on a summer day!" Trying to make a joke of it, I lay down my money and head out the door, running smack into the huge black mountain of a guard from Miss Lizzie's. He promptly collars me right there in broad daylight.

"Miss Lizzie done request yo' presence, suh," he growls without letting go of my sleeve.

I have no choice but to go with him or cause a scene and a lot of questions from my peers, which I would rather not do.

Hoping none of those peers would see me entering a house of ill repute, I quickly slip inside the door at her bidding. I have only been here at night, of course, and the place looks ten times worse when seen by daylight. All the shabbiness is visible, the tawdry lamps, worn furniture and Miss Lizzie is the worst of all. Good Lord, what a hag she is!

Now that Mary is gone, I know I won't be stepping foot in this place ever again.

I am jolted back to the moment by Miss Lizzie's shrill voice shouting accusations at me. "What have you done with Mary? Where is she?" she demands in a rapid-fire voice while advancing on me with a menacing look on her face.

Backing up toward the door, I reach behind me for the knob. I hold a hand up toward her and firmly and without raising my voice, say, "I had nothing to do with, nor have any knowledge of Mary leaving your employment. If girls are being held here against their will, then that is a police matter and should be looked into forthwith."

Upon my uttering this, she goes stone white under her layers of makeup, her jaw flops up and down a couple of times but no words come out. She drops heavily onto her throne-like chair.

Finally raising my voice to get my point across, I say to her and her man, "Now I believe you owe me an apology for having kidnapped me and removed me to this place, before I do go to the police."

Looking to her for instructions and receiving none, the guard does nothing as I turn and leave the way I came, quickly out into the fresh, clean daylight, looking right and left to make sure the coast is clear. My knees tremble though I try to act normal while making my way down Second Street to Centre Street.

My heart is still pounding so loudly from the encounter I can hear it inside my head and I am sure others I pass must hear it also. Thankful at last to reach my office, I close the door and drop into my chair without even shedding my coat. Closing my eyes, I envision Mary smiling at me ... sunlight shining on her hair ... on some tropical island ... a gentle breeze blows strands around her pretty face ... until at last my heart returns to a normal cadence.

I look back over last night and this morning's happenings and know that she is worth every minute. I am happy she made her escape from that wretched place and I only wish all the girls could do the same.

Divesting myself of my coat, I gather the ledgers together for tonight's council meeting and begin to assemble the reports. It takes a matter of almost two hours to complete the agenda and special reports and gives me just enough time to hurry home for supper and to freshen up for the meeting.

I barely am able to keep myself alert and awake and have never been so thankful a meeting has drawn to a close as I am at the end of this one.

Graciously declining the offer to have a drink with the other members afterwards, I hastily make my way home and am in bed the earliest I have been since I was a schoolboy at home.

There will be no tossing and turning this night, no disturbing thoughts to keep me awake. My body and mind are so tired, no lullaby will be needed; only the crisp, white sheets and soft downy pillow on which to lay my weary head and I am soon fast asleep.

*

What a difference a good night's rest can do for a man's body and spirit, I think to myself while mindlessly whistling a tune this beautiful, sunny day as I walk to work. Nothing could possibly go wrong or interfere with this mood I'm in, nor will I allow anything to do so.

Not even Katie Eppes, who is out early and is walking purposely toward me with a look of determination on her face.

"It's a nice morning for a walk," I say. I smile, tipping my hat in greeting while trying to sidestep around her at the same time, but she will not have it. How did I know this wouldn't work?

"No, it is not a nice day at all!" she nearly screams at me while her face becomes redder by the second. "Jeff was to be home on the early train but when I went to meet him, all I got was this message." She thrusts out her hand, showing me a crumpled piece of paper which until this moment had gone unnoticed. " 'Darling Katie,' he says, 'I will be home tomorrow night, due to a shortage in conductors.' I am so tired of meeting trains with no husband on them and spending endless days and nights alone in that one little room with no home to call my own, I could just scream!"

She starts to cry right then and there, and refuses the offer of my handkerchief.

She turns her back on me, and the last words I hear from her are, "I will make him pay attention to me, oh yes I will. Wait and see!"

I have a feeling like someone "just walked over my grave," as my mama used to say. I watch Katie strut away, her shoulders drooping less and back stiffening with every quick step. She holds her head high, as if on a mission.

Expelling the deep breath I have unconsciously been holding, I offer up a prayer for Jeff. There's no telling what she has in store for the poor man when he arrives home tomorrow. I know I would not want to be in his shoes, no siree.

*

"Don't take your coat off," I am directed by William as I enter the office and find he has his on and is ready to depart, along with David Yulee and Superintendent Maxwell of the Florida Transit & Peninsular Railroad. "We have been invited to ride along on the maiden trip to Callahan and back today on the two new locomotive cars, No. 19, Sumter, and No. 20, Hernando."

David Yulee

Glad for a respite from the hectic office of the last few days, I gladly turn around and go out the door for an adventure. I only wish I had known ahead of time so I could have brought my camera along.

The locomotives built by the Rogers Locomotive Works in New Jersey prove to be fitted out with the latest in improvements in air brakes and so on, and the ride proves to be not only comfortable but exhilarating as well.

We alight at the railroad complex building near Railroad Avenue and dine at Andres Restaurant.

In Callahan, I am pleasantly surprised. This town was named in honor of Daniel Callahan, an old Irish railroad gang leader and former resident of Fernandina who was favored by the inhabitants of the area. It has a number of hotels, restaurants, stores and even a social hall called the Boothe House, as well as a church, drugstore and liquor establishment— not at all the small cattle-crossing stop I had expected.

When we board the train again heading back toward Fernandina, it is getting late. But this works well with the last part of our day's itinerary to do some bird shooting along the way. It is best done at dusk when they come in to roost for the night.

What the engineer does is slow the train down while we jump off, with guns provided by Mr. Yulee, and run ahead to the edge of the woods or corn fields, shoot the birds, bag them up and then run and hop back on the train. We have even tried deer hunting like this in the past, but gave it up even though we had the luck once to bag a nine-point buck. The effort to lug the huge beast back to the train proved to be more than we had bargained for. The noise of the train covers the sound of hunters approaching and prey is not frightened off.

"All right, let's go!" William hollers over the engine.

We leap to the ground at a run for our first foray toward a copse of woods and in a few moments we each have bagged a number of quail.

Laughing and sprinting like schoolboys, we swing our trophies up into the open baggage car door to David. Due to his advanced years of seventy-three, he is not up for such physical activities, but gives us a hand up as we follow behind, rolling on the floor with glee.

We stand and dust ourselves off, and then pass the whiskey flask, fortifying ourselves in readiness of the next whistle call from the engineer to go again.

By the time we reach Fernandina we have bagged enough birds each for a number of tasty meals. The entire day's outing has been one of learning and camaraderie.

I am able today to become better acquainted with Mr. Yulee, U.S. senator, railroad pioneer and founder of the *Florida Mirror*. He was born on the Island of St. Thomas in the Caribbean to Moses Levy, who made his fortune in timber and then in turn moved his family to the Jacksonville area after purchasing nearly 50,000 acres there.

David was educated in Norfolk, Virginia, and studied law in St. Augustine. Having served in the Florida legislature, he was also a leader in the campaign for statehood and in 1845 became one of the new state's senators at the same time. In 1846, David married the daughter of

Kentucky's ex-governor, and renounced Judaism. It was during this time he changed his name, adding Yulee after one of his ancestors. He became a devout Christian; nevertheless, he tells me, he continues to be the object of anti-Semitic attacks.

Yulee supported slavery and secession and was imprisoned for nine months at Fort Pulaski as a prisoner of state during the Civil War. At that time he was considered a rebel and all his properties were seized, including the Florida House Hotel, which was built by the railroad in 1857.

Reaching into his satchel he pulls out a sheaf of papers whose edges are worn from constant viewing. "Here is a decree issued from Joseph Remington, United States Marshall, ordering the seizure as 'An Act to suppress insurrection, to punish treason and rebellion, to seize and confiscate the property of rebels and for other purposes.' I carry these with me to this day as a reminder of those dark days."

He returns the papers to the satchel and stows the satchel overhead. He sits and leans back with a smile of satisfaction while watching the countryside roll by as we near our destination.

"A lot has been accomplished in the years since the war," he says. "Look at the progress the railroads have made connecting cities coast-to-coast, reaching farther than I ever dreamed possible."

Tired and dirty as errant schoolboys who played hooky from school all day, we roll into the depot. Parting company I sling my sack of quail over my shoulder, tip my hat with a wink and head for home.

Miss Annie is pleased with my contribution of the quail and immediately sends it to the kitchen in preparation for the next evening's addition to the menu.

Her dinner menus are extensive, change every day and are printed by William's stationery shop. And in color, no less, for the guests to peruse upon arrival.

I have retained a menu from one of my first dinners at the Florida House in 1882 and show it to you now:

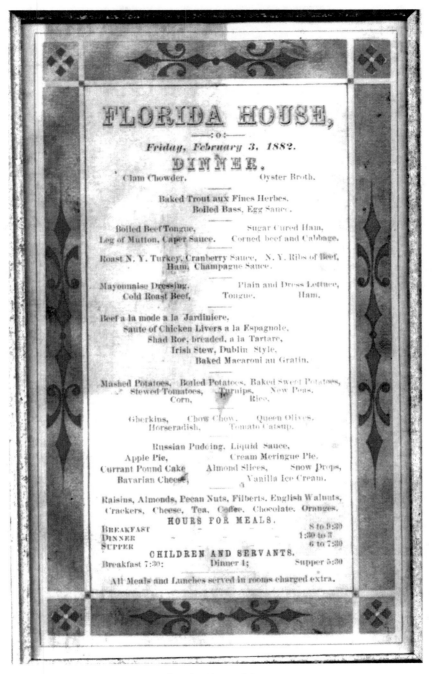

FLORIDA HOUSE,

—:o:—

Friday, February 3, 1882.

DINNER.

Clam Chowder.   Oyster Broth.

Baked Trout aux Fines Herbes,
Boiled Bass, Egg Sauce.

Boiled Beef Tongue,   Sugar Cured Ham,
Leg of Mutton, Caper Sauce.   Corned beef and Cabbage.

Roast N. Y. Turkey, Cranberry Sauce,   N. Y. Ribs of Beef,
Ham, Champagne Sauce.

Mayonnaise Dressing.   Plain and Dress Lettuce,
Cold Roast Beef,   Tongue.   Ham.

Beef a la mode a la Jardiniere.
Saute of Chicken Livers a la Espagnole,
Shad Roe, breaded, a la Tartare,
Irish Stew, Dublin Style,
Baked Macaroni au Gratin.

Mashed Potatoes, Boiled Potatoes, Baked Sweet Potatoes,
Stewed Tomatoes,   Turnips,   New Peas,
Corn,   Rice.

Gherkins,   Chow Chow,   Queen Olives,
Horseradish,   Tomato Catsup.

Russian Pudding, Liquid Sauce,
Apple Pie,   Cream Meringue Pie,
Currant Pound Cake,   Almond Slices,   Snow Drops,
Bavarian Cheese,   Vanilla Ice Cream.

Raisins, Almonds, Pecan Nuts, Filberts, English Walnuts,
Crackers, Cheese, Tea, Coffee, Chocolate, Oranges.

HOURS FOR MEALS.

BREAKFAST   8 to 9:30
DINNER   1:30 to 3
SUPPER   6 to 7:30

CHILDREN AND SERVANTS.

Breakfast 7:30;   Dinner 1;   Supper 5:30

All Meals and Lunches served in rooms charged extra.

Florida House Menu

As you can see, guests and permanent residents at the Florida House are offered an abundant selection and assortment of tantalizing foods to choose from and the table service is excellent; which is why, along with the convenient location, I choose to live here and shall remain until the day I marry and establish my own home.

On our many walks about town Pauline and I have daydreamed about different cottages and houses, seeing ourselves in them.

Pauline and I agree on most of the important aspects of our future, including the number of children, their education and the desire to remain in Fernandina, the place we both love so well.

I don't have wanderlust like some men I know. Take, for example, Joseph Higgins, who talks nonstop about the California gold fields and "the fortune to be made there!" Marie threatens him if he even dares step foot on a train or boat. "The rush is over!" she tells him. "There's nothing left out there but fool's gold for an old fool."

But I see the wandering look in his eye; especially when he has been hitting the bottle on a Friday night down at the Five Star or one of the other saloons, and he has been listening to the sea captains spin their tall tales of adventure.

Hard at work in his blacksmith shop from dawn to dusk, Joe never complains over the extra hours he put in on the addition in 1882 on the Florida House, nor the fact that he purchased the property for the addition, a fact unknown to most.

"It's what you do for family, laddie. And I promised Thomas on his deathbed, I would look after Annie and Gracie," he says, staring into the bottom of yet another empty glass.

"Did you know that Fred Lohman was granted a license by the city commissioners to sell wines and liquors at his store regardless of the vigorous opposition of the temperance people?" I ask him. "Now you can purchase a bottle there at a good price for home consumption. Steil's New York Sample Room was already selling wine but not liquor. If you ask me, folks need to have some whiskey in the pantry at all times—for medicinal use. My mother always gave me a teaspoonful with lemon and honey for a cough and fever, wrapped me up tight in a woolen blanket and by the next morning I would be on the road to recovery."

Looking around and covering his hand over his mouth so no one else will hear, Joe leans toward me and whispers, "Marie tells me there are some very influential, so-called temperance ladies, in town who take a 'medicinal dose' of elderberry wine every afternoon for their sinking spells—whatever that might be."

He tips his chair backward on two legs, hooks his thumbs in his suspenders and grins at me. "Temperance obviously doesn't include what these holier-than-thou sisters are doing behind their men's backs at home—or should we put a medicine label on wine?"

"I don't know about that, Joe, but if you've tried Brown's Bitters, which is reported to be the miracle drug of all time, curing everything from bad breath to worried nerves, watery blood, aches and pains, bad dreams, bad appetite, and even a bad disposition and has a god-awful taste, I think I shall stick to my mother's remedy for a cold or sore throat, with a shot of whiskey when my disposition is foul."

He laughs so hard he almost topples over, so we agree it's time to take our leave before Marie comes looking for her man and I am blamed once more for being the culprit who leads him astray.

We have not gone but a few steps before we encounter Peter Simmons, a young black laborer who has a reputation for being extremely unruly when drunk, as he obviously is now. Pushing and shoving, uttering obscenities as he staggers down the street, his strong arms and fists fly at anyone in his path.

Not one to allow something like this to continue and his brawny blacksmith's body equal to the task, Joseph steps squarely into Simmons's path, blocking his destructive forward motion.

Holding him back with one hand against his chest and jerking his head up with the other beneath his chin, Joseph looks Simmons dead in the eye, daring him to resist. "Go home, sober up, Peter, before you get yourself into something you can't handle," he says.

But Peter catches him off guard and comes at him swinging with all his might. His huge right fist catches Joseph a glancing blow on his left cheek, just below the eye, and blood spews forth.

"Now look what you've gone and done," Joseph says with a shake of his head and a narrowing of his eyes.

He is circling around Peter to get a better advantage and the fight is on. A crowd from inside the Five Star has spilled out into the dark street and is egging on the combatants, whooping and hollering and placing bets, furthering the intensity of the situation.

Lucky for Peter and to the disappointment of the crowd, the sheriff arrives in time to put a stop to the whole affair before serious damage is done. Joseph refuses to press charges and Peter is hauled away to sleep it off, courtesy of the city jail.

*

"It's too bad Peter is a drunkard," Doc says as he tends Joseph's cut. "His mother, Jane Bronson, is a hard-working widow woman and one of the finest cooks around. He has a nice young wife and I delivered a new baby for them just three months ago. Only twenty-two years old and he has already been in trouble numerous times due to his drinking."

Doc decides to give us a ride home "to keep us out of further trouble." Also, he has been summoned to the jail to tend to Peter's slight wounds, and the time has grown late.

Marie is waiting on the Florida House front porch with a stormy look on her face. It soon disappears on seeing the bandage on Joseph's cheek. An arm around her waist and a kiss on her lips stills her questions as they head across the street toward home and I to the peaceful quietness of my room.

Entering, I find several pieces of mail have been delivered while I was out: one, of course, from Pauline and the other of a script I don't recognize, with a foreign stamp but neither a return address nor a name.

Bone-tired though I am, curiosity gets the best of me when a scent of spices wafts from the envelope and drives me to open it at once. Much to my amazement a lithograph falls out onto my lap and staring up at me is Mary, in a pure white silken dress, with flowers in her hair. She stands on a sandy beach, surrounded by palm trees and close beside her is a man looking proud as can be, who obviously is her sea captain. He also is dressed in white, albeit linen and a straw hat.

She looks happy, I think with a pang of jealousy that stabs straight through my heart. Fool, I think again, isn't this what you wanted for her, a better life far from the terrible place she was in?

I steal a better look at the photograph, looking for signs that the smile is not genuine. But it is real. She is truly happy and I must be happy for her. Letting out a deep sigh, I rub my finger across her face and wish her well before putting the photo away to look at another day.

The next morning I awake from a troubled night of mixed dreams of Pauline, Mary, Katie Eppes and the Old Town witch Felippa standing over a boiling cauldron and chanting some sort of evil spell as she cackles and stares first at one, then at the other of us with her beady, dark eyes.

At breakfast I tell Miss Annie about the dream, not mentioning Mary, of course. Immediately my landlady makes the sign of the cross to ward off evil spirits and then advises me to seek out Felippa for advice.

"You can't be serious!" I say, startled by her reply. "Have you ever sought advice from the witch?"

"You should not call her that," she answers in a hushed voice. "She is a voodoo priestess with skills passed down from generation to generation. She can cure the sick, deliver babies and cast spells of all kinds. She makes potions with herbs right out of her garden and plants that grow in the forest, some of which I have seen Doc himself use. One time, a mother was bleeding badly from a birthing and Felippa stopped it simply with the use of a spider web and clean black soot from the back of the chimney. Not everything needs explanation or understanding in this world in which we live."

161

Miss Annie rises and resumes her daily chores as if we had just had a normal, everyday conversation about the weather or such. I am left sitting here staring after her in mute shock.

Saturday is laundry day and I have sent down my laundry for Dilsey Bascom, the washerwoman, to pick up in her little cart on her early morning rounds. She and her husband, Charles, live in a good-size house over on Seventh Street and take in a number of boarders. Dilsey likes to pick up the laundry herself in order to socialize and gossip while she goes about her business. Perhaps she, being upward in years, knows something about this so-called voodoo priestess, so I hang around near the stacks of laundry for her arrival, which is not long in coming.

Her small donkey pulling the cart stops on command behind the gate on Fourth Street and I offer my hand, to her surprise, as she steps down.

"Good morning, Dilsey," I say as she and her young helper begin to throw bags of laundry, including linens from the Florida House, into the cart. I hem and haw around, not knowing quite how to bring up the conversation and, to be truthful, I am embarrassed.

Eyeing me with a raised brow, she picks up a bag and then sets it back down with a thump for the boy instead, and comes over to me. "Just let it out, whatever it be, mister. Ain't nutn' gits told without askin.'"

"Well …" I then start over with a rush: "Can you tell me about the Old Town witch or as some people know her, the voodoo priestess?"

"Lawd have mercy, chile! Ain't dat a subject fo' so early on a Sati-day morning!" Her gaze is curiously searching my now sweating, flushed face and she invites me to ride along on her morning route.

I begin by telling her of my strange dream and of the little I already know about Felippa from Miss Annie and Doc. "Miss Annie thinks I should go see this witch," I add, and then laugh nervously. "What do you think?"

Dilsey stops at the next corner and turns to face me on the cart seat. The look on her face is serious. "Dis ain't no laughing matter or nutn' to be foolin' around wid."

The words she speaks feel like ice water running in my veins.

"I kin gib yo' direction to her place and yo' can git a conjure or juju for yo self."

*

Armed with the address, I order a horse saddled at the livery stable, much preferring to go on my mission during the daylight than in the dark of night. The ride to Old Town is short and I am soon passing Bosque Bello Cemetery where graves mark the resting places of those buried there as far back as 1798. Those such as Domingo Acosta, member of the Spanish militia, and Old Town's first postmaster; Amos Latham, Revolutionary War hero and Fernandina's first lighthouse keeper; and more recently, John and Regina Waas, our friends and partners in the supposed love triangle.

"Bosque Bello," the beautiful wood, sounds so lyrical in Spanish and is indeed as pretty a setting as one could wish for in a final resting place, with its giant old oaks and gentle breezes lifting the Spanish moss from their branches while pretty flowers nod their heads.

Turning down Franklin Street I begin to watch carefully for the address Dilsey gave me, but I am soon surprisingly and hopelessly turned around. Puzzled, I head back the way I came but decide to try one more back street and there it is! The tiny hovel of a house sits back against the wood as to not be immediately noticed to the untrained eye. The roof is of thatch, and garden to one side, exactly as Pauline described.

Dismounting, I tie my horse to the sadly leaning fence post and enter through the gate, which creaks loudly under protest and alerts a den of dogs. With lips drawn back over sharp teeth, they howl a message to their mistress of my arrival—as if the gate had not already done so. Still, she does not appear, which makes me more nervous than ever.

On slightly trembling legs I advance and rap lightly on the door, somewhat hoping at the last moment that she will not answer and I can escape, having changed my mind after all.

Turning to leave, I am startled to find Felippa standing still as a statue beside the well, appraising me from top to bottom.

Her eyes are hooded in the bright sunlight, her attire is as Pauline described; nothing has changed.

When she speaks, her voice is smooth as dark rum: "Dreams of the night bring seekers of truth by day." She motions toward the door, moves forward and I am powerless to follow.

The gloom of the interior is dispelled by fragrant aromas issuing from a steaming pot on the hearth. With a knowing smile, she murmurs, "My love potion of which you have no need."

I sit in the chair to which I am motioned. She settles across from me after selecting several bottles, bags and various other assorted and odd items I don't recognize and don't dare ask her to identify.

Rain begins to fall lightly and a mockingbird is whistling like a young turkey, causing Felippa to look up with a start from examining the jumble of bones, rocks and sticks between us on the table where she has thrown them.

"You hear that?" she asks almost fearfully, hooded eyes now wide-open and darting here and there peering in every corner of the tiny, awful place.

Felippa proclaims: "Before the year is over, your true love will fail you, one of your close friends will commit a foul and horrible deed and the Dark Angel of Death will follow all dear to you."

Falling back in her chair, her dark eyes become hooded again, unfathomable. She resists answering any of my questions.

Shaken and unsure about the whole scene, I take my leave. I breathe in gulps of pure fresh air while delighting in the feel of cleansing rain on my skin. I push the horse through his paces, hurrying to get as far away from her as fast as I possibly can.

I should have left well enough alone; the dream was not nearly as bad as the evil omens predicted by the witch—that is, if I in any way believe her predictions.

Laughing like a maniac as I gallop along, I must appear so to those whom I pass, for I truly must be losing my mind to have even sought her out, much less believe this foolishness!

The horse is wheezing and covered in froth when we race into the stable, kicking up hay. We have surprised Joseph, who has never seen me ride a horse in this manner.

He grabs hold of the bridle and strokes the horse's flanks, calming him down as I dismount.

Joseph looks at me curiously. "What ever has taken hold of your senses?" he shouts at me, for nothing else would have gained my attention, I am so lost in the strange mood of the afternoon.

Holding up my hand to still his questions, I unceremoniously drop down onto a bale of hay with my head in my hands to give myself time to gather my thoughts before I can even begin to try to explain it to him.

Being Irish, Joseph takes it all quite seriously and does not jest nor make fun of anything to do with magic, looking into the future and the subject of love potions. "In Ireland we have elves, trolls, pots of gold at the ends of rainbows, fairies and witches of our own," he says with a straight face that tells me he believes every word.

"You should have asked my advice, not Annie's, before you went seeking out the witch. 'Tis a foolish thing to meddle in things you know nothing about without first gaining knowledge or support from someone who does."

It is not from the lightly falling rain that the goose bumps begin to crawl on my flesh, but from his words and strangely fearful look on his face.

Laughing nervously, I try to change the subject to something lighter, but the feeling of doom and gloom lingers in the dark corners of the stable and in our minds while we curry the horse and prepare to close the livery stable for the night.

Chapter 8

The Murder

January is racing to a close with temperatures all off kilter; up one day to 70 degrees and down the next to 42 degrees. It seems to go right along with my churning waves of mixed emotions, which I cannot shake since that dreadful day at the witch's hovel. Her words disturb my working hours and haunt my dreams at night, causing hours of fitful tossing and turning.

Marie Higgins's worried frown and raised eyebrows are becoming morning fixtures as she bids me good day and passes the usual steaming cup of coffee my way.

I reach for it and my hands tremble from lack of sleep. The cup feels heavy. I ask myself how long I can continue like this.

Miss Annie has been taking in the situation. "You must seek out the witch again for a potion," she says as she dries her hands on her starched, white apron upon entering the kitchen, "before you wither up and die from lack of rest."

Startled by her words, I am shaken clear down to my boots by the mere thought of returning to that horrible place. The cup slips from my trembling hand onto the table, spilling coffee all over my freshly pressed shirtfront and right down into my lap. I jump out of my seat with a yowl, trying to get the steaming, hot, wet attire away from my most private parts before damage can be done.

"I do believe she has put a curse of the worse kind on me!" I declare over my shoulder while racing out of the kitchen to my quarters.

Muttering to myself as I change, I am no longer feeling fearful of the old hag, but am now angry. I look at the ruined shirt and pants crumpled in a heap on the floor beside the bed. I kick them aside. For the second time this morning I grab the shoehorn hanging inside the bureau and slide my shoes on. I determine that I will pay her a visit as soon as I leave work this very day and not a moment later.

*

Darkness has settled over the island like a heavy blanket. I carefully venture down the lane on which the witch's hut sits among oak trees. The low-hanging Spanish moss sways gently in the evening breeze.

Starting down the sandy path, I am caught off guard by the opening of the door. I quickly step behind the nearest tree. Thankfully, it is a large oak and conceals me completely. To my surprise, Katie Eppes is standing there outlined by the gentle glow of the hearth fire. Her head is bent toward the speaker, listening intently and nodding as she holds out her hand to accept something small that I can't make out from this distance.

I remain still as she passes within a hair's breath of me, and I watch her turn to walk farther into Old Town.

"You can come out now," the hag says right beside me, making me jump out of my reverie and let loose the breath I have been holding.

"You could make a man have a heart attack sneaking up on him like that!"

"Look at who's talking," she responds quickly, piercing my depths through veiled eyes. "I am not the one sneaking around spying on folks in the middle of the night, trespassing on their property, now am I?"

She has a valid point, but when I try to explain why I have come she holds up her leathery hand and points toward the door.

She ushers me to the same chair as before. I have no choice but to sit and before I can explain, she tells me why I am here.

She moves around the small room, from shelf to shelf while saying, "You can't sleep, nor eat …." She mixes things from tiny jars and bags into a small pot. "And you worry about the future."

Watching her work, I begin to feel my earlier anger resurfacing. I all but shout at her, "It's your entire fault. I was doing just fine until I came to see you!"

The look on her wise, old, wrinkled face as her head turns slowly toward me is enough to still my tongue once and for all.

Her voice is patient and sad as she speaks these words: "I do not make the future. I have been given the gift—or the curse, if you wish—to foretell the future and pass it on."

Gesturing around the room I ask, "Then what of these potions you sell so readily to the gullible ones such as Katie Eppes, whom I just saw leaving?"

Throwing back her head, she cackles, and then in a near whisper, says, "If I tell you my secret, you must promise never to reveal it to any other. Do you promise?"

After I swear myself to secrecy on my gentleman's honor, she tells me how it is done; the love potions are nothing more than herbs grown and mixed into a secret recipe which is then poured into a loved one's drink to make him or her more amorous of an evening. The same is true of the potion to increase the chances of pregnancy, to be taken at a certain time of the month.

"It all seems like voodoo and magic and certainly does have some powers of belief thrown in to help it along," she says with a sideways look while passing me a vial of shimmering liquid. "This is to help you sleep at night. You will need to place two drops on your tongue prior to getting into bed and you will sleep peacefully the night through.

There's no potion I can give you to stop the future events I foretold from occurring."

I reach into my pocket, lay down two dollars, turn and walk out the door for the final time, never to return.

While riding away I am saddened by her words. I had so looked forward to a new year of happiness. Now it seems it will be far worse than my mind can conceive and heart can bear.

*

Time seems to creep forward as if it understands my abject misery in its coming days of knowing something will happen. Yet I must bear this pain of not knowing what, when and who.

At least I am sleeping as promised, dreamless nights a dull void, only to awaken to countless hours of wondering if this will be the day.

Doc comes by the office today, dropping his abundant frame heavily onto the chair facing my desk. "Well, it finally happened." He breathes a heavy sigh of sadness and shakes his head in sorrow. "Peter Simmons shot and killed his wife, leaving their three-month-old baby to crawl around its mother's blood until Victoria was found by her mother-in law. He escaped across the river and was last seen in Callahan late last night. The boys down at the saloon said he had been drinking pretty heavily after work."

"Pistols are evil," I say in anger over the terrible tragedy. "I don't now own one, nor will I ever allow one in my home."

Doc rises slowly, pointing his finger at my face. "How will you defend your home against a burglar or any intruder if you don't own a weapon?"

Doc and I have had this conversation on other occasions and our points of view never change.

"I understand what you're saying," I reply, "but there must be put into law a system making it difficult for just anyone to own a pistol. There was an article in the Lancaster, South Carolina, *Ledger* recently, suggesting a tax on pistols, the same as is on the manufacture of tobacco and whiskey, and I for one am all for it."

The chiming of the mantle clock reminds us both of the dinner hour.

Doc says, "The Idle Hour is in full operation again and if you are so inclined, we can continue this conversation there." He gathers his hat and coat from the hall tree by the door.

I follow suit without any argument. Visions of fresh fish make my mouth water.

Watching Mrs. Sweeney work her way through the crowded room, I find it good to see the business is doing so well. With the help of the boys after school and on weekends, and hired help during the day, she should be able to make a go of it. But George's presence sure is missed. No more stories, and his loud, infectious laugh is a fading memory. Others come and try to fill the gap.

To our delight, holding center court today is Captain William Sharpe of the pilot boat *Agnes Bell*. He regales everyone with a story of his recent catch off Fernandina bar of seventeen fish in one haul, with one little hook and one line; to wit, two blackfish and fifteen sharks. They were landed as follows: one shark, six feet long, from which came forth fourteen young sharks and the two blackfish. Laying the fish down end to end, the catch measured twenty-two feet in all. His explanation of how this amazing feat occurred puts to rest at last all doubts of his credibility of the fish tale which has been circulating around town for the past few days.

It's good to see Mrs. Sweeney join in the good-natured laughter and fun; her eyes crinkle at the corners and she wipes the sweat from her brow with her apron. She checks each savory dish coming from the kitchen before it is allowed to be placed in front of her customers. Heaven have mercy on the cook or servant who sends out anything but the best-tasting and best-presented food at all times.

Platters of succulent steamed oysters and flaky fried flounder arrive at our table, served with boiled red potatoes and another round of lager.

Doc rolls up his sleeves, pulls on an oyster glove and begins to tackle the oysters in earnest. All conversation ceases for the duration of the meal other than sighs of contentment and exclamations of delight as each juicy oyster is unveiled in its glory.

Holding out an opened shell with a quivering, slimy mass upon it, Doc encourages me: "Here, try just one. They are sweet and salty at the same time."

I shake my head vigorously "no" at the mere thought of putting the thing in my mouth, and he pops it in his, laughing. After a lick of his lips he says, "You don't know what you're missing."

Pushing back my plate, and then my chair from the table, I say, "You can have your oysters, I'll stick to fish, my friend. I'm not missing a thing."

"Well, you better be eating something," he replies, looking me over, "you are beginning to look on the puny side lately. Do you want to come by my office for a checkup?"

"No, it's not anything physical that's bothering me," I tell him, "it's something else and I don't know quite how to explain it."

Leaning forward, I stare intently into his kind old face and search for answers to questions I can't even put into words. Clasping my hands behind my head I lean back again, eyes closed against the bright afternoon sun filtering through the chintz curtains. I'm trying to decide whether or not to share with Doc my venture into Old Town … and the old hag's premonitions. … No, I'll keep it to myself. The burden is too heavy to place on my friend.

Taking in a deep breath, then exhaling deeply, I force a smile on my face before steering the subject tactfully to something other than me.

"Have you seen the progress on T.J. and Katie's house?" I ask him.

"Yes," he replies while sitting up straighter in his chair, "as a matter of fact, T.J. and I rode by there last week and walked around the property.

He showed me the blueprints and is very proud of the home he's building for his bride. It will be quite the place with over three thousand square feet, a parlor, grand staircase, dining room and six fireplaces."

My eyebrows shoot up at his information. I had no idea the house was to be so large. "A project of this enormity should keep Katie busy and less fretful of being left alone while her husband is away on business," I say as we stand to leave.

Doc shakes his head in disagreement, looking at me as if I were some poor idiot not understanding women, at least not this one.

"I can see you have a lot to learn about women, my friend," he says, indicating the way to his carriage, "and I will not even begin to unfold the mysteries in the short time we have during our ride back into town. But one thing you can always be sure of, and that is men will never completely understand women and that is what keeps us on our toes."

With a hearty laugh he gives the horse a gentle tap with the reins and we are off again, our stomachs full and my spirit somewhat lighter than it has been lately.

*

January rolls uneventfully into February and as each day passes I begin to feel more like my old self and foolish for having believed any of that nonsense.

The day of the Calico Hop draws near; tomorrow is the big day. Sophie and I have made our final plans. I fear the excitement is too much for her to bear. The same is for Gracie, who is presently showing off her costume to accumulated family, boarders and guests in the front parlor, when the front door bursts open, admitting a wildly gesturing and jabbering Joseph, who makes no sense at all.

Grabbing him by both arms I shake him to try to calm him, all the while asking, "What's wrong, Joseph, tell us, what's happened?" The bad feeling of dread and doom returns to settle over me like a heavy, evil monster.

Waving his arms toward the door he is finally able to blurt out, "T.J. shot Major Suhrer over at the Mansion House. I believe he might be dead!"

No one breathes. Not a word is uttered from the mere shock of his words. It can't be possible, I think to myself. Why would he do such a thing? It must be a mistake.

Time stands still with the exception of the ticking of the grandfather clock which sounds inordinately loud somehow, in the parlor where no one moves while the terrible words of the messenger slowly penetrate our brains.

Coming to my senses I charge for the door and am followed en masse by a large portion of the parlor's inhabitants, all pushing and shoving to exit at the same time with one destination in mind, the Mansion House Hotel, scene of the supposed shooting.

The hotel is situated on the corner of Broome and Third streets, a mere three blocks away. The distance is covered in a matter of minutes in our haste to ascertain or disclaim the dreadful announcement.

The truth is obvious as we draw near and see the ever increasing crowd of onlookers surrounding the hotel entrance. People spill down the sidewalk and street in both directions.

The sheriff is unsuccessfully attempting to disperse the gathering. "Please go to your homes, back to your businesses," he shouts, but is barely heard over the noise.

I spy my friend, C. A. Key, standing on the west porch, and work my way through the crowd until at last I am able to climb over the railing to where he is quietly talking to another resident of the hotel, L. F. Smith, agent for the railroad.

"My God, C.A., tell me what has happened here," I implore, grasping his hand.

Turning toward me, his face is distorted in agony of the scene he has witnessed between two of his longstanding friends.

"I will tell you exactly as I told the sheriff as to the occurrence this afternoon: I was in the reading room and had finished going through my mail and was reading the newspaper Ferdinand had retrieved for me, as usual, at the train depot, when I heard a scuffle on the porch and loud voices. Looking out, I saw two men grappling with each other. Ferdinand and T.J. And I heard Ferdinand say, 'What does all this mean?' That's when I saw the flash of a pistol and saw Ferdinand stagger. I then arose and went to the door. T.J. was standing with one foot on the steps and one on the platform in front of the house, his face distorted in anger. Ferdinand was on the porch. T.J. had a whip in his right hand and Ferdinand was grasping the end of it. I saw T.J. strike Ferdinand once or twice with the whip after he shot Ferdinand and that's when I heard him ask T.J., 'What does all this mean?' T.J. told him, 'You insulted my wife one week ago today.' To which Ferdinand vehemently denied, saying, 'I may be a dead man, Jeff, but before God, I did not.' Captain Smith and I assisted Ferdinand to his room, where Dr. Pope is attending him now."

Pacing back and forth across the porch I shake my head in disbelief at all that has happened and I say in relief, "Thank God he is alive! Rumor has it he has died."

"The bullet entered his right chest just about here," C.A. says, and points to his own chest just below the collarbone. "He has lost a lot of blood. It will be touch and go through the night. It is hard to believe this has happened, and Ferdinand with a wife and six children. What will become of them if he does not make it?"

At that moment a murmur goes through the crowd and our attention is diverted to the hotel entrance as Eva Rosa, Ferdinand's wife, moves along the pathway made by the assembled friends and neighbors. Many of them reach out to touch her, imparting words of sorrow as she and her children hurry to the side of their fallen loved one.

What indeed will become of them, I ponder as we lose sight of the mother carrying the youngest, Joseph, who is crying on her hip, and the others trailing behind, clinging to each other with eyes solemn, downcast and frightened.

The hours wax on; the vigil is long. Most people return to their homes knowing word will come one way or another. The Catholic priest is summoned, and he gives the last rites. Children and friends are allowed to visit one last time while Eva Rosa sits stoically beside her husband, holding his hand, speaking softly to him. Sometimes she sings a gentle song in their native tongue as his life slowly but surely departs, until at last he breathes one last breath, sighs and is gone.

It is about one thirty in the morning of February 8, 1884, and the life of Ferdinand Charles Suhrer is no more. Snuffed out in a fit of jealousy and passion by a friend of many years over an insult Ferdinand supposedly committed against T.J.'s beautiful young wife.

I, like many others, am numb with grief, but none so much as Eva Rosa who lies prostrate across her husband's body, sobbing uncontrollably, refusing to leave. It is a heart-wrenching scene for those who slip quietly out of the room to give her these final moments with him.

Eventually the priest encourages her to leave with him, to return home with her children. "It is best, Eva Rosa. The children need for you to be strong for them now, to carry on as Ferdinand would wish you to do."

Nodding in agreement she pulls herself up straight, gathers the sleeping babe from the sofa in the corner and with the rest of her children, they kneel for prayer. Before departing, each one places a kiss on their father's forehead.

They trail out into the night knowing this will be the last time they will all be together.

"Now that the family has gone home, we must take care of business at hand." Dr. Pope instructs each one of us. "C.A., will you please inform the sheriff of the death, and you," he says, pointing his finger at me, "I need you to go fetch the undertaker. The post-mortem must be conducted as soon as possible." Shooing us out the door, he closes it to insure privacy for the deceased.

After completing my errand, I turn my weary feet toward home in hopes of finding some sleep before daylight ... and rest for my weary soul.

Miss Annie is waiting for me in the kitchen just as I should have expected: a pot of hot coffee sits on the stove and a bottle of whiskey on the table.

"I thought you might need a hot toddy to help you sleep," she says kindly, pouring a big helping of the whiskey in the cup and stirring as she stares into my face. "I can tell by looking at you the news is not good."

I don't know why the tears start, but when they do they won't stop. I haven't cried since my mama died, but tonight, seeing Eva Rosa and her children's sorrow and my friend Ferdinand lying there dead, and knowing that it was not a stranger but a friend to us all who caused this pain, took something out of me. The dam holding back my emotions broke loose.

I drop my head into my hands and cry and cry with deep, gut-wrenching sobs that seem to last forever until at last with a shudder they come to an end. Raising my head, I take the cup of coffee offered and drink the now tepid liquid down quickly, trying to ease my pain. I hold it out for a refill. Understanding my need, Miss Annie fills it again and even once more. Without the need for words she puts an arm around my shoulders and assists me to my room and into bed.

I hear her quietly pull the door to and moments later the creaking of the rocker on the porch keeps rhythm to muffled sobs of her own. As my eyes close, my heavy heart tells me the town of Fernandina mourns deeply tonight and will do so for a long, long time.

My sleep is at best fitful, filled with dreams of witches laughing with glee, flying and cackling all around my bed, stirring pots of evil-smelling brew in my fireplace, while I shiver in fright, watching from the corner by my bed.

Finding it useless to go back to sleep, at last I rise. I stir the embers in the small fireplace and add a couple of logs. Then I sit down at my desk to write the inevitable letter to Pauline.

The wound is too deep, the hurt too fresh; I am able to write only the briefest account of the affair, ready it for the post and myself for the new day before obtaining my usual cup of strong black coffee from the kitchen and bringing it back to my favorite place on the upstairs porch. I watch the town stir slowly and begin its new day.

But today is different—or is it my imagination? Does the milkman linger longer than usual talking to Miss Annie and does the sheriff do the same as he makes his rounds?

I am sure everyone is talking about Ferdinand, T.J. and Katie and what happened yesterday. T.J. turned himself in to the magistrate after the shooting. I wonder if he is still in jail and what has happened to Katie in all this.

Smells wafting up from the kitchen cause my stomach to grumble, reminding me I did not eat last night, and even though my appetite is not great I know I must eat something.

Of course tongues are wagging around the breakfast table as I enter the room; gossip had arrived before the ham and eggs were dished out by Marie.

"You were there right after it happened," Clay says to me. "Is it true what they're saying about T.J. being enraged over Ferdinand insulting Katie last week while he was away on business?"

Slowly looking at each one of them, I pick up my knife and begin cutting the thick, juicy ham on my plate before answering. "Every one of you in this room knows the fine, upstanding character of Ferdinand Suhrer. He has been a pillar of our community, holding numerous city and county offices as well as being a wonderful husband and father. Do any of you really believe he would do such a thing?"

Red-faced Clay leans forward in his chair, causing it to thump loudly. "Gosh, you don't have to get so upset. I was just asking you what everyone is saying."

"Then no, I don't believe in this gossip that is spreading like the plague around town, because that is exactly what it is, gossip! It will only serve to harm everyone involved, including Ferdinand's wife and children, if it does not stop."

Throwing down my napkin I stand up, saying, "No one has given Katie a chance since she arrived in Fernandina. Gossipers had it she was a poor farmer's daughter and a gold digger, when truth be told, her family came to Florida from Lexington, South Carolina, before the Civil War and are very rich planters owning considerable property—even owning a number of slaves prior to the war. Her mother was widowed during the war, leaving Katie, her mother, sister Mary and two brothers to be taken care of by her uncle, but her mother was left with the land and house. Katie is high-spirited and beautiful, but that does not give people reason to gossip about her, just because she is different."

Having said this mouthful, I interject another thought before stomping out of the room: "Let's leave the findings of the matter up to the sheriff, and gossip out of it. We will all be the better for it."

The walk to work is no better. People try to stop me along the way, wanting to talk about the murder but I refuse, reasoning I will be late for work and must hurry. Thankfully at last I am safe in my office, door closed to intruders, not a living soul to bother me. The humdrum daily tasks offer relief for once.

But keeping my mind on these tasks is more than I bargained for, and after attempting to add the same row of figures numerous times I rise and stand by the windows. I look down on Centre Street and the hustle and bustle of the people of Fernandina as they go about their lives, working, shopping and yes, gossiping. I can tell by the way they hold their heads together, their furtive glances up and down the street, and the way their hands wave and point in a certain direction. This will be fodder for conversation for months to come.

Standing there deep in thought, I had not heard anyone enter the room until William clears his throat.

Startled, I turn around stammering an explanation: "Oh, I'm sorry. I didn't hear you come in. I was just stretching my legs—taking a little break from the figures in the report."

He walks the length of the room to stand beside me. He looks down upon the scene, taking in the same thing I see and astutely knows what I am thinking.

The look of sorrow and compassion on his face as he stands quietly there speaks for him. I turn, shake his hand, go back to my desk and my work. No words need be spoken between this man and myself. We have worked side by side far too long.

After he closes the door softly behind him, I immerse myself in the reports, determined to complete them before I leave today, for tonight is the Calico Hop and I must have my head clear of work, at least, in order to do justice for Sophie. She deserves a good time even though my heart is not in it.

At last it is done: my desk neat and orderly, the oil lamp snuffed out and fire dampened for the weekend. The reports are neatly stacked, ready to be delivered to Mr. Wood on my way past his office and I will be off to dine and dress for the hop.

Lifting his head from his perusal of the newspaper that he reads every afternoon as a matter of habit, William accepts the reports with a nod. "Well done as usual. Do you have time to go over the reports or would you rather do it Monday morning?"

"Monday morning would be best for me. I am Miss Sophie's chaperone to the Calico Hop this evening and am in a bit of a rush to make it on time."

"The hop, yes indeed, Mrs. Wood and I are attending as well. I'm glad you reminded me. Calico is not my pattern of choice but the ladies seem to be having fun with this one."

Parting company until later, we head our respective ways home, me to don my pink shirt which surprisingly does not look so bad after all. I have chosen a white horse and carriage for Sophie's first "grownup" social and she squeals in delight upon my arrival.

"I feel like a fairy princess," she says, and sighs when I hand her up and wrap a soft, cozy blanket around her to ward off the chill. Her parents stand in the door waving goodbye as we turn the corner and head for Lyceum Hall and the night of her young life.

Some girls are gathered near the entrance when we arrive, and ooh and ahh over her conveyance (just what I had in mind). A young Negro takes the horse's reins and I assist her in alighting. Her head is held regally, to which I try to hide my amusement. But as soon as she reaches her consorts she is all giggles and girlish whispers.

With her arm on mine, we enter the hall and our eyes are immediately assaulted by every color and pattern imaginable of calico! It is large and small and everywhere, in dresses, shirts, parasols, banners, programs and table covers.

We skate until nine o'clock and then I am thankful the dancing will begin soon. Not that I don't like skating, but my ankles are beginning to ache terribly since Sophie does not let up, but skates every song with youthful vigor.

Excusing myself for a smoke break, with a huge sigh of relief I gratefully lower myself onto a chair on the porch and heave my legs up on the rail. Closing my eyes I take a deep drag on my Havana and slowly let it out, enjoying to the utmost not only the cigar but the relief for my poor feet.

But alas, this is to be short-lived when little Sophie comes tugging on my sleeve. "Come on, the music has started. It's time to dance and as my chaperone you must dance the first dance with me. It's the custom."

And away we go to dance the night away, until I deliver a very tired and half-asleep Sophie back to her parents just before midnight.

At the door she turns to me, giving me a big hug of gratitude and says in an uncharacteristically grownup Sophie manner, "Thank you so much for taking me to my first grownup dance. I know how hard it was for you to wear the pink shirt and how hard it was for you to try and be happy and smile and try to make everything nice for me when you are sad because your friend died." Planting a little kiss on my cheek, she smiles, and with a goodnight wave she enters the house, leaving me standing on the porch feeling honored to know such a lovely young person.

Joseph and I take chairs from the back porch to sit beside the old oak behind the Florida House, after the horse and buggy have been situated for the night, in order not to disturb the folks sleeping soundly behind the darkened windows.

Passing the inevitable flask to me, he fills me in on Ferdinand's funeral arrangements to be held at 9:00 a. m. tomorrow morning from St. Michael's Catholic Church, and his visit to the widow today.

"It was a terrible thing to behold so much weeping and wailing from the widow and children and the oldest boy, George, now fourteen years of age, trying to be the man of the house. One minute he is a boy crying and the next he is angry, threatening to kill T.J. himself for murdering his father—which upsets his mother all the more."

Joseph jumps out of his chair and leans against the tree. "It's a good thing T.J. and George are still locked up at the jail," he says. "The feelings of the majority of town folk are not very favorable toward them right now. In fact it would not take much for a lynch mob to gather," he adds, shaking his head sadly at the thought of his friends being strung up.

The vision conjured by his words sickens me as well. "What do you think happened, Joseph?" I ask, and then take another swig of whiskey from the flask.

"I hesitate to even guess. Nothing makes sense, it should never have happened," he states while vehemently slamming his fist against the age-old tree time and time again, punctuating each word and trying to make the pain go away. His fist begins to bleed from the impact of flesh against the unyielding tree.

Finally he drops into his chair with shoulders slumped and head bent. I can see tears roll down his weathered, work-lined face. There are no words left, none to be found between us; nothing can right this wrong, nothing will justify the killing of a friend.

Before turning in, we sit quietly for a while. Sharing the flask, we watch the cats go about their nocturnal duties, stalking smaller four-legged creatures. They pounce on them and occasionally bring one to drop at our feet for our approval of a job well done.

The town is eerily quiet this morning, with the exception of church bells ringing the death toll and hushed voices of the townspeople making their way to pay their last respects to their departed friend. Not a store is open, not a train or ship is moving. The wind does not even dare to blow on this almost spring-like day with the temperature reaching almost sixty-eight degrees and it not even eight thirty.

We move together, a crowd of black-garbed mourners clutching each other's hands. The church is filled to capacity, overflowing into the churchyard and surrounding streets. It takes hours for those who want to view him one last time, to file past his coffin.

He lies there, in state, a handsome man of only forty-five years, husband, father, and friend gone from us forever. Tears flow unabated throughout the ceremony, without shame by men and women alike. I myself have soaked the handkerchief now wadded up in my hand; I have given up keeping it in my pocket.

Finally, last rites are spoken. The priest sprinkles Holy Water over the now-closed casket and city council members acting as pallbearers gently carry him out of the sanctuary lined with statues of saints. The casket is bathed by sunlight filtering through stained-glass windows and the soaring tune of "Ave Maria." Outside, the black hearse with glass-windowed sides awaits. Flowers adorn all four of its corners. A pair of matching black bays will convey him to be laid to rest in Bosque Bello Cemetery.

The end has come at last. No business is conducted this afternoon. Neighbors attend the widow and children, providing food and comfort. Everyone speaks in hushed tones as if in fear of shattering the churchlike atmosphere which hovers over us all. Even the drinkers in the saloons and bars, which never close, do so in silence, toasting the fallen one in respect and honor when evening comes. But the whorehouses remain closed knowing it would be a dishonor to operate tonight.

Tomorrow will be another day. The sun will rise as usual and life will continue its same old cycle, yet somehow different, missing a vital link in our lives.

And life does go on day in and day out, but Ferdinand does not leave us. The speculations of how and why it occurred are on every tongue and in every mind continuously, especially after his obituary is posted on February 16 in the *Florida Mirror* as follows:

The Late Fernando C. Suhrer

The funeral of the late Fernando C. Suhrer, whose tragic death last week cast such a deep gloom over our whole community, took place from the Roman Catholic church on Saturday morning last, and was attended by the populace en masse, the members of the City Council, of which that body the deceased was president, acting as pall-bearers. After the ceremonies at the church the body was conveyed to the burying ground of that parish set apart in the Old Town Cemetery. The grief of the bereaved family, so suddenly and violently bereft of a protector, counselor and provider, was distressing in the extreme to witness, and many a strong man, to whom tears had been strangers for years, was seen to weep.

The deceased was a native of the Grand Duchy of Baden in Germany, and a graduate of the college at Tauber-Bischoffsheim. In 1856 he came to America, and lived several years in Milwaukee, Wis. From Milwaukee he went to Ohio, where he studied medicine under Dr. Luther L. Jenkins until the breaking out of the war, when he entered the army as a private in the 107th Ohio Volunteer Infantry, in which regiment he served until the close of the war, having raised to the rank of major. In July, 1865, he was mustered out, and came to Fernandina, where he has resided since. As stated in our last issue, he held many offices of public trust, Federal, State and municipal, during his residence here, and his genial and polite ways made him a host of friends, who sincerely mourn his loss, and extend their heartfelt sympathy to the bereaved widow and children.

Adding insult and anger to the citizens of Fernandina is the matter of bail set for T. J. Eppes and George Dewson in the amount of $ 6,000 each.

The *Florida Times-Union*, February 12, 1884:

The Suhrer Murder
Judge Baker Refuses to Change His Order Granting Bail

Yesterday the Mayor of Fernandina, as the representative of a large number of citizens of that town, came to Jacksonville, retained the services of Colonel John T. Walker and presented to Judge James M. Baker additional evidence in the Eppes-Suhrer murder, asking the order granting bail be vacated.

One of the papers presented was the verdict of the coroner's jury, which charges Eppes with felony murder and Dewson with being an accomplice. Another document was the affidavit of Conductor L. F. Smith, that fifteen minutes before the murder he met Eppes and Dewson on the street and Eppes asked witness if he had a revolver. Witness said he had not. Eppes said, "Mr. Dewson thinks he can beat me shooting, and want to try." He saw the affray, and Dewson was holding one of Suhrer's arms.

The object of the evidence was to show that the shooting was deliberated fully fifteen minutes and done deliberately and in cold blood, but Judge Baker declined to change his order and Eppes was upon Bay Street in this city yesterday.

Mrs. Eppes's statement made to her husband's attorneys, is that the alleged indignity to her by Major Suhrer occurred the latter part of January, in her room.

It appears that Mrs. Eppes never told her husband of this, but broached it to George Dewson's wife, who told George Dewson, who told Eppes and then went about with him borrowing pistols and finally assisted in accomplishing the murder. It will be interesting to learn very accurately the whole course of this indignity business. Not only did Suhrer with his dying breath deny it, but he particularly demanded the arrest of George Dewson. Major Suhrer was an old hotel man, a man of family, whose character was unblemished, and whose death was universally regretted. That he should have sought to ravish in his own house a newly wedded bride is not exceedingly probable on the face of it.

The *Florida Times-Union*, February 12, 1884:

Mr. Dewson Arraigned

February 11, 1884

The coroner's jury, sitting on the body of F. C. Suhrer, having found a verdict against George W. Dewson for aiding and abetting in the murder of Major Suhrer, he was arrested and arraigned before Magistrate Schuyler today, who held him to bail of $ 6,000, which was immediately furnished, and Mr. Dewson was discharged to appear before the Circuit Court.

Katie is noticeably absent from public view except for brief outings during all these goings-on, and when she is present her appearance is unusually pale, her demeanor quiet and withdrawn. If she had been treated with social tolerance before the murder, this attitude has now turned to suspicion and even disdain.

"Circuit court will not be held until May, a long time for folks to continue gossiping about who is to blame, was it Katie, T.J. or was it Ferdinand?" I say, exasperated one Saturday afternoon while fishing with Louis Horsey. He is home from Charleston and his studies at the medical college until commencement of the fall term.

Rolling up his pant legs to walk farther out into the still chilly Atlantic Ocean, he answers back over his shoulder, "You know as well as I do how hard this has affected the whole town, and the trial can't come soon enough for us all, when the truth will come out."

The truth, yes the truth. It seems to echo in my head but will it really matter in the end?

"Do you believe it was worth Ferdinand's life if he did forget himself for one moment and say something he should not have to Katie or even have touched her breasts, as some are saying he did?" I ponder out loud to Louis. "Do you think Jeff should have taken Eva Rosa's husband and the father of her children away from her for one indiscretion? Don't you think Jeff should have given him the chance to explain? After all, they had been friends for years."

Walking back in to shore we bury the ends of our rods in the sand, the lines remaining taut in the water. We are hopeful of catching something to show for our half-frozen feet and legs. We sit side by side and he cups his hands against the breeze in order to light our Havanas.

Louis takes another moment before answering my questions. "Put yourself in Jeff's place," he says, "fueled with Jeff's quick temper—not with your even temperament and logic—and you have answered your own questions."

With a deep pull on my cigar I stare out to sea and it dawns on me what Louis is saying; I now understand the heat of passion that could escalate into such an act, given the right moment in time.

Changing the subject he informs me of something I did not know. "The United States Fishery Department has sent Captain Hamlin to inspect several sites for the artificial propagation of shad fish along the St. Marys River." His expression and voice both show his excitement. "Each shad yields approximately 20,000 young fish, and Captain Hamlin aboard the Fishery Commission's schooner, *Fish Hawk*, hopes to start some 25,000,000 shadlets along their mission before leaving our area."

Laughing, I pull my now slack line in. The hook is empty of bait. I say, "I hope those shad grow fast so we can go fish the St. Marys with better luck than this!"

Time creeps forward, the inevitable trial looming over our heads. Ships arrive with their loads of cargo and tourists, Jay Gould's splendid yacht and steamship, *Atalanta*, arrives in all her glory, as does entertainment in the form of "The Goldens" at Lyceum Hall, another skating gala and a Necktie Party as well as the Leap Year Ball.

Mr. Mead Hunt now occupies the desk in the clerk's office at the Mansion House, which the newspaper reports is doing a fine business this season. I no longer am able to visit my friend C. A. Key there for an evening of cards but, rather, have him come here to my residence at the Florida House instead. Given time, I know this will pass.

There is an ad in the *Florida Mirror* for 88 acres of good, rich hammock land, partly cleared, with improvements for sale. For further particulars apply to: Mrs. E. R. Suhrer.

She is having a difficult time; there is no source of income to sustain a family of six children and the extended family is too far away to turn to.

Not much is known about Eva Rosa. Ferdinand once told me her elderly father, Peter Plotts, a cabinetmaker, had died and also her brother, Augustus, who served in 45th OVI during the war. Her mother and three sisters, Katherine, Elizabeth and Magdalena reside far away in Elyria, Ohio. She has spoken fondly of her younger brother, George, who died at the tender age of twelve at a Fourth of July picnic when the homemade firecracker he made blew up in his face.

A number of properties can be sold and a widow's pension applied for. Eva Rosa is smart and frugal, but proud. She has refused outright offers of loans and gifts, but some friends have made anonymous monetary gifts through the *Florida Mirror* which have been forwarded to her, and so she cannot refuse.

The cold winter months of February and March finally give way to the warmer ones of April and May and with spring comes the much-awaited, much-talked-about circuit court session that will bring an end to this endless gossip. You would think that after almost four months the talk would have died down at least a bit, but if anything it just seems to increase like a churning tidal wave lashing furiously at our island.

I myself make it a point not to discuss the death of Ferdinand, deferring the issue to the upcoming trial and its outcome. My father always told me there are two sides to every story but not necessarily a right and wrong side. I have never forgotten his many words of wisdom; they have stood me in good stead in numerous situations in my life, such as now.

Even though I wonder to myself who will speak for Ferdinand, who will tell his side, who other than Ferdinand himself really knows the truth and can defend his honor? Who will indeed, as tomorrow the trial begins.

EPPES-SUHRER TRIAL
MAY 27, 1884

The journey to Jacksonville is long and extremely arduous in this ungodly early summer heat unfit for either man or beast. My heart is heavy as I travel the long, tiring road, a trip I would rather not be making but one I must endure for the sake of both my friends, the one who stands trial and the one he murdered, snuffed out in a fit of rage of jealous passion. Daily, my thoughts often drift to his wife and six fatherless children.

Riding alongside me wiping the sweat from his brow with an already soaked handkerchief is Dr. Pope, another friend and acquaintance to us all, and physician attending the last moments of Ferdinand's life.

Pauline begged me to take her with me but I insisted that she not attend the trial. To my amazement her parents for once backed me up.

Arriving finally at our destination at the courthouse on East Bay Street we find it difficult to find a place to tether the horses. A cargo of gasoline has been spilt while being offloaded from a nearby ship, adding to the massive turnout. After finding a young Negro who agrees for a ridiculous sum to secure them at a nearby stable, we enter the unbearably overcrowded courtroom to find the stench from gasoline has added to the discomfort.

It is a curious mob that packs and jams the courtroom long before the trial is to begin. We can hear the whispering among themselves, between glances toward the side door where Jeff and George will have to enter. A baby cries in its mother's arms and the crowd forces her out. She balks at leaving. The bailiff orders, "Take the child out," and she does as he orders. There are many women in the audience. Pauline will be mad now, that I refused to allow her to attend. More people are begging to be allowed in, but there isn't an available spot. Spectators are in the windows, packed in, standing up against the wall, standing on chairs, sitting on tables and in the inner recesses of the court.

Women and men of all walks of life have come to gawk and stare at the accused in The State of Florida vs. Eppes & Dewson in the murder of Ferdinand Suhrer, and to hear all the titillating facts.

Pushing our way forward we find seats reserved near the front for witnesses, without a moment to spare before the bailiff issues the order, "All rise. This court is now in session, the Honorable Judge James M. Baker presides."

Entering the courtroom from his chamber door, the judge strikes an imposing figure and all is quiet for a moment. Taking his place on the bench he orders the accused be brought in and pandemonium breaks out when they enter dressed in their Sunday finery and take their seats at the defense table already occupied by attorneys T. A. MacDonell, Colonel John T. Walker and Judge H. J. Baker, a circuit court judge from Nassau County. It appears that I am not the only one curious to know why a judge is at the defense table; people consult each other, gesturing toward the one who bears the same last name as the presiding judge.

The gavel hammers down again and again and the call to order by the bailiff is barely heard over the uproar. The judge is fast losing his patience with the disrespectful crowd.

Finally gaining their attention he offers this ultimatum: "If there are any more outbreaks of this kind I will have no choice but to clear the courtroom of all spectators for the duration of the trial." Scanning the room with eyes of steel he sees it sinks in, and court is allowed to resume.

It is now ten o'clock in the morning, an hour past time for court to commence, with the first order of the day being selection of a panel of twelve jurors. State's attorney A. W. Owens announces to the judge that the State is ready in the case of Eppes and Dewson, charged with murdering Ferdinand C. Suhrer, which case has been transferred from Nassau County. Colonel John T. Walker, of counsel for the defendants, then announces they are also ready, and the clerk proceeds to call the jury.

A special venire of seventy-five jurors has been ordered and return made to the court. Juror after juror, when asked, owing to the prominence of the case and it having been discussed a great deal throughout the county, are honest to admit they have already formed an opinion on the subject of guilt or innocence of the defendants, or when asked by prosecution or defense attorneys, they fail to qualify for various other reasons.

After exhausting the special venire and regular panels, three jurors are still lacking. The judge orders another special venire for thirty jurors and a recess until four o'clock, giving those jurors already sworn in, the usual instructions to jurors in a murder case.

"What do you think?" I ask Dr. Pope as we work our way through the crowd. Since the afternoon session will begin so late, we seek some sort of repast to tide us over through the rest of the day, not knowing how long the judge intends to hold court.

Looking cautiously around him, he says, "I would rather wait until we have privacy before I offer an opinion on the subject, seeing as how I am a witness."

Exiting a side door we walk quickly to a little restaurant I have frequented in the past and settle into a quiet corner for coffee and a hot meal before continuing our conversation.

"Do you recall or did you read the *Times-Union* article dated February 19?" he asks while pulling it out of his satchel.

He spreads it out between us on the worn oak table. It is an editorial entitled:

THOU SHALT NOT KILL

The following editorial from the *Gainesville Bee* is reproduced, not because of any intrinsic importance it possesses, but because it is a characteristic expression of the views of a class whose influence is steadily declining in Florida through the growing respect for law and order.

It has been the policy of the *Bee* to desist from comment in any case similar to the killing of Major Suhrer at Fernandina last Thursday by Mr. Eppes whenever the courts have taken the matter in hand. But a leading newspaper of the state has so far transgressed journalistic propriety as to try to create a prejudice against the prisoner in this case. Under such circumstances, therefore, it may be admissible for others to express opinions in the premises.

All who read the testimony before the coroner's jury were doubtless convinced that Mr. Eppes was at least guilty of manslaughter in its most aggravated form. None will deny, however, that the sworn statement of Mrs. Eppes places her husband in an entirely different attitude before the public. None, we dare say, will deny that Mr. Eppes was entirely justifiable in killing Suhrer, provided he was satisfied that the alleged insult was extended. That is simply the question. Not whether Suhrer was guilty of the charge of attempting to seduce Mrs. Eppes, but whether her husband honestly believed him to have been. We have no reason to doubt the wife's statement, and admitting its truth, it is difficult to see how Eppes could have honorably acted otherwise.

We believe a jury of his countrymen will promptly acquit him.

For the lesson in "journalistic propriety," the editor of the *Times-Union* is, of course, appropriately grateful. The young man who edits the *Bee* has had such a large experience of journalism, has enjoyed such extensive acquaintance with journalists whose example and practice prescribe the etiquette of the profession, and holds a position of such dignity and importance, that any pronouncement he may make as to "journalistic propriety" must be listened to with respectful attention. The editor of the *Times-Union* not only accepts the lesson for himself, but passes it on to those other editors of leading newspapers who are constantly violating "journalistic propriety" by commenting on the current events in which the people of their respective localities are most keenly interested.

As to the doctrine propounded by this punctilious stickler for the proprieties, let us see what it means when reduced to practice. Mr. Eppes, according to doctrine, "was entirely justified in killing Suhrer provided he was satisfied that the alleged insult was extended." Whether or not Suhrer actually offered the insult to Mrs. Eppes is of no consequence;

the question is "whether the husband honestly believed him to have" done so and holding this view "a jury of his countrymen will promptly acquit him."

If this means anything, it means that when anybody comes to a man and tells him that his wife has been "insulted," that man, without even taking the trouble to ascertain the nature and extent of the wrong, is "entirely justifiable" in borrowing a friend and a revolver and going out and killing the person accused of committing the offense. Supposing this doctrine to be generally accepted, let us watch its practical operation. Some unscrupulous man has a grudge against the editor of the *Bee* and wants to put him out of the way. He therefore arranges with an unscrupulous friend to come and tell him that his wife has been "insulted" by the editor of the *Bee*, and the two hunt him and shoot him down. The perpetrator will be "entirely justifiable" and will be "promptly acquitted" of the crime, provided he can convince a gullible jury that he "honestly believed the editor of the *Bee* to have been guilty." Or the deadly doctrine can be worked still more adroitly. The man having a grudge against the editor of the *Bee* can pick out some excitable acquaintance, tell him that his wife has been "insulted," put a revolver in his hand and rush him off to kill the editor of the *Bee* without giving him time for remonstration, explanation or denial.

Under the operation of this doctrine, every man in the community holds his life subject to the condition of having no unscrupulous enemy; and it is only necessary to contemplate its practical working in order to see its monstrous iniquity. The true doctrine is that when a man who commits such a crime is defended on such a plea, the jury should consider very carefully whether he took proper steps, really to "satisfy" himself that a deadly offense had been committed. If he took no such steps or if he accepted untrustworthy evidence when conclusive evidence was at hand, the full penalty of the law should be inflicted upon him in the interest of law-abiding members of society.

Another point raised by the *Bee* is worth considering a moment. Where public morals and welfare are concerned, a newspaper is not bound by the decisions of a court. The court has its jurisdiction, and administers a code of laws full of technicalities and pierced with loopholes. The newspaper has its jurisdiction and appeals to the voices of public sentiment. The verdicts of the two tribunals do not always agree. Aaron Burr was acquitted by the courts, but branded with infamy by public opinion. The murderer, Dukes, was declared innocent by a jury but pronounced guilty by the unanimous voice of the press and public.

As regards the *Times-Union*, it holds that no part of its mission is more important than that of denouncing and bringing into disrepute those deeds of lawless violence that have cast a stain upon the fair name of the South. So far as its utterances have influence, the man who kills another save in self-defense shall go forth with the brand of Cain upon his brow. And if the Divine command, "Thou shalt not kill," has any meaning, the curse of God shall pursue him.

"No, I had not read this particular article, but I find it to be similar in context to many others written over the past months," I say wearily, handing it back to Dr. Pope. "This is why juror after juror is being dismissed and our town has been split in two over this damn mess."

AFTERNOON SESSION

Entering the courtroom we find a number of spectators had not left during the recess in fear of not being able to reclaim their seats. The rush is on for others to occupy the empty spaces before the chamber is filled to capacity once more.

To the left and slightly behind us are seated newspaper reporters from far and wide, some busily writing and others sketching the scene at hand. Seated with and behind us are witnesses to be called for the defense and to the right are witnesses for the prosecution.

With an "All rise" order from the bailiff, the judge enters the courtroom and is followed by the thus-far selected jury who take their places in the jury box. By their sunburned looks and attire, the majority of them are obviously farmers.

Thirty more prospective jurors are called to come forward and be seated. The task of selecting the remainder of the panel begins.

The first man, when questioned—much to our dismay—has indeed already formed an opinion, and is dismissed. And so it goes until W. W. McCall, the twenty-two-year-old son of a local attorney, is called, and when queried he duly swears that even though he has followed the case in the newspapers this will have no bearing on his opinions in the case. He says he can objectively view all evidence and form his own opinion, and he is approved by both prosecution and defense attorneys.

This having been done, the rest goes quickly. With the selection of two more jurors, the panel of twelve reads as follows:

Walsh Silcox	Farmer	age 52	married	7 children	
W. W. McCall Jr.	student of law	age 22	single		
E. T. Acosta	Merchant				
Prudentia Hartley	Farmer	age 26	married	1 child	
F. M. Richard	Farmer	age 45	married	0 children	wife, age 20
E. B. McCuen	Bookkeeper	age 28	single		
E. Harrison	Farmer				
T. W. Dansler	Merchant				
Albert Hartley	Farmer	age 30	married	3 children	
Thomas Hogan	Farmer				
G. H. Fleming	Broker	age 34	single		
David Holmes	Grocer	age 23	single		

It is interesting to note that the majority of the jurors reside in Mandarin, this of course being the largest area of Duval County; and none of the jurors are women due to the fact that one of the requirements is to be a registered voter, and though women are allowed to own property they are not allowed to vote. Susan B. Anthony and Elizabeth Cady Stanton have been instrumental in the women's suffrage movement since beginning their news publication, *National Woman Suffrage*, in 1869, and did in fact coerce their way into voting during the presidential election of 1872 by citing the 14th Amendment, but their vote was indeed thrown out. Anthony was fined $100, which she never paid.

Also of interest, the Negro is allowed to vote, which causes major difficulties, as you can imagine.

Though the hour is late, the judge has no intention of losing any more time. Mr. Owens, who had been conferring with United States district attorney E. M. Cheney, commences to read the indictment and instructions to the jury, to which the jury listens intently, taking their civic duty seriously.

"Preliminary instructions. Ladies and gentlemen of the jury, you have been selected as the jury to try the case of the State of Florida vs. Eppes and Dewson. This is a criminal case. Eppes and Dewson are charged with the crime of murder. The definition of the elements of murder will be explained to you later. It is your solemn responsibility to determine if the State has proved its accusation beyond a reasonable doubt against Eppes and Dewson. Your verdict must be based solely on the evidence, or lack of evidence, and the law. The indictment is not evidence and is not to be considered by you as any proof of guilt.

"It is the judge's responsibility to decide which laws apply to this case and to explain those laws to you. It is your responsibility to decide what the facts of this case may be, and to apply the law to those facts. Thus, the province of the jury and the province of the court are well defined, and they do not overlap. This is one of the fundamental principles of our system of justice.

"Before proceeding further, it will be helpful if you understand how a trial is conducted. At the beginning of the trial the attorneys will have an opportunity, if they wish, to make an opening statement. The opening statement gives the attorneys a chance to tell you what evidence they believe will be presented during the trial. What the lawyers say is not evidence, and you are not to consider it as such.

"Following the opening statements, witnesses will be called to testify under oath. They will be examined and cross-examined by the attorneys. Documents and other exhibits also may be produced as evidence.

"After the evidence has been presented, the attorneys will have the opportunity to make their final argument. Following the arguments by the attorneys, the court will instruct you on the law applicable to the case. After the instructions are given, you will retire to consider your verdict. You should not form any definite or fixed opinion on the merits of the case until you have heard all the evidence, the argument of the lawyers and the instructions on the law by the judge. Until that time you should not discuss the case among yourselves.

"During the course of the trial the court may take recesses, during which you will be permitted to separate and go about your personal affairs. During these recesses you will not discuss the case with anyone nor permit anyone to say anything to you or in your presence about the case. If anyone attempts to say anything to you or in your presence about this case, tell him or her that you are on the jury trying the case and ask him or her to stop. If he or she persists, leave him or her at once and immediately report the matter to the bailiff, who will advise me.

"The case must be tried by you only on the evidence presented during the trial in your presence and in the presence of the defendant, the attorneys and the judge. Jurors must not conduct any investigation of their own. Accordingly, you must not visit any place described in the evidence, and you must not discuss the case with any person and you must not speak with attorneys, the witnesses or the defendant about any subject until your deliberations are finished.

"Murder, First Degree. There are two ways in which a person may be convicted of first degree murder. One is known as premeditated murder and the other is known as felony murder.

"To prove the crime of First Degree Premeditated Murder, the State must prove the following three elements beyond a reasonable doubt." Holding up one finger in front of the jury, he states, "Number one, Ferdinand C. Suhrer is dead." Holding up two fingers, "The death was caused by the criminal act of T. J. Eppes and George Dewson. Or," and holding up a third finger, "there was a premeditated killing of Ferdinand C. Suhrer.

" 'Killing with premeditation' is killing after consciously deciding to do so. The decision must be present in the mind at the time of the killing. The law does not fix the exact period of time that must pass between the formation of the premeditated intent to kill and the killing. The period of time must be long enough to allow reflection by the defendant. The premeditated intent must be formed before the killing.

"The question of premeditation is a question of fact to be determined by you from the evidence. It will be sufficient proof of premeditation if the circumstances of the killing and the conduct of the accused convince you beyond a reasonable doubt of the existence of premeditation at the time of the killing.

"If there are not any questions as to these instructions, gentlemen of the jury, we will then proceed with our first State's witness."

Owens scans the jury members one by one, eye to eye, and almost in unison they answer "nay." The trial is on.

Called to the witness stand to the right of the judge, Dr. Pope solemnly places his left hand on the Bible, raises his right and swears to "tell the truth, the whole truth and nothing but the truth, so help me God" and is seated.

Owens faces the doctor and begins his examination of the witness. "Dr. Pope, will you please tell the court in your own words, the events of

Thursday, February 7 of this year, beginning with your name and place of residence and occupation, for the record."

Sliding forward in the chair, Dr. Pope says, "My name is Dr. W. H. Pope, I reside in Fernandina, Florida, and my occupation is that of family physician. On the day in question, I was called to the Mansion House Hotel to attend one of my patients, Ferdinand Suhrer, whom I was told had been shot. On arrival I found he had a gunshot wound to the right side of his chest just below the collarbone; and just shortly after my arrival he began coughing up blood from his lung. Major Suhrer continued in this condition for a matter of approximately five hours, until his death."

"Do you then consider this to be the cause of death, Doctor?" asks Owens, turning to pace back and forth in front of the jury.

"Yes sir, I do. Though upon autopsy I found other evidence on his body. Marks and bruises on both arms of the deceased, just above the elbow, apparently made by a blow."

"Thank you, sir, that is all for now."

Cross-examined by defense attorney T. A. MacDonell, Dr. Pope further states, "The ball entered at a point under the right collarbone, passing through the left lung and was lost below the left armpit. The lung was in a state of collapse. The ball traversed through the body from right to left. The bruises on the arms, in my opinion, were made by forcibly grasping the arms, or possibly, blows from a stick. It is hardly possible they could have been made after death."

The witness is excused and R. M. Henderson, undertaker and officiator of the funeral of Ferdinand, is sworn in next, following the fashion of swearing in of Dr. Pope.

"I arrived at the Mansion House just after the post mortem had begun, and assisted Dr. Pope, who was conducting it. I made a thorough examination of the body and found a mark on each arm. That aside from these marks, the arms were pure white. That on the right arm presented a mottled appearance, the color not all being the same. It was about an inch square. The mark on the left arm was about the size of a ten-dollar gold piece and was midway between the elbow and shoulder. The mark on the left arm was on the inner side and that on the right was on the outer surface."

Excused, Mr. Henderson rises stiffly and steps down from the witness stand.

Now the interesting testimony is about to begin; we can feel it in the air all around us, the way the crowd leans forward in their seats and out into the aisles when C. A. Key is called. They crane their necks to get a better look; some even stand as he strides purposefully forward.

"C. A. Key, teacher. Resident at the Mansion House Hotel, Fernandina, Florida. At about four o'clock p. m. according to his custom, Major Suhrer went to the depot on the arrival of the train. He returned to the hotel and did some writing, then went to the post office after the mail. Around five o'clock he returned to the reading room in the hotel and gave me my mail and papers. After a while I noticed him go out the west door and take a seat on the porch. About ten minutes later I heard a noise, as of a scuffle, and heard Major Suhrer exclaim: 'What does all this mean?'

"Looking up, I saw two men grappling with each other, heard a pistol shot and saw Suhrer step back, then saw Jeff Eppes strike the Major twice with a whip. I rushed over to the porch and saw Suhrer standing near the west steps, while Eppes had one foot on the porch and one on the step. Suhrer then repeated his question, 'What does all this mean?' and Eppes replied: 'You insulted my wife a week ago today!' Suhrer replied, 'I did not, I may be a dead man but before God, I did not do it.' "

"Did you see or hear anything after this, Mr. Key?" questions the State's attorney.

"George Dewson ordered Suhrer to 'let go of the whip' he had grabbed and wrapped around his hand during the fray and as soon as he did, they went away."

On cross-examination by defense attorney Colonel John T. Walker, C.A. is asked: "Are you sure you heard the gunshot first and then saw Mr. Eppes whipping the Major afterward? Think hard about this. It is very important to get the facts in the correct sequence."

Without flinching a bit, C.A. restates his previous testimony reaffirming the pistol shot came first.

Colonel Walker pauses, strikes a pose looking first at his right hand, then his left and asks, "Which hand was the pistol in?"

To which C.A. answers, "He was holding the pistol in his left hand and the whip in his right."

"And, sir, to your knowledge, is Mr. Eppes right-handed or left-handed?"

C.A. gives a moment's thought and answers, "I am not a close friend of Mr. Eppes and have no knowledge of that information."

"Thank you sir, I have no further questions of this witness."

The State calls Mr. L. F. Smith, railroad engineer, residing in Fernandina, Florida, at the Mansion House Hotel.

Being duly sworn in, he states: "I was also reading my mail in the reading room when the murder occurred—"

"Objection, Your Honor!" shouts the defense attorney, jumping up from his seat. "Please instruct the jury to overlook the use of that word."

"Objection sustained," rules the judge. Turning to the jury he asks, "Do you understand what just happened?" At their nods he turns to the witness and asks him to refrain from usage of the word and to continue his testimony.

Looking paler and more ill than when he first took the stand, Smith hurriedly continues: "I heard a noise, looked up and saw two men in plain view scuffling. Saw Eppes and Suhrer standing about a foot apart, holding each other and Dewson a little to one side holding Suhrer's right hand. Apparently they were not doing anything but talking at this point. I could not hear what they were saying."

Owens, seeing Smith's state of health and nervousness, attempts to calm him down. "It is my understanding that Mr. Eppes came in on the four o'clock train. Were you also on that train?"

"No sir, I was not, but I did see him and Mr. Dewson in the superintendent's telegraph office about ten minutes to half an hour before the shooting, and passed the time of day with them."

"And what would you say was his frame of mind at that time? Did he appear upset or agitated that day, to your way of thinking?"

Looking over at the defense table where Eppes and Dewson are intently staring at him, Smith quickly looks down at his trembling hands and begins to talk. "I met them again a bit later between Centre Street and the Mansion House. Centre Street terminates at the depot. I met them between Kydd's store and the Mansion House on Third Street, two blocks from the depot. They were coming from the Mansion House and I was going to the Mansion House. Mr. Eppes asked me for a revolver, saying that Dewson had said he could beat him. I don't carry one on me, and told him so."

"What was Mr. Dewson saying or doing during this conversation?"

"Nothing."

"What happened next?"

"I left them there, went on to the Mansion House to the reading room to open my mail and that's where I was when it happened."

"Thank you sir, that will be all."

Colonel Walker rises, strides toward the witness stand and the now very pale Mr. Smith.

"Mr. Smith, I will not keep you long, as it is apparent you are not well. I just need to clarify a couple of points. First you say you later met my clients coming from the Mansion House as you were heading to the Mansion House just prior to the unfortunate event of February 7, is that correct?"

"Yes, sir, that is when Mr. Eppes asked me about a revolver," Smith replies, shaking his head affirmably.

"Okay, that is fine, but you also stated this was just minutes prior to the shooting and that he did not appear to be angry or upset?"

"Yes, sir, that is also true. In fact he acted a little excited about showing Dewson off."

"Thank you sir, that is all the questions I have for you."

Next witness for the State is W. H. LeCain, route agent for the railroad, residing at the Mansion House Hotel, whom being duly sworn in, states: "As the route agent I was on the train with the accused Eppes. The train arrived slightly ahead of schedule, at 3:50 p.m. I reported to the post office, delivered the mail and at the time of the shooting, was in my room at the Mansion House dressing for a dinner engagement at 6:00 p.m. On hearing it, I looked out my window for a moment, then at my watch and observed the time to be about 5:20 p.m."

Owens asks, "When you looked out your window, were you able to see anything?"

"No sir, my room is on the east side of the hotel. Therefore I only took note of the time of the pistol shot and went about my business."

"Thank you, that is all I need to ask of you at this time."

The defense team sits huddled in heated conversation until their attention is caught by the judge's loud, hammering gavel.

"Please forgive us, Your Honor, we would like to question the competency of this witness."

The courtroom buzz escalates dangerously as Colonel Walker approaches the witness stand and Mr. LeCain appears unsure as to what this is about.

"Mr. LeCain, is it not true you are convicted in Marion County of embezzlement?" he asks, his back now to the witness as he pivots to face the stunned jury and now the judge.

LeCain's mouth drops open, words won't come for a few moments, until at last he jumps up, angrily pounding on the railing. "What does any of that have to do with the time I heard a pistol shot?" He is so angry his face has flushed blood red and sweat beads up on his forehead in the already stifling room. "Yes, I was tried and convicted, but a new trial was ordered and I was acquitted. The railroad knew all this when I was hired. Did you dig into every witness's background or just mine?" he all but yells at the attorney.

The judge orders him to silence. The smug look leaves Colonel Walker's face, the witness is excused and the State calls John C. Rutishauser, a barber residing in Fernandina.

"Tell us, Mr. Rutishauser, in your own words, where and exactly when you saw the accused the day of the shooting."

"They come into my barbershop sometime between four and five o'clock for a shave," he states in his thick, broken Swiss brogue that is barely understandable by most everyone in the room.

"How long did it take you to shave them, and please be more specific as to the time, and sir, please speak more clearly and slowly if possible," Owens asks of the witness.

He sits straighter in the chair. You can tell by the way he is dressed and his hair is combed he takes his court appearance seriously. He begins again. "I try, but my English it not so good. I shave Mr. Eppes at about four o'clock, they both went away and come back again in about ten minutes with a carriage whip and borrowed one of my shaving knives from my boy and cut off about a foot and a half to make it shorter."

"So if I understand you correctly, they came in around four o'clock, you shaved Mr. Eppes but not Mr. Dewson, they left and came back, let us say about four thirty, cut a carriage whip down with one of your shaving knives and left again. Is this correct?" he asks.

"Yes, sir. That is correct," he answers, obviously relieved to have it over with.

"That is all, thank you for your time." He seems anxious to dismiss the witness but the defense is having no part of it and rises before Rutishauser can take his leave.

"Just a moment, sir," Walker calls out, "the defense has a couple of points to clear up. Do you remember a discussion between the two defendants pertaining to shooting Mr. Suhrer or anyone at any time?"

Looking startled, Rutishauser is quick to answer, "No sir! They never did. Mr. Dewson told Mr. Eppes if he used the whip, to use it lightly, else he would be sorry next day. Dewson said, 'Come on,' and they went away again."

"Okay, good. Then, one more thing. Which direction did they go the first time they left your establishment?" Walker leans on the witness box searching the barber's face for any sign of uncertainty and finding none, presses on. "Well, which way did they go?"

"Sir, the first time they left they went down Third Street toward Noyes's or Hoyt's store," he says, nodding his head vigorously as if to reassure himself of his memory.

"And did you see where they went the last time they left?"

"No, sir, I did not."

"Were you not at all curious as to what this was all about?"

The witness sits mute. Minutes tick slowly by; the only sound is the striking of the clock on the wall. Finally the judge orders him, "Answer the question," whereupon Rutishauser looks helplessly at Eppes and Dewson before speaking.

"Your Honor, the two of them was making plans how to beat Major Suhrer for insulting Mr. Eppes's wife. I have a beautiful wife thirty years younger than myself," he says, his voice growing louder with each word, "and to tell the truth, I would do the same if some man insulted her!"

Pandemonium breaks out in the courtroom; no one hears the judge's gavel hammering over the deafening noise for at least five minutes. The black-garbed judge stands behind the bench the better to see, banging his gavel so hard it breaks in two, leaving him to hold only the handle.

Shouting over the clamor and running up and down the aisles, the bailiff finally gets everyone's attention. "Be seated and shut up now or the courtroom will be cleared of spectators once and for all by order of the judge!"

This does the trick; the silence is so sudden as to hear a pin drop in the stillness.

With a stern glare, the judge reprimands Mr. Rutishauser for his outburst and excuses him from the witness stand.

Nudging Dr. Pope with my elbow I offer him a peek at my pocket watch. The hour is drawing near six o'clock and the judge does not seem inclined to draw the day's proceedings to a close.

The State calls Frank Hughes, a colored sometimes-handyman (most often unemployed), to the stand. He looks wide-eyed and nervous, twisting his worn, stained hat in his calloused hands. It is obvious Mr. Owens will have to lead him through his testimony as he is barely able to get through his swearing in.

"Mr. Hughes, if you will just repeat to the gentlemen of the jury what you told the coroner's jury and me of the day in question, about what you saw and heard." Owens holds up a statement signed with an X for all to see.

"Well, suh, it happen like this. Me and Lewis Jenkins was standing on the sidewalk in front of Reynolds's shop when Mr. Eppes and Mr. Dewson done come along. At first I thought they was arguing but then I heard Mr. Eppes say 'I gwin' shoot him' and Mr. Dewson took hold his arm, he say 'No, no, let us go so you can think on it' but Mr. Eppes he say 'Damn him, I will shoot him!' "

"What happened next?"

"I followed them to Yulee's Corner and turned down the cross street, while they kept on. When I got to Mr. McGiffin's place I heard a pistol shot and I knowed he done what he said he was gonna do. Yes, Lawd."

"And how long did it take you to walk to Mr. McGiffin's place?" Owens asks Hughes.

"Well, suh, I don't got no pocket watch 'cause I cain't read," Hughes replies while scratching his nappy head, one eye squinted closed, the other looking toward the ceiling as he thinks and calculates, "but I figure it to be about thirty minutes by the way the sun sets."

Suddenly a loud noise startles everyone. It is the scraping sound of a chair overturning and upon investigation it is found that Thomas Oliver, the court clerk has fainted dead away. The judge calls for a temporary suspension in the proceedings while Dr. Wiginton is called to assist, and Mr. Oliver is soon revived.

"It is no wonder more folks have not succumbed in this heat and the length of time the judge is keeping court in session," says Dr. Pope as we take a brief break in the practically empty hallway to stretch our legs while all this is happening. Most everyone else, it appears, are afraid of losing their seats and remain rooted in their places.

Darkness has not come quite yet but the afternoon sun filtering through the windows makes me think today's session should be over soon.

Hearing the "call to order" we slip back into our seats for the defense's questioning of Mr. Hughes.

Colonel Walker is pretty slick and knows how to work on the nerves of an already nervous witness, to his clients' best interest. Approaching Hughes, Walker attacks without mercy: "Mr. Hughes, it seems there are a couple of discrepancies between your testimony here today and the one you gave at the coroner's jury in February. Let's start with the coroner's jury statement where you stated you were at the corner of Mr. Huot's lot when you heard the pistol shot, not Mr. McGiffin's. There is a significant distance between the two properties. Now, which was it?"

Hughes appears almost terrified of Walker but shakily denies that he ever said he was near Huot's lot.

"Also, you stated at the coroner's jury that Major Suhrer had been shot by Mr. Eppes after you heard the shot, is that also untrue?"

Again Hughes denies making any such statement, to which Colonel Walker turns the tables on him by asking, "Which statement, then, do you propose the jury believe, Mr. Hughes? The one given here today or the one given at the coroner's jury?"

"... Uh, suh, I believes it happen the way ... I mean I be sho' ..." he falters.

"Your Honor, gentlemen of the jury, I ask that all testimony given by this witness be stricken from the record, as he appears not to know what actually happened nor what the truth is." Colonel Walker points his gold-headed cane at Hughes in disdain.

Frank Hughes, not sure what has just occurred, exits the stand to lean heavily against the far wall, waiting like the rest of us for what is yet to come.

To our relief the judge orders a recess until tomorrow morning at nine o'clock a.m., at which time the State will continue presenting its case.

The jury is given its usual instructions to not discuss the case among themselves or anyone else, and is adjourned for the night.

Before turning in, Dr. Pope and I head for our night's lodging and a passable meal. The discussion, of course, is of today's testimonies. The table has been cleared and fresh lagers poured.

Relaxing in my chair, I say, "I would have thought Katie would be here, you know, the injured flower draws sympathy from the jury and so forth."

With a look of surprise Dr. Pope informs me, "I guess you don't know she is expecting a baby late August or early September. The stress of all this has been very difficult for her in her condition and of course there is no question about her traveling at this time, and attending the trial is definitely out of the question. It would be far too much. I would have thought the town gossip had spread this juicy tidbit around."

Now I understand why Jeff was shaking his head "no" to Katie at the docks when Pauline left for school. It all falls into place: the paleness, the change in attire and attitude. I must tell Pauline. Apparently she does not know either, or she would have said something.

"No," I say, "I did not know, and Jeff said nothing to me last time we spoke. But of course, our relationship has been, to say the least, very strained. It has been difficult for all of us. You do know someone set fire to George and Mary Dewson's house, don't you?"

"That's his story," Dr. Pope responds heatedly. "According to Fire Marshal McGiffin, the fire started in the kitchen from a defective flue. It occurred around noon while no one was home. Everything was lost including the outbuildings and fence. If it had not been for the valiant efforts of the fire department and the new chemical engine, the adjoining properties would have gone up in flames as well."

The scars on my hands validate all too well the truth of his words.

"As it was," Dr. Pope says, "several homes and firefighters suffered damage and injury. I can't see how Dewson could possibly think anyone would burn his house, knowing the whole town would more than likely suffer as well."

"You have a point of course," I reply. "George obviously feels the town has it in for him and Jeff over the killing of Ferdinand and believes the fire was intentionally set."

"Sounds like a guilty conscience if you ask me," he says with a snort. He rises from his seat to call it a night.

I am surprised by his comment, he usually being a quiet-spoken individual not prone to debating politics or religion with the rest of us on those occasions we do so for hours on end.

I bid him good night, order another lager and settle nearer to the warmth of the inn's fire to sit and mull over our conversation and the day's events.

So engrossed am I in my thoughts I am unaware of the presence of anyone or anything else around me until a tug on my coat sleeve startles me out of my reverie.

"I did not mean to give you such a fright," Jeff says, laughing nervously and pointing at an empty seat, seeking permission to join me.

Turning his chair to face mine he leans forward, elbows on his knees, hands clasped together, his gaze searching my face for a sign of our friendship, I suspect.

"I saw you sitting here alone and thought to take the opportunity of speaking to you privately while I had the chance," he starts off, selecting his words carefully.

I do not move nor flinch. My eyes remain on his face, on this man who has been my friend since he first came to Fernandina in June of 1880 as a baggage master for the railroad. I can still remember seeing him swing his satchel down from his shoulder in the Florida House lobby the day he came by seeking room and board.

Miss Annie had no rooms to let at the time and I offered to escort him to the Mansion House where I knew my friend Ferdinand had rooms available. Somehow I feel all this began on that fateful day.

Leaning forward I take hold of his hands, look him squarely in the eyes and say, "Jeff, you know we have been friends from the beginning and so have Ferdinand and I. This damned mess has caused a rift between folks who have been friends and neighbors for years. The whole town and two, maybe even three counties, have been torn apart taking sides."

"Damn it, John!" he all but shouts, shaking loose my hands.

People turn to stare at us.

He tones down his voice but a fraction, saying, "Don't you think a day doesn't go by that I don't play that day over and over again and again in my head wishing it could have turned out differently? Don't get me wrong, I still would defend Katie's honor to the end, but I never meant to kill Ferdinand. I only meant to shame him in public for what he did and that is what I wanted you to know. It is important that you as my friend understand this."

And without giving me a chance to respond he rises quickly and is gone.

THE TRIAL
DAY TWO

The trial resumes pursuant to adjournment of yesterday. First witness called is P. W. O. Koerner, a civil engineer residing in Fernandina, who has an office in this city. A map of Fernandina is shown him, whereupon he has marked the locations and given the distances of places indicated in diagrams of yesterday.

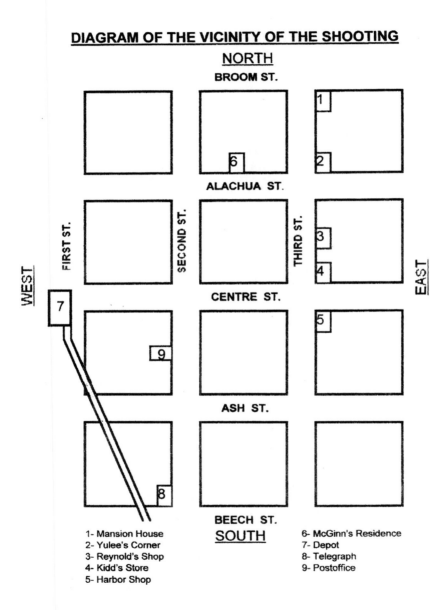

DIAGRAM OF THE VICINITY OF THE SHOOTING

NORTH

1- Mansion House
2- Yulee's Corner
3- Reynold's Shop
4- Kidd's Store
5- Harbor Shop
6- McGinn's Residence
7- Depot
8- Telegraph
9- Postoffice

Duncan Cobb (colored), sworn: His testimony is substantially the same as that of Hughes and no questions are needed by the defense. Therefore he is excused and exits the witness stand.

At this point, this being the last witness, the State rests its case.

OPENING OF DEFENSE

The defense is ably represented by T. A. MacDonell, Esq., assisted by Walker & Walker and Judge H. J. Baker.

Colonel John T. Walker, counsel for the defense, rises to his full height, right hand in his pants pocket, left one leaning on the ever-present, gold-handled walking stick (more of a stage prop than a necessity). He walks over to the jury box and commences to make his opening statement.

"Gentlemen of the jury, let us put ourselves in the place of my client, Mr. Eppes. Think how you would feel if your wife had been verbally and physically insulted by a man, any man, and especially if that man were your trusted friend of many years. An upstanding citizen of the community—someone you should have trusted. You and I know without a doubt we would defend her honor! The witnesses I will produce today will prove without a doubt, that is in fact what happened, and will clear my clients of murder."

The defense opens by placing Thomas J. Eppes, one of the defendants, on the stand to make a sworn statement. It's obvious he is nervous by his rapid, unintelligible speech, his words tumbling out so fast, not the jury nor anyone else can keep up with him. The judge orders him to "Slow down, start over again."

"Yes, Your Honor. Well, as I said, I came in on the four o'clock train and was met by Dewson at the depot. We went to the railroad office to make my customary report and talk about an occurrence that happened that day on the road and from there we went to the corner of Centre and Second streets to continue the conversation with Mr. Gambrell. It is customary for me to get a shave before going home from one of my long trips. Therefore we continued on to the barbershop for that purpose."

Walker turns to face the now calmer witness. "Mr. Eppes, please tell the jury at what point Mr. Dewson told you about the indecent overtures Major Suhrer committed against your wife."

"Objection, Your Honor!" shouts Cheney, leaping up from the prosecutors' table. "There has been no evidence submitted to prove that such an incident ever occurred."

"Objection sustained," rules the judge, admonishing Colonel Walker to "Watch yourself," and the jury to "Strike the last statement."

"Let me rephrase myself then," Walker says to Eppes. "Please tell the jury in your own words your conversation with Mr. Dewson just after leaving the barbershop."

"We were walking toward the Mansion House when Dewson stopped, turned to face me on the street and said, 'I have to tell you something that will upset you badly.' I could tell he had something heavy on his mind and I said, 'Go ahead, George, spit it out. Tell me what it is.' That's when he told me his wife, Mary, had confided in him what my wife had told her over a week prior, and that was that Suhrer had made indecent advances toward her, even going so far as to touch her breast."

"And how did this make you feel?" Walker asks, looking at the jury at the same time for their reaction.

"How do you suppose it made me feel? I was madder than hell! I wanted to beat the living daylights out of him! So I told Dewson, 'Let's go to Hoyt's store and get a whip.'"

"Go on, tell the court what happened next," Walker instructs his witness.

"We went to Hoyt's, bought a buggy whip and trying it out on the sidewalk, I determined it was too long to suit my purpose. So we went back down to the barbershop to cut it down some. When we arrived at the Mansion House I spied the Major sitting on the west porch and called him to come to me. It was no doubt he could see I was angry and he asked, 'What does all this mean?' when he rose and came toward me.

"All the time I was slapping the whip on the steps near the top. When he got near I began whipping him hard as I could about the body. Then he asked me again what this was all about, and I shouted at him for all to hear, 'You insulted my wife!'

"He grabbed hold of the whip, wrapping it around his hand, drawing me near to him and we began grappling with me trying to push him away. I was getting angrier by the minute when suddenly he pushed me away and I reached into my coat pocket, drew out my pistol, held it against his chest and fired before I knew what had happened."

Much to the surprise of everyone in the room, Colonel Walker picks the pistol up, hands it to Eppes and asks, "Mr. Eppes, would you please demonstrate exactly how you held the pistol that day? I am about the size of Major Suhrer, so you can come down and stand beside me for the demonstration."

The difference in height of the two men is very noticeable, Jeff being a good four inches or more shorter.

Returning to the stand, Jeff continues: "After the shot was fired he let go the whip, and Dewson and I left ..." His voice trails off to an unintelligible soft mumbling; his head is bent and turned toward the jury in a mixed attitude of anger and something bordering on regret.

"Mr. Eppes, please speak up and tell us what happened next," instructs the judge.

"Yes, Your Honor. We left and immediately went to Mr. John Edwards's office seeking to turn ourselves in to Mr. Ellermann. After telling him I had shot Major Suhrer, he sent us to Mr. Swann's office to turn ourselves in to Mr. Schuyler instead, which we did."

"I have no further questions of this witness," states Colonel Walker. He returns to the defense table and sits with one long leg stretched out and the gold-headed cane leaning against it casually.

Now it's time for the State to have a go at Jeff and all eyes and ears are intent upon Owens as he rises to the occasion.

Posturing himself in front of the jury, he looks perplexed before turning back to Eppes.

"Now, sir, we have witnesses stating you went about town seeking to borrow a revolver prior to going to the Mansion House to call the Major out."

"No, I don't recall doing that," he replies almost too strongly. "I always carry a pistol while on duty and had mine with me in my left coat pocket that day."

"So it isn't true, you did not ask Captain Smith to borrow a revolver, and that gentleman sat here and swore under oath, committed perjury and made up a fabricated story as to how you wished to show Dewson you could beat him at shooting?"

Owens holds up a hand. "Don't even bother to answer the question, Mr. Eppes, I think we all know the true story here." Going over to the State's table he picks up several papers and, shaking them at the jury, he continues: "You also stated that you reached into your left coat pocket, withdrew the pistol while still holding the whip with your right hand and shot the Major. Is this the pocket?" he asks, pointing to the inner one above his left breast.

"Yes, sir, that is correct," Jeff answers.

Reaching over to pick up the whip, Owens strides purposefully toward Jeff, all the while fumbling in his left pocket with his left hand trying to extract a pistol he has stashed there.

"Gentlemen of the jury, as you can see, it is extremely difficult for me to extract this pistol from my left coat pocket with my left hand, as the defendant stated happened. So what really happened? Did Dewson hand you the pistol, Mr. Eppes, or did you shoot Major Suhrer first, as another witness has testified, then beat him unmercifully? It is my opinion you went there to kill him and kill him you did!"

To which Colonel Walker jumps up shouting that "Owens is badgering the witness" and seeking the judge to require the State's attorney desist this line of questioning. The judge does so and Owens smiles a polite pardon of the judge. Eppes is excused with no more questions.

The other defendant, George Dewson, now nervously takes the stand, mainly corroborating Eppes's statement, only adding: "That day was one of my layover days and during the day my wife told me she had something to tell me, but only after extracting a promise to secrecy did she tell me that on a visit to her sister, Kate Eppes, she found her crying, and when asked what was the matter, Kate replied that Major Suhrer had grossly insulted her by coming into her room about a week before then, and putting his hand on her bosom and making indecent approaches to her."

"Mr. Dewson, how long have you known Mrs. Eppes?" Colonel Walker asks.

"Mrs. Eppes is my wife's sister. She lived with us for a number of years prior to her marriage to Mr. Eppes, and I hold her in the same regard as one of my own sisters. I told Jeff if he didn't take it up and chastise Suhrer, I would do it myself!" he replies with vigor.

"Have you ever known Mrs. Eppes to make a false statement or to treat anyone unkindly?" he asks.

I can see where his line of questioning is going and am surprised when George becomes almost angry at his own attorney's apparent accusation.

"No sir, and if you want to question her or my wife, they both came into the courtroom just a few minutes ago!"

The buzzing in the room is like that of a beehive as everyone turns looking for the ladies in question. They are easily found standing, two solitary, wan figures dressed appropriately in black, just inside the double doors at the back of the court. When the court refuses the application for their testimony, they depart as quietly as they had entered.

I myself am shocked to see Katie there, knowing what I do after last night.

Having accomplished exactly what he meant to do, Colonel Walker turns the witness over to the State for questioning.

Pouncing without mercy, Owens lowers the boom on the witness. "In your own words you stated that"—he rereads the testimony back from his notes—"you would have chastised Suhrer yourself had not Mr. Eppes done so, is this not so, Mr. Dewson?"

"Yes, sir, I would defend any lady under the same circumstances, would you not also?" he challenges back to the solicitor.

"I am not on trial here and do not have to answer the questions, sir, you do," responds Owens with a dissenting look.

He resumes. "It seems to me you encouraged Eppes, maybe even excited him, to overreact to the accusation prior to seeking an explanation from Major Suhrer. Did not either of you think to seek an explanation? After all, the gentleman was not a stranger in your midst, but a well-known friend to the both of you."

Leaning forward, grasping the witness box rail the better to be heard, Dewson states evenly: "No sir, it did not occur to either of us because friend or not, he had no right to do what he did!"

With that, Dewson is dismissed.

Robert Belcher, baggage master on Eppes's train, is sworn in: "I, Robert Belcher, had been residing at the Mansion House for about two months when the shooting occurred and had been at the hotel all week. I saw Mrs. Eppes frequently going to and from her meals. Her room was upstairs. One day I came out of the dining room from a meal just ahead of Mrs. Eppes and passed into the reading room, off the hallway where Major Suhrer was settling some accounts with two drummers. As Mrs. Eppes passed up the steps, Major Suhrer leaned out the door for a better look and remarked to us: 'How would that go?' or 'How would you like a piece of that?' He laughed and further remarked that she was looking hearty and well and that Eppes was looking thin. Perhaps he would have to call someone in to help him."

It is hard for spectators to keep the snickers and gasps of surprise quiet at this shocking, titillating testimony.

"I reproached the Major for speaking insultingly of Mrs. Eppes. That's no way to speak of a lady."

Colonel Walker says, "Your Honor, I object to any reference the witness has to make as to his remarks to the decedent and ask that his last statement be struck from the records."

"So be it," orders the judge. "Mr. Belcher, please confine your testimony to only what was said by Major Suhrer."

Belcher continues: "Suhrer replied to me that Eppes would not have to go outside the hotel for this purpose, as the Major usually attended to that himself."

The audience by now is well on its way to completely losing its barely contained control and being ordered out by the judge.

Cross-examination of this witness is by United States district attorney E. M. Cheney.

Cheney poses a striking figure of a man. His white linen suit has refused to show signs of a single wrinkle in the heat of the day, his starched white shirt still fresh and crisp and not a drop of sweat dampens his brow as he marches directly up to the witness box.

"Mr. Belcher, did Mrs. Eppes come into the office at any time while you were there?"

"No sir, she passed directly from the dining room through the hall and upstairs."

"Do you know who the two drummers were or where they were from?"

Again he replies, "No sir, I do not know them nor have I seen them since. They were in the office settling their bills prior to leaving the city. The Major made those comments to them in my presence. They were registered at the hotel. Maybe the hotel records show who they were."

"Most importantly of all, Mr. Belcher, did you tell Mr. Eppes about this conversation prior to or after the shooting? Now think carefully and answer honestly," he instructs the witness.

"I swear on my mother's grave I never told Mr. Eppes about that conversation until after the shooting. And he got mad all over again, knowing he had done the right thing."

"Did he tell you that?" Cheney asks.

"No sir, but I could tell how mad he was. His face was red and his mouth got all tight and then he cursed him again and again."

"Thank you, you may step down. I don't have any more questions of this witness."

The defense now calls Millard N. Gambrell: "I, Millard Gambrell, am in the employment of the railroad in the capacity of conductor, and reside at the Mansion House. On the day of the shooting, I went on my train early in the morning to Jacksonville and arrived back in Fernandina shortly after Mr. Eppes arrived on his. I saw him at the railroad office, where we talked about something that occurred on the Transit Road that day and then later, just prior to my train leaving again at 4:30 p.m. at the corner of Centre and Second streets. Eppes requested me not to mention what he had said earlier until further developments, referring to what occurred on the Transit Road. There came near being an accident on the road that day. I then left on my train and I did not see him again."

The State has no question of this witness, and he exits the witness stand.

The defense now calls Mr. Temple, another employee of the railroad, who corroborates Mr. Gambrell's testimony as to the times Mr. Eppes was seen and where by both men.

The State does not have any questions of this witness.

The defense calls Mr. John A. Edwards, sworn: Is clerk of the circuit court for Nassau County, residing in Fernandina.

Colonel Walker asks the witness "to state the events of the day in question for the jury."

To which Edwards replies, "I was in my office on the afternoon of February 7 at about five o'clock talking to Dr. Robert Harrison and Judge

H. J. Baker when Eppes came in enquiring for the sheriff. I noticed he had a peculiar look on his face, indicating something was wrong."

"Go on."

"I asked him what he wanted with the sheriff, and he looked at the judge and doctor and asked me to come outside so we could speak privately in the hallway, which we did. At that time he told me he had shot Major Suhrer and was looking for the sheriff to surrender himself."

"What happened when you heard this?" the Colonel asks.

"Of course I was shocked, but I told him he did not need the sheriff but rather Justice of the Peace G. W. Scuyler, and directed him to Mr. Swann's office farther down the hall where he would find him."

"And did he go to Mr. Swann's office?" queries Colonel Walker.

"Yes, sir, he did. I watched him go in the door before I went back to my office where I gave the bad news to the other gentlemen waiting there."

The State has no questions of this witness.

Next the defense calls George W. Scuyler, justice of the peace residing in Fernandina, who being duly sworn, is asked by Colonel Walker: "Sir, the previous witness has stated that on or about five o'clock of the day in question, Mr. Eppes surrendered himself to your office in the shooting of Major Suhrer. Does this in fact agree with your recollection of the events and time?"

"Yes sir, it does. As a matter of fact I recall it being no later than five fifteen standard time when Mr. Eppes entered Mr. Swann's office looking very shaky and pale and told me he had shot the Major and wished to surrender himself up."

Colonel Walker asks the witness to "Please continue," to which Scuyler states, "I asked Mr. Eppes if he thought he had killed the Major and he shook his had 'no,' and said he had 'shot him in the shoulder,' to the best of his knowledge. I took him to my office, left him there and went immediately to the Mansion House to see how Suhrer was. When

I came back I admitted Eppes to bail, wrote out and executed the bond for that purpose, and it was executed before candlelight."

"Now, sir, this question is very important and pertains to the testimony of a previous witness, Mr. Frank Hughes, who testified at the coroner's jury to which I understand you acted as coroner, is that not correct?"

"Yes sir, I did in fact act in that office."

"Did or did not Mr. Hughes state that when he heard the shot he went into Huot's store and say that a man had shot Ferdinand Suhrer?"

Scuyler seems surprised by the question. "Yes sir, Mr. Hughes did testify, and his statement was written down at the coroner's jury to that exact statement."

The State has no questions of this witness.

The defense calls Rev. Edward G. Chandler, pastor of the Methodist church and resident of Fernandina.

"Reverend Chandler, please tell the court what occurred, just as you told me, in a late January visit to Mrs. Eppes at the Mansion House."

Bringing in a man of the cloth and so late in the trial is a surprise to the spectators, and I look questioningly at Dr. Pope, who looks back at me with an "I don't know" shrug to his shoulders.

The Reverend begins to speak in the same monotone he does every Sunday behind the pulpit, but not enough to put this congregation to sleep. "Late one afternoon in January, Rev. C. A. Fullwood, a presiding elder and myself called on Mrs. Eppes, a member of the church, at the Mansion House and were met at the door by Major Suhrer. He invited us into the sitting room to wait there and left us under the impression he had gone to notify her. We talked for about five to fifteen minutes, when Major Suhrer came back and said Mrs. Eppes was not at home but had gone to see her sister, Mrs. Dewson. We left, went to the railroad office, and then made a call on Mrs. Dewson. We told her we had been to see her sister, Mrs. Eppes, but that Mr. Suhrer had informed us she was at her—Mrs. Dewson's—house."

"That is all, Reverend Chandler, thank you for your time."

We are surprised when after not questioning witness after witness, the State decides to question the good reverend.

Colonel Cheney steps forward and politely asks, "Reverend, what did Mrs. Dewson say when you told her Major Suhrer said Mrs. Eppes was not at home but had gone to visit her that afternoon?"

Reverend Chandler looks confused and a little embarrassed, but answers, "I don't know."

Cheney stops dead still in his pacing to and fro, spins around and looks quizzically at Reverend Chandler. "What do you mean, you don't know? You remember everything else so clearly, why don't you remember what Mrs. Dewson said?" he asks a little too harshly.

"You will have to ask Reverend Fullwood what she said," he responds indignantly. "I can't remember what she said, that's all there is to it!"

"That's all the questions I have for you, sir."

The reverend exits the stand without a backward glance at the attorney.

"The defense calls Reverend Fullwood to the stand."

Not a movement is made in the courtroom; no one stirs with the exception of heads turning this way and that, looking for the absent Reverend Fullwood.

The defense asks the judge to allow Reverend Fullwood's testimony to be admitted since he has not arrived from St. Augustine in time to testify, and the State agrees. The testimony corroborates that of Reverend Chandler's, with the addition that Mrs. Dewson told him in reply to his remark of her sister's visiting her, that she had not come there and in fact had not seen her that afternoon.

This closes the case for the defense.

The judge orders a recess until three o'clock, it now being 12:45 p.m. and the jury is given their usual instructions.

After almost four hours of sitting still as stone, trying to be quiet as church mice, the room bursts forth in an ever increasing roar as people try to voice their opinions to each other of the proceedings and the various possibilities of outcomes.

"I don't know about you," Dr. Pope says, "but I need to get some fresh air and stretch my legs, maybe get a cold drink of some sort."

Hearing my joints crack as I stand and stretch, I laugh in reply, "I'm with you. Our seats are safe. Not like some of these other poor folks who are afraid to go take a leak for fear of losing theirs. I'm afraid it's going to be a long afternoon, with closing arguments from the defense and prosecution and no telling how long the jury will be out. Let's go while we have a chance."

People around us wisely are overheard asking others to "save their seats" as they make a mad rush to relieve themselves, promising to repay the kindness on return. Women pull retinues from under the benches, filled with jars of tea, water and assorted libations and linen napkins, which they pass around, having learned from yesterday that to leave for one of the nearby, overcrowded restaurants or inns could cost them their places.

Several street vendors just outside the courthouse are vocally peddling their wares. I select an orange and a meat pie while Dr. Pope opts for a small cake. We stroll over to the nearby wharf to sit and devour our repast whilst enjoying being outside in the balmy sea air instead of the stuffy, overcrowded courtroom. Sea gulls hover overhead waiting expectantly for any tidbit we might drop accidently or on purpose.

"There is so much conflicting testimony," I muse out loud while peeling the orange. I offer a piece to Dr. Pope, who takes it, popping it all at once into his mouth. The juices dribble out into his beard, causing us both to laugh for the first time in two days. A much-needed sense of relief from all the stress that has built up flows over the two of us and we sit there in compatible silence for the rest of our break.

A dipper of cool fresh water from a nearby artesian well, surrounded by other witnesses and spectators arguing and speculating on whether or not Jeff should be charged with murder and whether or not Ferdinand was guilty of adultery, satiates our thirst on the way back.

"You would think Ferdinand is on trial here," Dr. Pope states angrily as we make our way through the crowd, "and he has no one to defend his character!"

Finding our places occupied by two very large, beefy-faced, overall wearing, rough-looking country types, we are at a dilemma as to how to go about asking them to vacate our seats, when the bailiff thankfully sees our predicament and comes to the rescue.

Stepping aside we allow him the opportunity to execute the duties of his office and we are soon seated, albeit the curses and glares from the country boys bode us no goodwill on their part, as every seat has by now been taken and the call to order given.

CLOSING ARGUMENT FOR THE STATE

Colonel Cheney steps forward, hands clasped behind his back as he paces back and forth before the jurors. He comes to a stop in front of the foreman before beginning this speech: "Gentlemen of the jury, for the past two days you have heard State's evidence showing without a doubt that the accused, Thomas J. Eppes did, willfully and with forethought, murder Ferdinand C. Suhrer, and that George Dewson did, willfully and with forethought, act as his accomplice in this murder and should be charged as such. Now there are various degrees of murder, i.e., Murder in the First Degree, Murder in the Second Degree, and Manslaughter. These have been previously explained to you.

"We know without a doubt Mr. Eppes fired the shot that killed Major Suhrer. He admitted it to be the truth but he allows he is justified in doing so due to a supposed indecent advance made against his wife by the deceased, who cannot stand before you today in this court to either deny or admit to this allegation."

His speech gathers momentum and passion. The only other sound is the steady, angry droning of a wasp trapped against a windowpane.

"Witnesses came before this court and swore under oath Mr. Eppes intended to kill Major Suhrer and did indeed go about town seeking a pistol stating 'I will kill him' only minutes prior to the shooting. Another witness swore he first heard the pistol shot, then looked and saw Eppes beating the deceased with the whip.

"Gentlemen, the law charges you to find Thomas J. Eppes and George Dewson guilty of one of the charges of murder as described or of manslaughter. It is your duty, given the testimony presented. None other is acceptable!"

With this final statement Cheney turns with a slight bow, looking directly at each juror before taking his seat.

CLOSING ARGUMENT FOR THE DEFENSE

An eloquent speaker, Colonel Walker is first up for the defense, beginning with "the theme that the law governing cases of this type and character are not written down in human statute, but rather are unwritten in the breast of every brave man who has a wife, and its language is that whoever attempts to defile the marriage-bed, in making his attempts, takes his own life in his hands. A man is permitted to kill the would-be assassin who is trying to murder him, and shoot down the burglar who invades his home. The law permits this. What are these, compared to the invasion of the marriage-bed? From Edward to Charles I, 360 years, there was no penalty for a man's thus vindicating his family's honor, and it was not until the dissolute reign of Charles II, that England was humiliated by having a king, courts and lords who looked upon a beautiful woman as their prey. Then it was attempted to fetter the virtuous husband in defending the honor of his wife. For the last thousand years there has not been a solitary case of this kind where juries have convicted a man for slaying the destroyer of his domestic happiness."

Colonel Walker arraigned "certain apostles of a higher morality" for advocating a legal solution to difficult problems of this kind. He then cited the Bible, Greek and Roman law and other codes which prescribe death to the adulterer.

I am in awe of his oratory skill, as are the rest of the spectators. I can hear the almost simultaneous expulsions of withheld breath.

Colonel MacDonell is next to speak for the defense, reviewing the evidence carefully, dwelling upon the fact that Suhrer, instead of sending a servant, went up to Mrs. Eppes's room in the third story of the hotel to announce the visit of the two preachers, his prolonged stay there and after leaving her there in an excited condition of mind, thought it safer to tell a lie to them saying "she is not at home."

"This probably was the time referred to of his going to her room and making indecent advances to her," he says, to conjure up an image in the minds of the jury. He adds, "Fifteen or twenty-five minutes was not sufficient cooling-off time, as the State would like you to believe."

Picking up the buggy whip he crosses in front of the jury panel arguing, "Furthermore, it was Eppes's first impulse to horsewhip Suhrer, and holding the whip in his right hand is proof positive on that point. Had he intended to kill him, at first he would have held the pistol in his right hand."

He lays the shortened, almost harmless-looking buggy whip on the jury box railing. The desired effect is uncanny and immediate as the eyes of the jury stare at it.

"Gentlemen, the burden of proof lays heavy in your hands today that justice shall prevail in finding Thomas J. Eppes innocent, perfectly justified in shooting Suhrer."

He sits down to the silence of a courtroom quiet as a church. The stillness belies the certain undercurrents churning, eager to burst loose.

The judge does his duty, charges the jury and excuses them to make the most momentous decision the majority of them will ever have to make in their lives. Their decision will not only affect the lives of Eppes and Dewson but also the lives of the widow Suhrer, her children and countless others.

They must be aware of the many eyes upon them as they exit the courtroom, but not a one turns around. Looking straight ahead as they go forth to face the challenge with heads held high and backs straight, they remind me of soldiers marching off to war.

"Better them than me," I remark to Dr. Pope as we both stand for the first time in almost four hours.

The clock on the wall shows it is well on the way to seven o'clock. No wonder my body is stiff and my head is pounding unmercifully.

"Do you have a potion in that bag you carry everywhere, to cure this god-awful headache of mine?" I ask.

"The heat, lack of water and exercise are more than likely the reasons you are unwell," he responds, reaching into his bag to hand me a folded paper filled with a fine white powder.

He directs me to place it under my tongue. "This will make you feel better shortly and it works better than Brown's Iron Bitters and doesn't taste near as bad," he adds with a laugh, seeing the awful look on my face after I empty the packet in my mouth.

"Good God, I must find water—that is horrible!" I exclaim, bolting for the side door and the nearby artesian well.

With a cool, wet handkerchief wrapped around my neck, the pounding in my head has blessedly abated upon my reentrance a mere ten minutes later. The jury is also filing back in.

What is going on, I wonder.

As I hurry to take my seat the judge hammers his gavel for "Order in the court" and the bailiff barks out, "This court will come to order!"

Studying each man in the jury panel I notice a strange thing: none of them are looking at the prosecution attorneys. They are all turned slightly away from the prosecution table, facing the judge.

The foreman hands a piece of paper over to the judge, who reads it without any expression and passes it back to the foreman to be read out loud.

"Mr. Foreman, has the jury reached a decision?" asks the judge.

To which the foreman responds, "We have, Your Honor. We find the defendant, Thomas J. Eppes, not guilty in the charge of Murder in the First Degree, Murder in the Second Degree or to the charge of Manslaughter."

The decision for George Dewson is the same, but cannot be heard over the deafening shouts of anger mixed with those of jubilation as the crowd grows dangerously out of control.

We are pushed and shoved, spilled out into the street along with the rest of the unruly bunch by the court bailiffs. The last look I have of Jeff and George: they are all smiles, shaking the hands of the attorneys and witnesses.

AFTERWARD
SUNDAY/JULY 25, 1886

Little Jeff Eppes hangs fearfully onto his father's hand in the doorway of his mother's darkened bedroom. The tears roll uncontrollably down his chubby little cheeks. Papa said Mama is going to heaven to be an angel with his little brother, Douglas, and Jeffy doesn't want her to go.

Suddenly breaking loose he runs to the high four-poster bed, climbs on the small stool and slips onto the pillow beside her. She's so pretty lying there; her long black hair spreads out across the pillow and down across one slender arm.

"Mommy, Mommy …" he says, gently placing little kisses on her cool brow while trying to wake her from the deep drug-induced sleep she has been in since Doc left this morning.

Her eyes flutter open to the sound of her babe and he claps his little hands, chortling gleefully. "Papa, see, Mommy not go to heaven!" He bounces on the bed.

Katie winces in pain and Jeff strides forward to remove Jeffy, but she holds up her hand, shaking her head "no." She whispers, "Please let me hold him one more time, feel him against my breast, smell the sweet baby smell of him before I go. Please?"

It is almost more than he can bear, watching her lie there slowly slipping away. The birth of Douglas last December 22 was such a joy. They named him after her brother, Douglas Shaylor, but the baby never thrived and after his death on June 18, Katie began pining away. She would not eat, no matter what Maum Salley fixed special for her and no matter how hard Jeff pleaded with her. She kept saying God was punishing her, but wouldn't explain.

Maum Salley takes Jeffy away, kicking and screaming for his mother, while Jeff sits gently on the bed stroking Katie's hair and arms. He utters tender words of love, and silent prayers for God to take this away from her, to bring her back the way she used to be.

Katie turns her head to him. Her beseeching eyes look into his and a flicker of life, a spark ignites between them. Jeff's heartbeat picks up. Hope beyond all hope swells in his chest … only to be doused by, "I lied, Jeff, please forgive me. I lied."

He cries in anguish, "What do you mean, Katie, I don't understand!"

He has to lean close to her lips to hear her tormented words, her death-bed confession. "I lied to you because I only wanted you to stay home more, to pay more attention to me, so I lied. Major Suhrer never touched me. He was always the proper gentleman. I am so sorry." Tears flow down her cheeks as she sobs out the words, "God has punished me by taking Douglas. Now he is taking me away from you and little Jeff."

Pulling away to look at the woman he has loved and defended, Jeff can't believe what she is saying. "It can't be true!" he cries out. "I killed an innocent man, oh my God!"

Author's Note

This is a true story based on real events, people and places, and it has been this author's intent to research to the best of my ability in order to provide the reader with an accurate accounting. Since history is sometimes misconstrued, as we all know, when it is passed down from one generation to another, some things may not be as accurate as desired. Good examples are the stories published in the *Amelia Islander Magazine* and the *Amelia Now* magazine in reference to the story about T. J. Eppes's wife, Celeste. Her name was not Celeste, not even as a nickname; nor was she a Creole from Louisiana. I myself fell victim to accepting this story verbatim as one of my ghost stories until research revealed the truth. This was a valuable lesson to me to not accept information as given, but to research before writing. I have done so with this book and therefore it has taken me over four years to complete.

Old newspaper stories and census reports often spelled names phonetically rather than correctly, so please forgive those errors. Also, there are a few places where a name was unavailable, so I used an author's liberties in providing those names. If perchance you happen to know those names, I would love to hear from you!

CPSIA information can be obtained at www.ICGtesting.com
Printed in the USA
LVOW13s0345080714

393258LV00001B/5/P